## *BEAUTIFUL WOMEN, TOP SECRETS, FAST DEATHS . . .*

**GINGER LOUIE:** She was seventeen, half-Oriental, all beautiful—hooked on the bad side of LA. Lujack gave her a ride home from the Betty Ford Center. A few days later she was dead . . .

**CHASE FIELD:** The Hollywood modeling agent scouted gorgeous women and rich deals at LA's sexiest nightspots—until someone stabbed him through the heart . . .

**LAWRENCE BROWNELL:** His Brownell Industries was developing an ultra-secret new supersonic bomber—while he took pleasure cruises in a super swank yacht and got his own kind of kicks . . .

**DEBBI ARNOLD:** The blonde, smart TV news anchor was the woman of Lujack's dreams—until she started spending time with a U.S. Senator who had friends in too many wrong places . . .

**DOLPH KILLIAN:** The former Navy man was a God-fearing patriot who made millions from the government and the defense industry. When he got angry, he called in his own armed defense force . . .

**KAZUO YOSHIDA:** The billionaire Japanese banker worshipped the code of the samurai and owned half of California. And Lujack's tie

mob called the Yakuza . . .

---

PRAISE FOR D

*THE GC*

"A crackling good, gritty Southern California mystery in the best hardboiled Chandler tradition."

—Jim Murray, *Los Angeles Times*

"Has a taste of the underworld, the Hollywood rich, and a few police (local and FBI) that are doing their jobs . . . a page-turner all the way . . . extremely entertaining."

—*Mystery News*

**Books by David Thoreau**

The Book of Numbers
The Good Book

Published by POCKET BOOKS

# THE BOOK OF NUMBERS

DAVID THOREAU

POCKET BOOKS
New York London Toronto Sydney Tokyo Singapore

This book is a work of fiction. Names, characters, places and incidents are either the product of the author's imagination or are used fictitiously. Any resemblance to actual events or locales or persons, living or dead, is entirely coincidental.

An *Original* Publication of POCKET BOOKS

POCKET BOOKS, a division of Simon & Schuster Inc.
1230 Avenue of the Americas, New York, NY 10020



ISBN: 0-671-64526-9

First Pocket Books printing April 1990

10 9 8 7 6 5 4 3 2 1



Printed in the U.S.A.

*To Doris*

## *Acknowledgments*

The author would like to thank Eric Tobias, Margaret and H.D. Thoreau, and Michael Johnson for their editorial assistance.

# THE BOOK OF NUMBERS

# Chapter One

## *At Seventeen She'd Just Begun*

Not likely, Jimmy Lujack thought to himself as he saw the "P.S. I love you" sign when he turned onto Palm Canyon Drive. It was a little after eight in the morning and already Palm Springs was too hot for tennis, even the way the local geezers played. Dry heat was high on his most overrated list, just after New York pizza and Dodger pitching. What could a guy expect from a city that elects Sonny Bono as its mayor?

Admittedly he wasn't in the best of moods. Picking up people at the Betty Ford Center was a job for a limo driver or an agent or a relative, not a bookie. Lujack's partner, Tommy Chin, had roped him into the job.

"Ginger has caused great dishonor to our family. None of her aunts or uncles will get her," Tommy had confided the previous day.

"You're her uncle. Why don't you go?"

"I don't like hospitals. They make me sick."

"The Betty Ford Center isn't a hospital, it's a place where rich people go to get rid of bad habits."

"Ginger was such a pretty girl. Beautiful. She

started modeling when she was fifteen. Already she's on the cover of many magazines."

"I know all about your niece, Tommy. Remember, I was the guy who helped her get an agent."

"Maybe she'll listen to you, Jimmy. No one else can talk to her. My sister only cries when she hears Ginger's name. She can't even go shopping in supermarkets because she's afraid she'll see Ginger's picture on the magazines."

"Better than on milk cartons."

Tommy didn't laugh. There were times when Chinese logic became irrefutable. Lujack understood it would be pointless to argue, much less reason. That was why he was making a left turn on Frank Sinatra Drive and following it to the Eisenhower Medical Center.

On each side of the street large bougainvillea-covered walls blocked the view of passersby. Lujack wondered why people needed eight-foot walls in the middle of the desert. Probably to discourage roaming Bedouin tribes or roaming bikers from San Berdoo.

Anyone who read *People* didn't have to be told about the Betty Ford Center. It was uniquely American. If the royal families of Europe went to Baden Baden for gout in the nineteenth century, America's royalty, the rich and famous, went to Betty Ford's for twentieth-century American gout . . . alcoholism and drug addiction.

The place looked nothing like he'd imagined. More like a modern minimum-security prison than a spa. Lujack pulled his Shelby Mustang into the visitors' parking lot in front of the white, no-frills, one-story Firestone Hall. Sitting among the rest of the modern multistoried medical buildings in the Eisenhower Center, Betty Ford's place looked like a poor relative, which didn't jibe with the hefty tuition Lujack heard the place charged.

A sixtyish leather-skinned man in a ridiculous red, white, and blue outfit came out the door to greet him. The man's shirt had little red circles with white stars and blue centers. He looked like a colonial flag. The fellow checked out Lujack with a practiced eye. Drunk? Coke freak? Heroin junkie?

"How are you doing?" Lujack smiled amiably.

"Can't complain," the old man drawled in a desert tongue Lujack recognized from his days in the LAPD. A lot of the guys in the department used to buy small places out in the desert. A place to get drunk, shoot off your gun, and not worry about the neighbors.

"What can I do for ya?"

"I'm here to pick up Ginger Louie."

The man nodded. "Come inside. I'll tell her you're here."

"My name's Lujack, James Lujack. I'm a friend of the family."

The man gave Lujack a look that left little doubt about just how good a friend he thought Lujack was.

Lujack followed the man into the center's entry. There was a picture of Betty Ford on one wall, Dwight Eisenhower on the other. He thought about the wives of recent Republican presidents and why the country needed drying out.

The man in the Old Glory suit conferred with a similarly dressed woman working at the admitting desk. He motioned Lujack to an uncomfortable-looking couch. The woman behind the desk picked up a phone, and the man disappeared down a long hall. Lujack was halfway through an old issue of *Forbes* when he heard the clicking of heels on the tile floor.

Ginger Louie sashayed down the hall looking every

bit the gorgeous, precocious, outrageously self-possessed seventeen-year-old girl he remembered. She was a fourth-generation Chinese-American who wouldn't know a panda from a polar bear but who could take you on a tour of LA nightclubs blindfolded.

When she saw who was picking her up a pout formed under her nose. Ginger's features were a perfect mixture of Eastern delicacy and Western recklessness. She was wearing a leather skirt with a red top. Her tall, lithe figure was as exquisite as her face. Lujack assumed that Ginger looked just as saucy walking out as she had walking in.

"What are you doing here, Lujack?"

"What happened to *Mr.* Lujack?"

"What happened to the limo that was supposed to pick me up?" she countered, spotting Lujack's Mustang in the parking lot.

"Your uncle sent me down here to get you. You don't like the car, you can walk."

The old man smiled wryly as he handed Lujack Ginger's bag. Ginger ignored them both and pushed open the glass doors. Lujack followed her back out into the heat. Her suitcase fit into his fastback trunk on the first try.

"Good luck, Ginger," the old man said.

"Fuck off," Ginger snapped, climbing into the shotgun seat.

Lujack turned on the ignition and the big engine kicked over like an angry stomach. He and Ginger didn't say much until they were out of the city going north on Highway 111 past the tram.

The desert without man's intrusion was truly spectacular. The smallest hills became dramatic mountains in the stark, lifeless terrain. It was the spiritual quality of the desert that attracted people as much as the weather. Man's respect for nature. Right.

Like all of Southern California, Palm Springs was dependent on other people's water, and it seemed the more dependent people became, the more water they used.

"Do you ever wonder why they have more water rationing in Portland, Oregon, than they do in Palm Springs?" Lujack asked.

"All the time," Ginger said, looking out the window at the mounds of sand and dirt.

Lujack followed her gaze to a pair of off-road vehicles tooling down an adjacent wash.

"How long have you been down here?"

"Four weeks," she said, laughing to herself. "Mark said I was getting crazy, but Molly and Janis, they did as much as me."

"As much what?"

"As much everything. Blow . . . ludes . . . men."

Lujack didn't give her the satisfaction of showing surprise. After five years of working LAPD vice he had been around more girls like Ginger than he wanted to remember.

"Who's Mark?" he asked.

"Mark Lyman."

"Mark Lyman from Marina Shores?"

"You know Mark? He's totally happening," she said with enthusiasm.

Lujack knew Mark Lyman well enough to know better. Lyman ran a spiffy development in the Marina, LA's answer to Turnberry Isle in Florida. A place where wheeler-dealers could park their yachts, buy condos, and hobnob with politicians, defense contractors, and all the beautiful models Lyman could supply. And from everything Lujack had heard, that supply was impressive.

"Does your uncle know you hang out with Mark Lyman?"

"Mark wanted to pay for my treatment but Uncle Tommy wouldn't let him. Tommy and Mark are like buddies. I guess you're a buddy too, huh, Lujack?"

"Like not at all, Ginger."

"The place cost six grand."

"I hope Tommy got his money's worth."

"I've been straight for thirty-one days."

"You've been at Betty Ford's for thirty-one days. Now comes the hard part."

"I can do it. One day at a time," she said without conviction.

"You didn't seem too friendly with that man at the clinic."

"He's a jerk. He used to be a drunk, now he's a lech."

Lujack smiled to himself. Women, even seventeen-year-old women, had their own unique sensitivity.

"Are you going back to work?"

"Work is the best thing for an addict," she said rotely.

"You going to stay away from your friends at Marina Shores?"

"Some of them," she said, this time a little defensive.

"But not Mark Lyman."

Ginger didn't answer. Lujack figured Mark Lyman had some hold over her. The kind of fraudulent, reflective power handsome, wealthy, middle-aged men often have over young, impressionable women.

"He's a creep, Ginger. No matter how many nice parties he invites you to."

"Fuck you, Lujack."

"If you're going to insult me, kid, call me Jimmy."

"Nothing personal. I just don't like being told who I can see and who I can't see. I mean, like if it were up to my mother I'd still be in school learning to make brownies."

"Liz just wants you to slow down . . . before you crash."

"I already crashed. How do you think I got out here?" she said softly.

"Tell me what happened."

She hesitated. Lujack thought he heard her clucking her tongue over the murmur of the Mustang. She was still a seventeen-year-old girl, no matter how many magazine covers and silk sheets she'd been on. The clucking stopped and she turned on the radio. Lujack found himself listening to a station he didn't know his radio received.

Ginger crossed her legs, and the black skirt caught her midthigh. She was no rookie. One of the rules she lived by was, when in doubt, show thigh.

"Tommy says you've got an apartment up in the Hills," Lujack said.

"Up on Beachwood. The place is a trip."

"Seventeen is awful young to have your own place."

"Seventeen isn't what it used to be, Lujack."

What is? Lujack thought to himself.

They drove the rest of the way in silence. If listening to a disc jockey by the name of Pet Rat playing rock 'n' roll could be considered such.

It turned into a typically ugly summer day as Lujack followed Interstate 10 down the San Gabriel Valley toward the Civic Center. The hills on his left were occluded by a light brown haze some pundit had named after the combination of smoke and fog. The contraction *smog* was now more famous than its parents.

Tommy had asked Lujack to take Ginger back to his restaurant, the Chin Up, in the Pico-Robertson section of West Los Angeles. Tommy, as the head of the Chin family, supposedly had the final word in these family matters, but Lujack had a sneaky hunch that Ginger didn't kowtow to the Chin family traditions.

"Your uncle is waiting for you at the restaurant. I think your mother will be there too."

"No way, Lujack. I'm not seeing her."

"She's your mother."

"She's a bitch. Drop me off at Zodiac, I'll go home with Molly."

"What's Zodiac?"

"It's a club on Melrose."

"I thought Molly was a user. Aren't you supposed to stay away from people like her?"

"Molly's my roommate. She's part of my support group."

"Great," Lujack said without enthusiasm.

Lujack stopped in front of a one-story bungalow on Beachwood. The sun was already behind the hills, and the canyon was beginning to cool. Ginger seemed happy to be home. She bounded up the concrete walkway. Lujack followed with her bag. She had the exuberance of youth, the beauty of the ages. He wondered what was in store for her.

She fumbled for her key, then pushed the door open.

"Molly. Mol . . . Hey, bitch, you in there?"

There was no answer from inside the cool, dark room.

Ginger gave Lujack an appraising look. She was tall for a Chinese-American, about five-feet-ten, but Lujack was still half a head taller.

"I guess nobody's home," she said without taking her eyes off him. "Maybe you'd like to come in."

"I think I should get going, Ginger. I promised your uncle I'd come by."

"Out at Betty's they don't let you do anything. Know what I mean?"

As she said it, she moved her hands along the sides of her hips and let her hair fall over her eyes. It wouldn't have worked for most women, but for Ginger, a very professional, very beautiful, and very young model, it seemed perfectly natural.

"I thought you had to call your counselor. To be sure you get off on the right foot."

"Step. Everything at Betty's is in steps. Twelve steps—just like AA."

"Steps. Right. Steps."

"I'm only giving up drugs, Lujack, not men."

"Good luck, Ginger," he said.

"You could have made her come with you," Tommy said unhappily.

Lujack was sitting in a booth at the Chin Up with Tommy, his wife, Jackie, and his sister, Liz. The two women looked at him as if he were a round-eyed pariah. Lujack was no stranger to Jackie's dark gazes. Jackie tended to blame Lujack for many things, mostly having to do with the Good Book, Tommy and Lujack's sports betting operation. Notably it was the not inconsiderable profits Jackie resented.

"You mean I should have trussed her up and thrown her in the trunk?"

"She's a minor, Lujack," Jackie said. "There are ways to persuade minors to do as they are told."

"I'll be sure to remind Lionel of that the next time he borrows the Mustang," Lujack said, referring to the Chins' number one son.

"You let Lionel borrow your car? He's only fifteen!" Jackie said in horror.

"We had to tell the admitting office that Ginger was

eighteen. They don't take minors," Liz Louie said, on the verge of tears.

Liz was shorter than her daughter and not nearly as attractive. She was a nurse at Cedars Sinai. Lujack remembered Tommy telling him that Liz had the brains to be a doctor but instead had married Ray Louie. Lujack had never met Ray, but he'd heard enough about the Reno blackjack dealer to know where Ginger got her looks and her wildness.

"I'll be glad to drive you up to your daughter's apartment, Mrs. Louie," Lujack offered.

"You've done enough already, Jimmy," Jackie said dryly.

"That's all right, Mr. Lujack. She wouldn't open the door anyway," Liz said, staring into the cruet of soy sauce on the table. "During her last week of treatment I went out to Betty Ford for the family support group. Ginger wouldn't even talk to me. Her counselor said she'd been doing so well . . . then I came."

"That girl needs to learn some manners," Tommy said sternly.

"She needs more than manners, Tommy, she needs a father," Liz said quietly.

"Maybe Jimmy and I could take a trip to Reno and talk to Ray," Tommy suggested.

"I called him when Ginger had her . . . when Ginger was hospitalized. He said he'd be down as soon as possible. I called him three days later, and he said he was on a hot streak and couldn't leave. I haven't heard from him since," Liz said.

"Sounds like Ray could use a few manners himself," Lujack volunteered.

"Ray Louie is a no-good bum. He always was and always will be," Jackie said emphatically. Her sister-in-law said nothing, just kept staring sadly at the soy sauce.

"Knowing Ray," Tommy said, "he gambled away his ticket in the Reno slot machines. Ray's the only Chinese I ever met who gambles to lose and drinks to remember."

"Half Chinese. It's Ray's Chilean blood that makes him crazy," Liz pointed out.

Lujack had always assumed that Ginger's looks were a mixture of something more than hamburger and chop suey.

"His mother was Chilean. Blond, tall, very beautiful. I've seen pictures," Liz said, then looked up at Lujack, circling her finger around her ear. "But very cuckoo. You know. Always having tantrums."

"That's not all she had," Jackie Chin said snidely.

Tommy gave his wife a sharp cease-and-desist look which temporarily subdued Jackie.

"Did she ask about me? Did she want me to call?" Liz asked, either unconcerned or unaware of Jackie's dig.

"She said she'd call you tonight after she unpacks and calls her counselor for the address of her AA meeting."

Liz nodded. Lujack wondered if she knew he was lying. She probably did but wouldn't admit it. Chinese-Americans were very good at seeing what they wanted to see, hearing what they wanted to hear. A lot like everyone else.

"I better go home then. I don't have to be at the hospital until ten," Liz said. "Did she say what time her meeting was?"

"I don't think she knew. Maybe you should call her."

Liz made a motion to move. Lujack got up to let her out of the booth. Jackie jumped up and offered to drive her home. Liz nodded. She already seemed to dread picking up the phone to talk to her daughter. Or sitting by the phone waiting for it to ring. Lujack expected it would be a long wait.

"Thank you, Mr. Lujack, for picking up Ginger," she said weakly.

Lujack almost said "Anytime" but instead told Liz it was his pleasure.

"So what do you think?" Tommy asked after the women left.

"I think seventeen-year-old girls shouldn't be allowed to make two thousand dollars a day, get their own apartments, or hang out at Marina Shores."

"With teenagers what should be isn't always what is. It hasn't been easy for Liz or Ginger."

"It isn't going to get any easier."

# Chapter Two

## *P.S. I Love You*

The Crocodile Cafe in Pasadena was one of those clean, cozy, high-tech, low-intensity restaurants that were currently sprouting up like so many daisy weeds around California. There was nothing wrong with the place, Lujack admitted. It was just that it seemed too . . . happy, too self-satisfied. Restaurants were supposed to be for eating. This one seemed to be for watching. Maybe that was the problem.

Anna was waiting for him on the restored nineteenth-century bench in front of the entrance. She smiled benignly as he approached. She was wearing an open-collared shirt and a full skirt. The pale blue eyes he loved seemed strangely serene. Her hair was shoulder length, he noticed she had touched up the few gray streaks since she'd been out of the clinic. Now it was the luxuriant chestnut color it had been when they were first married. All in all she looked great. It had been almost two years since Lujack and his ex-wife had talked about the night Marty Kildare was shot, almost two years since Anna had decided to rejoin the human race.

"I know you hate places like this," she said with a slight smile. Lujack was happy to see her smile.

"Did you give him our name?" Lujack asked, nodding toward the tall, blond twenty-year-old host.

"I gave him both our names, just in case."

Lujack nodded. When Anna had left the clinic she'd taken her maiden name, Dole, not Lujack's or that of the man she'd left him for, his former LAPD partner, Marty Kildare.

"Just in case I didn't show?"

"Just in case you did," she said lightly. "Bookies have been known to miss appointments."

Lujack raised his eyebrows. His new profession was something they'd never talked about. Lujack was finishing his fifth year as a sports bookie. He'd made over a million dollars in those five years when combined with his fees as an ombudsman for people in trouble.

"How'd you find out?"

"Todd told me that you were paying twenty-five hundred dollars a month to keep me in the clinic. Police pensions don't pay that much. I asked Jackie, she told me about you and Tommy."

"I meant to tell you, but . . ." This was a George Bush sentence. He didn't finish it. Lujack wasn't sure why he hadn't told her. He wasn't ashamed of what he was doing. But maybe he wasn't proud of it either.

"You don't have to tell me everything, James. We're not married anymore."

It had been six years since she had left him for Marty. Then, after Marty's death, she'd spent four years staring at a wall in the Sierra Madre Clinic.

Now, in this last year and a half, she'd come back to the so-called real world. He wasn't sure if that wasn't the reason he hadn't told her.

"But you don't have to shield me either," she continued as if reading his mind. "When I chose to reenter this world, I didn't come back on the stipulation that I be treated like a crystal goblet on a sound stage."

Before Lujack had a chance to react, their blond host interrupted and showed them to one of the outside tables below the sidewalk level. It was a warm Saturday afternoon in Pasadena, and the table along the deserted downtown street wasn't unpleasant. Like most older California cities Pasadena was undergoing gentrification.

Lujack ordered a hamburger and looked up Lake Street.

"I remember when Pasadena was where the old money hid out," Lujack said when they'd been seated.

"We looked for a house here once. You said it was becoming a ghetto," she reminded him.

"Now it's a shopping mall. The circle becomes a line."

"Always, James. Look at us."

Lujack had been looking at them because in the back of his mind he knew that's exactly why she had asked to meet him.

"That's why we're having lunch today? To make the circle into a line?"

She didn't answer so he continued: "That's what you want, isn't it, Anna? To put us in the shopping mall category. Like a pair of shoes that don't fit."

"We didn't fit, James. No one tried to make us fit more than I did."

She was right, nobody had tried harder than she

had. Now he wanted to try but he knew she had made up her mind. The circle was closed. He didn't believe it. He knew she still loved him. She had to. He still loved her.

"So what happens now?" he asked with a dumb smile. "Do we see each other twice a month and talk about the weather?"

"I'm not sure that would be appropriate under the circumstances."

"Under what circumstances?"

"I'm getting married."

"What?"

"You heard me," she said, meeting his eyes.

Lujack felt like he'd been hit by a Mike Tyson hook in the solar plexus. Ten minutes ago he'd considered proposing to her himself. Again.

"Can I ask his name?" he inquired feebly.

"Todd Barnes."

"Jesus Christ. Your fucking doctor! You're marrying your shrink."

"Todd isn't my shrink. He was the director of the clinic I was in. Now I'm out."

"You've been out for nine months. Isn't there a law or something that says doctors can't marry their patients until a certain amount of time passes?"

"I told Todd you'd react this way."

"React what way? My wife is marrying a shrink with a shoe fetish. How do you want me to react?"

"I'm not your wife anymore and Todd doesn't have a shoe fetish. Just because he dresses well and has a legitimate job, trying to cure sick people."

Anna's lower lip began to tremble. He wasn't sure he didn't want her to break down so he could hold her in his arms and tell her everything would be all right. That was how it used to be when they were first married, living in a little apartment in Santa Monica.

He was a westside patrolman, she was a waitress who didn't like cops. She was the sexiest girl he'd ever met. Sexy in a feminine, helpless sort of way. It had always amazed him that she could be so passionate. Their marriage those first years had been something he treasured. Then when he changed, when the job changed him, that treasure became lost. The harder he tried to find it, the more lost it became. For both of them.

"Anna, the guy's a leech. He lives off sick people, he doesn't cure them."

The moment he said it, he knew it was wrong. Like a curve ball that the pitcher knows isn't going to break.

"I don't know what I should resent more. What you said about Todd or implied about me."

"I didn't mean that . . . I know you're okay now."

"Do you? Maybe I might shoot you, James. Like I shot Marty?"

"Hiram used to tell me never get in a pissing contest with a woman. They got bad aim."

She was either gonna laugh or push the table over on him. When she smiled he let go of the gum he was hanging onto underneath the table.

"Hiram was one of a kind."

"He was that," Lujack said.

"He was shot too."

"By a man," Lujack said, remembering.

"None of Todd's friends are dead, James," she said, her voice rising. "They're normal people with normal jobs. Doctors, lawyers, teachers. They have families and own homes. They even go to church."

The waiter brought some sort of a brown bird's nest for Anna and a hamburger for Lujack.

"What's that?" Lujack asked, happy for any change of subject.

"Chinese chicken salad," the waiter volunteered pleasantly.

"I didn't ask you, Flash," Lujack said curtly. The waiter winced and retreated.

"Sorry," Lujack apologized.

"No you're not. You've never been sorry."

"Never."

"You're a jerk, Jimmy."

"I love it when you sugarcoat things."

"You're also a bad lover."

"Maybe we should get a check," he said, looking for the banished waiter.

"Maybe you should eat."

"It's hard to eat after your wife of six years has called you a bad lover."

"It could have been worse. You could have been a bad lay."

Lujack laughed to himself.

"What's so funny?"

"I was actually looking forward to this lunch."

She laughed. "You know something funny? So was I."

She stuck her fork into the salad. He grabbed his hamburger. They each took careful bites, watching each other as they chewed.

"A bad lover, eh?"

"Selfish might be a better word."

"And Todd?" Lujack sputtered. "Todd, he's not selfish?"

"All men are selfish," she declared between bites.

He was tempted to ask what made her such an expert but the conversation was risky enough as it was. He wondered about Marty. He'd always wanted to ask her about Marty.

"You're all right, aren't you? I mean really all right?"

"If by that you mean I don't stare at walls anymore, yes, I'm all right."

"Then I guess you can marry anyone you want."

She watched him carefully. "You didn't put up much of a fight."

"What did you want me to do? Make a counteroffer?" he asked plaintively.

"I'm not sure," she said pleasantly, as if they were negotiating over a used car.

"But Todd is sure."

"Yes," she said, "Todd is sure."

The way she said it he knew she wasn't sure. There was still hope. There was still history. That was the problem with reconciliation. There's always the doubt that split you up in the first place. She blamed him for her miscarriage. He blamed her for Marty.

"I don't want you to marry Todd, Anna."

"I know you don't, James."

"I love you, Anna."

"I love you too, James."

He nodded. Now that they were agreed, he could finish his hamburger. The bite was barely in his mouth when she finished her sentence:

"But I'm still going to marry Todd Barnes."

# Chapter Three

## *Nothing Is for Free*

Lujack was dreaming about a football game. He was playing wide receiver, running down the field under a long pass. The ball was thrown by Phil Hubner. Phil had a great arm and often overthrew him. Lujack was running as fast as he could down the field, at the last second he dived headlong for the ball . . . felt it on his fingertips, hit the grass with the ball balanced on his outstretched hands . . . then it popped up and fell harmlessly to the turf.

It was only when Lujack dropped the pass that he realized the phone was ringing. He reached for the receiver, noticing it was 3:20 A.M.

"You made me drop the ball," he said sleepily, figuring it was a client calling in with results of the Hawaiian Islanders game.

"Is that you, Jimmy?" asked a woman's voice. Not Hawaiian but close.

"Of course it's me. Who else would answer my phone at three-thirty in the morning?"

"This is Jackie Chin. Tommy wanted me to call you. It's about Ginger."

"Ginger," Lujack repeated, sorting out the name and his own consciousness. The good news was he hadn't been drinking, the bad news was the timbre of Jackie Chin's voice.

"What about her?"

"She's dead."

Lujack drove slowly across town. He was in no hurry. Tommy had gone to pick up his sister and together they would identify the body.

He crossed La Brea, and the parking lot of the all-night market was half full. This was a part of LA that never slept. When he'd worked Hollywood vice, they would routinely cruise the market parking lot if they needed a quick bust before the end of the seven P.M.–three A.M. shift. There wasn't a crime listed in the LAPD handbook of vice—prostitution male and female, gambling, kiddie porn, drugs—that couldn't be found between midnight and dawn in that parking lot.

Hollywood had a smell all its own. Even at four in the morning there was the mixture of jasmine from the gardens in the hills and the acrid aroma of desperation and drugs from the streets below. He had enjoyed working vice in Hollywood but he didn't miss it.

Lujack followed Franklin to Beachwood. One week before, he had driven Ginger Louie up this street. Now she was dead. She had seemed sincere about cleaning up her act but obviously had no intention of reconciling with her family. At the time Lujack had attributed her reticence to that of a prodigal daughter. Lujack knew enough about the Chinese family to know that a child, especially a daughter, did not go against her family's wishes without risking great emotional and spiritual distress. Ginger was not immune to those fears, no matter how tough she talked and how much money she'd made modeling. She had not wanted to face her family because she was both afraid and ashamed. She was also determined to live her own life as the ultimate American dream girl.

The too familiar sight of flashing police lights broke the blackness as he drove north on Beachwood Drive. He parked on the east side of the street. Ginger's house was on the west side. She had told Lujack that she and her roommate got the place for a steal, fifteen hundred dollars a month, because the landlord liked them. Lujack hadn't asked what the landlord would have charged if he hadn't liked them.

Lujack crossed the street. It was still warm, the jasmine smell even stronger now. He looked farther up the hill toward the Hollywood sign. There was just enough moonlight for him to see the last two letters: OD. The Hollywood Hills were no stranger to death by overdose, but in the case of Ginger Louie he doubted drugs had been the culprit.

Liz Louie was in the driveway crying on her brother's shoulder. Tommy looked uncomfortable. He also looked mad. Lujack could always tell when Tommy was mad. He rocked back and forth on his heels. Now Tommy was rocking, holding his sister in his arms, rocking her back and forth.

Two uniformed cops were in the driveway. A third cop was busy putting police tape around the crime scene.

Lujack and Tommy exchanged nods. He wanted to talk to Tommy, but now was not the time.

"I'm sorry," Lujack said when Liz looked up. The

sight of him was enough to start her on another crying jag.

"I'm going to take her home," Tommy told him. "They want to see you inside."

"They want to see me?"

"That's right. You," said a familiar voice behind him.

Lujack turned and saw Kyle Thurgood in the doorway. The homicide detective looked like he'd gained a few pounds since their last meeting—if that was possible. As usual, Kyle was impeccably turned out, even at four in the morning.

Tommy escorted Liz down the driveway. Thurgood motioned Lujack to follow him inside. It was against police procedure to let Lujack into the crime scene, but Lujack figured the lieutenant had his reasons.

"Tommy says you knew the girl."

"She was his niece," Lujack said, checking out the living room. The walls were covered with pictures of Iman, Christie Brinkley, and other famous models, including a recent cover of *Elle* featuring Ginger Louie. There were also pictures of Southern California's beach volleyball players who he knew were top male models. Lujack wondered how many other teenagers had the same pictures in their rooms.

"You saw her last Saturday," Thurgood said.

"I picked her up at the Betty Ford Center. I dropped her off here sometime after four. Does that make me a suspect?"

He continued to follow Thurgood into what he assumed was Ginger's bedroom. Lujack wasn't anxious to see Ginger Louie's body. And when he entered the room he didn't see her body. He saw only her head.

Ginger's head was lying on the pillow on her bed. It

was a grotesque sight, and Lujack, who had seen more than a few dead bodies in his life, felt a wave of horror break across him. There was a very real terror in looking at the head of a human detached from a human body. Especially the beautiful, hideous head of someone you knew.

"You didn't know?"

Lujack said nothing. He stared at the face, the dark stump that had once been connected to Ginger's body.

"You made her mother look at this?"

"The roommate called her. She called Tommy. Tommy called me. The crime scene's not worth a shit."

Lujack looked below the head. There was no bulge under the bed covers.

"Where's the rest of her?"

"Beats me. The roommate said she came home and looked in to say good night. The head was lying on the pillow."

"Jesus! That must have been some look."

Thurgood didn't smile.

"The roommate, Molly Blair, is in the other room. She's pretty shaken. Says she got off work at two and drove home. She works in a nightclub on Melrose. She says Ginger came in earlier, left with a guy. Local coke dealer. Dave Mason. Lives up on Beverly Glen."

"Sounds like Ginger didn't stay with the program."

"What program is that?"

"The Betty Ford program. I thought there was a chance."

"From the looks of her I'd say drugs and booze were the least of her problems."

Lujack took another look at the head. Ginger's beautiful black hair was spread out on the pillow like an Oriental Judith. A crime lab photographer snapped off a few more pictures. Ginger's last shoot.

"That face was worth millions of dollars," Lujack said.

"I know," Thurgood said, pointing to the framed magazine covers of Ginger arranged on the walls. "Big-time model. Looks like she had a pretty nice body too," he said, showing Lujack a picture of Ginger in a bathing suit.

Lujack watched as the medical examiner and his assistant secured the evidence. The gloved assistant lifted the head by the hair while the white-haired senior staffer opened the plastic bag. All that was left on the pillow was a red stain. Lujack felt another shudder of horror.

"From the looks of the angle and the cleanness of the cut, this wasn't done by the Texas chain-saw murderer," Barney Milch, the senior man, told Thurgood. Milch was something of a macabre legend around the department. He'd been at more murder sites than most of the police force combined.

The crime lab biologists put the pillow in a bag to take to the lab.

"Don't stick your neck out, Barney," Thurgood replied without smiling.

"Very funny," Milch said, handing the bag to his assistant. "My guess, and at this point that's all it can be, is a very sharp blade, either an ax or a sword. It would be difficult to make a cut that clean with a knife. You'd have to cut back and forth, to get through the muscle and bone at the back of the neck."

"Ax or a sword. That narrows our list of suspects. Either a woodsman or a knight."

"Get me the rest of the body, Lieutenant, and I'll narrow it further. I can put a laser beam on the neck for prints but don't expect much. There's not much skin to work with. It's too dry in Los Angeles to get good latent prints off such a small area. Besides the head was carried here. There's not enough blood for the murder to have been done here."

"When we find the rest of Miss Louie you'll be the first to hear about it, Barney."

Milch and his assistant left with the white bag.

Molly Blair was sitting on her bed. Her dyed white-blond hair was spiked. Her face was very pale, helped by a pancake makeup Lujack had seen on other LA children of the night. Molly didn't look much older than Ginger. Lujack thought she might have a very beautiful face under the twin layers of artifice and shock.

"Molly, this is James Lujack."

"Did he do it?" Molly asked weakly.

"No. Lujack is a lot of things but he doesn't go around decapitating pretty girls. He picked up your roommate at the Betty Ford Center last week."

"You hang with her Uncle Tommy. Lujack the cop," Molly said rotely.

"Ex-cop," Lujack and Thurgood said simultaneously.

"Ginger was straight. She went to her meetings every night, man," Molly said, defending her friend's honor, then stopping.

"This guy, Mason, he's no AA counselor, sweetie," Thurgood said.

"You got that right," Molly said, forcing a half-hysterical laugh. "But he didn't . . ." Molly looked toward Ginger's room. "He couldn't have done that. He's agro but he's harmless."

"That's not what his yellow sheet says. His yellow sheets say he's very agro indeed. Three arrests, one conviction for selling."

"He's a drug dealer, not a murderer," she said.

"A lot of people don't think there's much difference."

"They don't know Dave Mason," she said, pulling at her hair, wrapping it around her finger.

"I guess we'll have to introduce ourselves to Mr. Mason," Thurgood said with contempt. "Unless you have any other names you want to give us."

"Like I told you before. Everyone liked Ginger, she was a happening lady. I mean, who would want to kill her?"

"Maybe she was a little too happening."

"That's the way it is in LA. You snooze, you lose. You want phone numbers, call her agency."

"We haven't been able to roust her agent," Thurgood explained. "Chase Field, supposed to be one of the best in town. When he finds out what happened to his meal ticket, he's going to be one of the most unhappy in town."

"He'll get over it," Lujack said.

"Can I go now?" Molly asked.

Thurgood looked at Lujack to see if he wanted to ask any questions. Lujack hadn't played good cop–bad cop in a long time, he didn't want to start now. Not with an eighteen-year-old girl who just discovered her roommate's head.

"Do you have some friends you can stay with, Molly?" Lujack asked softly.

"Yeah. There's a guy up the street. He said I could crash there."

"I offered to give her a ride to her parents but she says she doesn't have any," Thurgood added for no apparent reason. Unless it was to prove that he cared, which he probably didn't.

"How old are you, Molly?"

"Old enough."

"Her license says she's nineteen. It also says she grew up in La Mirada. Bet we could dig up her yearbook with her picture in it, 'Most likely to secede,'" Thurgood said.

"Had Ginger seen Mark Lyman since she came back?" Lujack asked. The question caught both Thurgood and Molly by surprise.

"She told you about Mark?"

"Just that she used to hang out at Marina Shores."

"They were just friends," Molly said. "She had lots of friends."

Lujack let the subject drop. Mark Lyman was Thurgood's responsibility now. No sense in losing good clients if you didn't have to.

"One more question. How did you meet Ginger?" Lujack asked.

"I met her at Chase Fields's. We modeled together. I quit a couple of months ago. Chase said I didn't have the look."

Lujack noticed a picture of a very pretty California blonde on the dressing table. She was hugging an All American–type guy in a Corvette. The picture looked like it was taken in Newport Beach or Laguna Beach. Molly looked stunning.

"Everybody looks like that in California," she said, following Lujack's gaze. "Ginger was lucky—she had a different look."

Thurgood asked Lujack to tag along with him to Mason's house. They rode in Thurgood's unmarked unit. Lujack hadn't been in a police car since he and Thurgood had worked on the Randolf murder case. Ironically Kurt Randolf had also lived up Beverly Glen. Sometimes LA was smaller than it seemed. Lujack didn't consider that he and Thurgood were friends. After all, Lujack was still a bookie and Thurgood was still a cop, but Lujack felt a grudging respect for the homicide lieutenant. Maybe because he still was a cop. Maybe because he was a good cop.

"Do you mind telling me why I'm part of this investigation?"

"I need a witness. You know how I am when I get around drug dealers."

"Liz was pretty shaken up. So was Tommy."

"Do you blame her?" Thurgood asked. Then, getting no reaction, "I don't want you and Chin to start up with any Oriental vendettas. We'll get the guy who did this."

"So that's why I'm along. So I can vouch for your professionalism to the Chinese-American community."

"It's no secret that the Chinese don't appreciate the methods of our police departments."

What Thurgood said was true enough. The Chinese, even second- and third-generation Chinese, tended to solve their own problems their own way. Although Lujack doubted Tommy would be going straight to the Chin Family Association to find out who murdered his niece.

There was a patrol car parked down the street from Mason's apartment midway up Beverly Glen, next to the old general store. The Glen, as it was called by the locals, was one of LA's leftover pockets of hippiedom. Something of a rustic ghetto. A cluster of old wooden houses and apartments that had somehow escaped Los Angeles's newest sport: the home improvement loan.

Thurgood and Lujack parked behind the patrol car. A young officer came over to talk to Thurgood. His partner stayed in the car, talking on the radio. The patrolman couldn't have been more than twenty-five. Lujack remembered his own enthusiasm. It seemed a long time ago.

"His place is three up on the other side of the street. Looks like the front stairs are the only way in. There's a lot of growth up on the hill and it gets pretty steep behind his apartment. There's a light on inside, looks like a TV," the patrolman finished.

"Our man's an insomniac," Lujack said.

"More likely a base freak," Thurgood said. "You've been off the job too long, Lujack."

The young patrolman gave Lujack a look of recognition. Even the young cops had heard of Jimmy Lujack.

"Blondell, you get above the house. Tell Reese to stay down on this side. We don't want Mr. Mason going anywhere."

Lujack followed the lieutenant up the street. Thurgood waited while the two patrolmen took their places.

"Just like old times, eh, Lujack?" Thurgood said.

"An hour and a half ago I was sound asleep. Now I'm about to drop in on a deranged killer without a badge or a gun. That's my idea of a nightmare."

"Maybe we should have a little side bet, just so you'll feel like the night's not a complete waste. Even money this creep inside is our man. A hundred bucks."

"You're on," Lujack said.

Lujack followed the beefy lieutenant up the steps. Halfway up, Thurgood stopped. Both of them could see the flickering light from the television screen. The low murmur of voices, probably from the TV, could also be heard. Thurgood continued up the steps. Lujack followed, still not sure why Thurgood wanted him along. The story about the lieutenant being worried about Tommy and his relatives taking the law into their own hands didn't strike him as full disclosure.

Thurgood pounded on the wooden door. There was a glass peephole without any glass. The rest of the old wooden building didn't look much better. An ideal fixer-upper, but Lujack didn't think Dave Mason was the fixer-upper type. Thurgood pushed away the cloth hanging over the peephole with a pen.

"Mason, you in there?"

"Go away, I'm asleep," came a grumpy voice.

Thurgood peered through the peephole and reported to Lujack: "The guy's lying on the couch holding a Bud. There must be two grams of coke on his coffee table. And people wonder why the Japanese are taking over the country."

Thurgood knocked again. "Open up, pal. We want to talk to you."

"I don't want to talk to you. Go away."

"We can't go away, asshole. We're the police."

There was a sudden nonsilence. After ten seconds, they heard a shuffling sound. Thirty seconds later the door opened and they were facing Dave Mason, or what was left of him. Mason had the bloated look of a man who'd seen the bottom of too many parties. His skin was the color of skim milk and the circles around his eyes would make Little Orphan Annie jealous. He probably wasn't more than thirty, but he wasn't going to enjoy forty.

"What do you want?"

"We want to come inside and talk."

Mason hesitated, then backed away. "I'm beat, man. Make it quick."

Lujack followed Thurgood into the apartment. The place looked like the inside of a fraternity house just before it was kicked off campus. Beer cans were all over the table. The carpet was stained with blotches of red wine. The glass coffee table was covered with smudges and scratches from would-be coke snorters. There were the remains of a joint in the ashtray and a half a pack of Marlboros sitting on last month's issue of *Playboy.* The host reached for the Marlboros and plopped down on the couch. He was wearing a pair of boxer shorts and a UNLV T-shirt.

"How the hell can you live like this? When's the last time you took the garbage out?"

"Did you wake me up in the middle of the fuckin' night to critique my housekeeping?"

Thurgood reached under the couch and pulled out a mirror with a mound of coke on it. "What do you think, Lujack, this look like about two years' worth?" Thurgood asked rhetorically. Then, judging Mason's fear: "We heard you were out with Ginger Louie tonight?"

Mason was still drunk and high, but he wasn't completely out of it. He tried to be cool, but it was a struggle.

"I might have. What's it to you?"

"It's not a whole lot to me, but it might make your life a little difficult being that she's dead."

The dealer's eyes moved quickly in the direction of the hallway behind him. "That's impossible!" he blurted out. "She can't be."

Thurgood had picked up on Mason's eye toss immediately. The lieutenant was already in the hallway. Lujack followed him toward the door. There was a bad odor, and it wasn't the smell of rotting garbage. Lujack knew that smell and was preparing himself for the worst. Mason followed behind him.

"Don't you need a warrant for this, copper?" he protested.

"You let us in, jerk," Thurgood said, pushing open the bedroom door.

The body was lying on Mason's unmade bed. Lujack thought he was prepared but he wasn't. Not for the blood.

"Is she in there?" Mason asked, unable to see the corpse.

"As if you didn't know, creep."

Mason pushed himself past Lujack and found himself staring at a headless corpse on the bed. The sheets were covered with blood. The walls were splattered.

"Jesus fucking Christ!" Mason said before losing his cookies on the floor next to the bed.

The room had the look of a satanic ritual. Lujack hadn't been around during the Manson murders but knew cops who had. What kind of a human being would cut a beautiful girl's head off and then mark the walls with her blood? Kyle Thurgood thought he knew.

Thurgood cuffed the drug dealer while he was retching on the floor.

"You have the right to remain silent. Anything you say . . ."

"What the fuck are you doing? I didn't do this," Mason protested as Thurgood continued Mirandizing him. "She wanted to go home. I was too fucked up to drive so I gave her my car keys. The last time I saw her she was alive, I swear to God."

Thurgood waited, then said wearily, "Lujack, go out and tell Blondell to call the lab. Looks like Barney got his wish. A whole body to play with."

Lujack took a final look at the naked, blood-smeared corpse, then looked down at the sniveling doper on the floor. Lujack didn't get a match.

"You're making a big mistake. I got friends. Mick Jagger. Richard Pryor. Chevy Chase."

"Those aren't friends, asshole. They're customers," Thurgood said, putting his Italian boot in Mason's hip.

The last thing Lujack noticed before leaving was the wall. There was a series of markings, single marks in a row—////////—then about the same again, then three. The killer had dipped his or her finger into Ginger's blood and written some kind of number!

# Chapter Four

## *TV and Gore*

Every station in town had a camera at the funeral. The beauty of Ginger Louie and the macabre nature of her death were too much for the local press to pass up. The fact that Dave Mason was the son of a Brentwood surgeon and had gone to a local prep school just added to the frenzy. "Preppie chops model . . . cult drawings, drugs at scene."

Lujack watched the picture of Liz and Tommy pushing their way to their limousine. Ginger's father, the infamous Ray Louie, had missed another plane. It was just as well. Tommy would have killed him.

Debbi Arnold, the blond girl-next-door crime reporter from Channel 7, stuck a microphone in Tommy's face: "Do you think the police have the right man?"

Tommy pushed the mike away, and the shot was cut before Tommy's response was heard. Tommy had told the reporter what to do with her microphone. She had pretended to be offended.

"I never liked that bitch," Tommy said, looking up at the screen, after serving Lujack an iced coffee.

He and Tommy had come back to the Chin Up after the funeral. Death was the most important event in both the Taoist and Buddhist religions. It was a time for sons and grandsons to show their affection and respect. When a daughter died, a beautiful young daughter like Ginger, the Chinese traditions seemed inappropriate. By coming back to the Chin Up, Tommy was honoring an old American tradition: when in grief, throw yourself into your work.

"How's Liz?"

"Jackie's with her. Liz is a very strong woman."

"It's a shame Ginger and Liz weren't getting along."

"I didn't tell you. They had lunch the day before Ginger was killed. Ginger apologized to her mother for causing such dishonor. She said she was thinking of moving back home. Said she was off drugs and wanted to prove to her mother that she'd grown up."

"No, you didn't tell me," Lujack said, wondering if it were true. It wouldn't be the first time a grieving parent had imagined reconciliation.

"You don't believe it?" Tommy asked, looking at him.

"Do you?"

"Maybe," he said, busying himself behind the bar. It was baseball season, and the Good Book was pretty quiet. Most of the players liked to bet football or even basketball ahead of baseball. Tommy pulled a glass out of the sudsy water and asked the sixty-four-thousand-dollar question: "Do you believe Dave Mason killed her?"

"Do you really want to know?"

Tommy hesitated. "Yes. She was part of my family. Her father has no honor. It is my duty to see that her soul is resting comfortably."

"You think that by nailing her killer, her soul will rest more comfortably?"

"It is very important for the soul to be respected. If Ginger's murderer walks free, the evil spirits will haunt all the Chins."

Lujack had known Tommy for over ten years but had never heard him speak with such deep feeling about Chinese tradition. Tommy was the head of the Chin family. He took his duties very seriously, but this was something else.

"I don't think Mason killed her, Tommy."

"Then we must find out who did."

"It's not going to be easy. The police are happy with Mason. If he didn't do it, they'll want to know who did."

"What do you think?"

"I think whoever could cut off a girl's head and drive it four miles across town is more than strange and maybe very smart."

"Very smart? Why?"

"First, he created two crime scenes. The crime lab doesn't know if it's coming or going. Milch put Ginger in one of those plastic chambers full of super glue fumes to try and get a print. So far all he's got is a headache. I don't think he even knows where it happened."

Tommy didn't react, so Lujack continued: "Second, all the cult crap on the walls brings out every kook and psychic in town. Finally, by involving a drug dealer like Mason you raise the possibility that if he didn't do it his enemies did."

Tommy scratched his head. He pulled out a pack of cigarettes then put them back in his pocket. Tommy hadn't smoked in years, which showed how out-of-sorts he was. "But somebody must have seen whoever it was leave the man's apartment."

"That street's very secluded. The light is horrible. People went in and out of Mason's place all the time picking up drugs. That part of the Glen is a little like Chinatown—nobody sees nothing."

"So it could have been anybody?"

"Not anybody, Tommy."

"Where do we start?"

"What do you mean, we?" Lujack smiled.

"I can't do it alone, Jimmy. I need your help," Tommy said gravely. It wasn't easy for him to ask.

"Who's going to take care of the business?"

"Susie can handle things during baseball season," Tommy said of the Good Book's one-woman phone bank, Susie Katz.

"So what are we waiting for?" Lujack said.

"Where are we going?"

"To see a man about a yacht."

Marina Shores was a monument to opulence. Even by LA standards the place was gaudy. A cluster of glass condominiums, reputedly valued at a half-million a pop, located on the Marina del Rey harbor, each with its own berth and two-car garage for those who needed their cars and yachts in one place. Lujack gave his name to the uniformed gate attendant and drove past the swimming pool and the putting greens to the administration building.

"This place reminds me of a hotel," Tommy said as they entered the airy lobby.

"Except that here you can't rent the room, you have to buy it."

There was a sunken bar to their left and beyond that a dining room overlooking the water where meals were served to members and their guests. The latter included Lujack and Tommy, who had wangled an invitation out of Mark Lyman. Lyman was an old customer of the Good Book and during football season put tens of thousands of dollars' worth of bets through Lujack and Tommy. Of course, they knew he was making the bets for various Shores residents with a small commission for himself.

Lujack and Tommy stopped to study a model of the Shores. It seemed the Shores was in the midst of expansion. Four new condo towers were being constructed, and you too could get in on the ground floor of LA's hottest development for a cool seven hundred and fifty g's . . . for a two-bedroom condo.

"Do you get a bathroom?" Tommy asked, looking at the model, a collection of miniature glass buildings on a green and blue backdrop. Lujack noticed that the toy cars in the model were Rollses and Mercedeses.

"Yeah, a tiny little toilet," Lujack answered.

"I promise you, Tommy, the toilets are full-size and they flush on command," came a self-assured voice behind them.

They turned and faced Mark Lyman. As usual, Lyman was the picture of Southern California cool. Sandy hair, great tan, purple polo shirt, vanilla slacks, no socks inside his monogrammed loafers. Lyman was probably in his mid-forties but affected a much younger image. Only the fine lines around his eyes and the hardness of his look told a deeper history. A history that Lujack knew stretched from the Trafficante mob in Miami to the political and financial movers and shakers of the Bohemian Grove. One time or another, most of America's heavyweights ended up spending a night at the Shores.

"I was sorry to hear about your niece, Tommy," he said seriously, showing his usual flair for diplomacy. "Ginger was a special girl. So beautiful."

Tommy mumbled something Lujack took for agreement.

"Actually, Mark, that's why we're here. About Ginger."

"I didn't think it was to collect on the Dodgers. My players have been pretty hot lately. They love Orel."

Lujack smiled painfully. Lyman and his clients had been on a mild hot streak to the tune of seven or eight thousand dollars. By arrangement Lyman took care of his customers until the amount reached twenty thousand dollars owed or due.

"Come on out on the deck, we can talk there."

Lujack and Tommy followed Lyman out through the restaurant to the outside bar which was a huge deck built out between two of the docks. It was a languorous, warm evening, and the combination of the lilting, pale water of the harbor, the smell of the ocean, and the luxury of the complex itself made Marina Shores hard to resist.

Lyman guided them to a table right above the water, stopping to chitchat with a table of regulars—all men, Lujack noticed—back on shore after a hard day of sailing or fishing or whatever it was people did out on the water.

A gorgeous cocktail waitress wearing a loosely tied halter top and very short white shorts came to take their orders at the moment they were seated.

"Good evening, Mr. Lyman," said the waitress, who didn't look more than three or four days over twenty-one.

"Hi, Denise. Do you like the new uniforms?"

"I love 'em," Denise said with a sexy turn, not oblivious to Lyman's two friends.

"I'll take a scotch and water," Tommy ordered gruffly, the sight of Denise adding to his depressed mood. Lujack hadn't been sure bringing Tommy was a good idea. Now he knew it wasn't.

"Make that two," Lujack seconded.

"Perrier and lime, Mr. Lyman?" she asked intimately.

"Thank you, Denise." Lyman smiled. Lujack knew the smile. Unfortunately, so did Tommy.

"I told the police everything I know. They seem convinced that they have the killer," Lyman said, anticipating the reason for their visit.

"The police always think they have the right man," Lujack said smoothly.

"You should know, eh, Jimmy?" Lyman asked with a twinkle.

"When was the last time my niece came here?" Tommy asked abruptly.

"I told the police that I hadn't seen Ginger since she came back from the Betty Ford Center. I was so proud of her doing what she did. Not many girls have that kind of strength."

"Maybe she wouldn't have had to be so strong if she'd stayed with her family instead of coming here every night for parties," Tommy said.

"You don't really believe anyone *here* got Ginger mixed up with drugs," Lyman said, trying his damnedest to act offended.

"Perish the thought," Tommy said, watching a large white motor yacht pull up to the mooring. Two swarthy crew members in pristine white uniforms secured the lines.

"That's some boat," Lujack deadpanned.

"The *Southern Cross,* she belongs to Lawrence Brownell. The most beautiful yacht in Southern California. She's built by a European group, Feadship."

"Brownell Industries, the defense contractor?" Lujack queried.

"That's the man. He's had a place here for about a

year. Men like Brownell—it's more convenient to have a condo and mooring here than it is to join a yacht club."

"With a boat like that, why do you need a condominium?"

"Taxes, a place for the crew to stay while you're in port, a hideaway from the hideaway." Lyman smiled.

A white-haired man came out of the rear cabin onto the fantail. The man was heavily jowled, not tall, certainly not handsome, but with an unmistakable manner, an aura of power and money, an aura Lujack had long ago recognized as attractive to women. He also recognized the man as Lawrence H. Brownell.

A second man emerged from the cabin. He was shorter than his host, more muscular, his black hair graying at the temples. He moved with a compact, formal abruptness as he followed Brownell out to the open rear deck for a look at the softly lit harbor.

"I must say, Mark, you have a very impressive clientele indeed," Lujack said. "Two of the richest men on the Pacific Rim."

Tommy made a growling noise. Like most Chinese he had no love for the Japanese, especially Japanese of the stature of Kazuo Yoshida, president of the Pacific National Bank.

"I'm impressed, Jimmy. Most people wouldn't recognize Mr. Yoshida, and I must admit that's the way he likes it."

"It's not every day I get to see one billionaire, much less two," Lujack said, watching the two men chatting on the fantail. "What do you think men like that talk about?"

"Japanese politics, U.S. politics? The next takeover target?" Lyman suggested.

"Where's the next party?" Lujack said as a stunning

redhead in a stunning bikini walked out to join the men. She seemed at ease in their company. She also couldn't have been more than twenty.

"Don't tell me. That's Yoshida's granddaughter," Tommy said.

"Come on, Tommy, give the guy a break. He works hard. He runs the biggest bank in the state."

"That's not all he runs," Tommy said blackly.

"So tell us more about Ginger," Lujack interjected. "We hear she used to come to your parties. We want to know if there was anyone special in the last few months, before she went to Betty Ford's . . . or after."

"I told you I hadn't seen Ginger since she came back."

"But you talked to her?"

"Did I?"

"You said she was clean. On the straight and narrow. You must have talked to her."

"That's right, I did," he admitted. "She called me. It was probably a couple of days after she got out."

"But you didn't tell her about any parties you were having? Or about any of your clients asking after her?"

"What are you getting at, Tommy? You think I run a pimp service here?"

"He's not saying that," Lujack said smoothly. "We just want to know if Ginger had any particular friends."

Lyman took a second. Lujack decided the developer-promoter wasn't trying to remember, he was remembering who to forget.

"Ginger was a very outgoing girl. She had a lot of friends here. I hope you don't think anyone from the Shores is involved with her death."

"How did Ginger first get to know about the

Shores? Do you go through magazines and call up the models you like?" Lujack countered, using the old ploy of answering a question with a question.

"That's not a bad idea," Lyman said easily. "Actually I met Ginger through Chase Field. Chase was one of the original owners here and still likes his models to socialize at the Shores. He thinks it gives them sophistication."

"How convenient for both of you," Tommy said tartly.

Denise returned with the drinks before Lyman could be offended again. It was a definite mistake to bring Tommy along. He had many excellent qualities but tact wasn't one of them.

"Mark tells me the parties here can get pretty outrageous," Lujack said to the waitress.

"Sometimes I think I'm working in a big fraternity." She laughed. "There's a party every night."

"A very wealthy fraternity," Lyman added for Denise's benefit.

"Who organizes these bashes?"

"Nobody really," Denise volunteered. "They usually just start in the lounge and end up in someone's condo."

"For a little Scrabble or Password?"

"More like scramble and pass out." She giggled.

"That will be all, Denise," Lyman said quietly.

"Yes, Mr. Lyman," Denise said, moving off toward a table of yuppie businessmen who had recently arrived. Lujack also noticed the arrival of two very attractive girls at the deck bar.

"You're right, Mark. It does seem sophisticated around here. No wonder. I don't see too many wives on the premises."

"Come on, Jimmy. We have a lot of couples living

here. It's just that many of the condos are owned by corporations who use the place like a hotel or by very wealthy men who like to be near the water. Most wives hate the water."

"You've done polling on the question?"

"Informally," Lyman said, tiring of Lujack's humor.

"Let's get out of here, Jimmy," Tommy said before Lujack had even raised his glass. "Mark isn't going to be of any help."

"Is that true, Mark?" Lujack asked, taking a quick gulp of his scotch. "You're not going to be any help?"

"I told you the same thing I told the police. Ginger came to our parties. She used to have fun here. It's nice for a girl in a high-pressure job like hers to get away and enjoy herself once in a while."

"Nice for somebody," Tommy said.

"Tommy, I know how you feel, man. But you have to believe me. No one here would ever hurt Ginger."

"All we want is a name. Better you give it to us than we start asking around. We wouldn't want to embarrass anyone," Lujack said.

Lyman looked out at the water. Another girl had joined the Messrs. Brownell and Yoshida on the fantail. They were sipping cool drinks and looking at the sunset.

"If I give you the name you can't say you heard it from me."

"Our lips are sealed."

"Dolph Killian."

"Dolph Killian? The weapons analyst? Does a lot of consulting for the Senate Armed Services Committee?"

"There's no reason to drag the Senate into this," Lyman said a little too quickly.

Tommy and Lujack exchanged looks. A little flour had just been added to the plot.

"I hope Killian doesn't have a yacht named *Monkey Business.*"

"I'm serious, Jimmy. We've never had a hint of scandal in this place. I want to be helpful but I want you to be discreet."

Tommy grunted and looked at his watch. "I'd better check in with Susie. The Dodger game starts in fifteen minutes. Is there a phone around here?"

"Sure, Tommy. Just go back the way you came. There's a bank of phones against the far wall."

Tommy excused himself. Lyman gave Lujack a conspiratorial smile. "Poor guy. It must be hard having a family member taken like that."

"You mean getting her head cut off and driven across town?"

"Hey, Jimmy, I didn't want to say anything in front of Tommy, but that niece of his was no saint. She liked to party. China Doll, that's what we called her. Old Dolph said she goddamn near broke it more than once."

"Old Dolph, he was pretty fond of Ginger?"

Lyman laughed.

"Get real, Jimmy. Dolph is a happily married man. A war hero. A millionaire. President of the Del Obispo Country Club."

"Jack Kennedy was president of more than that, and don't think his love life didn't make a lot of people uncomfortable."

"Girls like Ginger don't make men like Dolph uncomfortable. No way. Very few people make men like Dolph uncomfortable."

"Is that a warning?"

"Let's just say you better hope that it was the drug dealer that cut Ginger down to size."

"You didn't like Ginger much, did you?"

"Not much, no."

A peal of laughter rang out from the *Southern Cross.* The redhead was laughing at one of Mr. Brownell's jokes. Those billionaires were a riot.

## Chapter Five

### *Still Live at Five*

Dave Mason was formally charged with Ginger Louie's murder eight days after her torso was found in his bed. The only question asked by the local TV crime reporters was why it took so long to charge him. Deputy DA Ross Toomey answered their questions with more humility than usual. A sure sign to Lujack that Toomey himself wasn't totally convinced of the validity of the case he had. Toomey didn't back off from TV reporters or TV cameras unless he thought they were booby-trapped. Kyle Thurgood answered most of the tough questions concerning the case.

After watching the news Lujack took a drive to the Nightwatch, a made-to-order cop hangout in Eagle Rock. If you ever needed a homicide detective in LA after six P.M., the Nightwatch was the place to go. The bartender, Slats McGrath, was a New Jersey native and former LA beat cop who, for some strange reason, never could get it through his thick skull that he'd left Newark. After shaking down half the merchants on his first two beats, McGrath couldn't understand why his partners and watch commander testified against him in his disciplinary hearing.

"I was trying to set up a little Christmas Club like my uncle had going back at the Ironbound. You'd think from the way these pussies reacted I was hitting them up for contributions," he once complained to Lujack.

It was generally agreed that Bob was better off as a bartender where the accepted quid pro quo of free drinks for big tips was better appreciated by his fellow officers.

"You owe me five hundred bucks, Lujack," McGrath bellowed as Lujack walked through the door. Lujack saw Thurgood and three other detectives standing at the far end of the bar.

"Thanks for the advertisement, Slats," Lujack said, "but I don't need it right now."

McGrath followed Lujack's gaze to the end of the bar. One of the detectives with Thurgood was LA's top vice detective, Captain Norm Pelitier. Stormin' Norman was one of the LAPD Christian mafia, a group of born-again believers who had slowly but surely worked their way up the ladder of bureaucratic success. What a straight shooter like Pelitier was doing at the Nightwatch Lujack couldn't figure.

"Don't worry about Ol' Norm, he found out last week he didn't pass the deputy chief's test, been drowning his sorrows ever since," McGrath explained.

"That's what happens when those believers get to the essay questions," Lujack said. "True and false, multiple choice, they're okay. But never give a zealot a blank page."

McGrath put a scotch and water in front of Lujack. Lujack slid five one-hundred-dollar bills across the bar. McGrath picked up the money and kissed it.

"Love those Mets," he cooed.

"Only reason you won the goddamn bet was because of a balk. You should be lovin' the umps."

"Drinks on the house, buddy," Slats said graciously.

"I'll thank the owner when I see him."

"Fuck you, Lujack," the bartender said, pocketing his money and moving to another customer.

Lujack was halfway through his scotch when Kyle Thurgood motioned him to join him at the other end of the bar. Lujack wasn't dying to reminisce with Norm Pelitier, but he did want to talk to Kyle.

"Well, if it isn't?" Pelitier said with a pronounced slur as Lujack approached. McGrath had been right, Norm was bombed.

"Long time no see, Norm."

"My favorite bookie," Norm said, putting his arm around Lujack and facing the two young robbery-homicide detectives with Thurgood. "This guy used to work for me. Then he went into business for himself. Didn't ya, Lujack?"

"Anything you say, Norm."

"I heard you made over three hundred grand in one game last year, Lujack. That's not bad for a scum-sucking crook."

"Take it easy, Norm. Lujack's here to drink, not fight," Thurgood said evenly. "Aren't ya, Lujack?"

"Anything you say, Kyle."

"Always the smart mouth. Everybody in town knows he's garbage, but we can't touch him. What is it, Lujack? You got something on the chief? Or is it the mayor? You take the mayor's action?"

"Give it a rest, Norm," Thurgood said with a little more edge.

"Hey, Lujack. We picked up a buddy of yours yesterday. Vinnie Paxton. We had a tap on the creep a week. He must not know the people you do. When we broke in, Vinnie was taking a shit. One of our guys puts a gun to his head and says he's under arrest. You know what Vinnie asks? Is it all right to wipe? When I get you, Lujack, you ain't gonna have time."

"It's your upholstery, Norm," Lujack said calmly.

"Twenty-two years I work for these bastards. Never miss a shift and what do I get for it? Politics."

"I know what you mean, Norm. Politics, secular humanism, they get you every time."

Norm's swing came from the bar, and by the time the forty-five-year-old teetotaler advocate got his fist anywhere near Lujack's jaw, three cops had Norm's arm.

"Why don't you boys give Norm a ride home?" Thurgood suggested.

"Let me go, assholes. I want that creep. Remember who's in charge!"

The two detectives escorted the captain out the door. McGrath watched the proceedings without regret.

"Old Norm seems to be slipping."

"Norm's an asshole. But he's proof of one thing," Thurgood said.

"What's that?" Lujack asked.

"You can be just as big an asshole drunk as when you're sober."

"Amen."

Thurgood motioned McGrath for a refill.

"Put 'em on my tab, Slats," Lujack said. McGrath grumbled and brought two more drinks.

"Something tells me you didn't drive out here to see Norm," Thurgood said, grabbing his drink.

"Something tells no lies. I saw you on the five o'clock news."

"I'd love to fuck that Debbi Arnold. Every time she

crossed her legs during the briefing my Johnson did pushups off the lectern."

"I guess Barney must have come up with something for you to charge Mason."

"You know Barney came up with zilch. There wasn't a latent print on either piece of the girl. The blood was all hers."

"What about the ax?"

"The deadliest weapons we found in Mason's place were the razor blades he used to lay out his lines. One of the blades we found under Mason's couch. It had blood on it . . . Ginger Louie's blood."

"You don't think Mason spent the night of the murder cutting off Ginger's head with a one-inch razor, then drove across town and dumped her head with a roommate?"

"Can you see it?" Thurgood smiled, making little chopping motions with his hand.

"You heard what Milch said about the cut. One chop. The blood was on the walls, not the bed. Not on either bed."

"Upon reflection Barney's changed his opinion."

"Upon whose reflection? The mayor? Chief Bane?"

"What's it to you, Lujack? The girl's dead. The kid's a loser."

"Since when did becoming a drug dealer also make you into a murderer?"

"Since the polls started telling politicians people had stopped making the distinction. Not to mention the fact that he was the last person seen with the victim. Not to mention the fact that he said he gave Ginger his car, but we found the keys in his pocket. Now, do you want to drink or fight?"

"Neither. I want to find Ginger's murderer."

"You think maybe the guy's drinking in the Nightwatch tonight?"

"I think maybe you don't have any leads and you're trying to make the kid roll over on someone, except you know he can't because he doesn't know who killed Ginger any more than you do."

Thurgood finished his drink.

"First, I've got to listen to the chief, then I have to suck spit with the so-called media. I come in here to relax and what do I get? A mean, drunk Christian and a righteous bookie."

Lujack laughed and figured maybe Thurgood had a point.

"McGrath, take good care of this man, he's had a long day." Lujack slid off the bar stool and walked out.

"Lujack," the lieutenant called after him, "try the girl. Molly. She won't talk to me, but then I'm not as good-looking as you are."

"You think she knows something?"

"Maybe not about the murder, but she knows something about Ginger. There was a speck of dried semen on Ginger's pubic hair. Barney couldn't tell how old it was. But he got a DNA readout, it wasn't Mason's."

"What's that have to do with Molly?"

"I have a sixteen-year-old daughter. She talks to her friends. She never talks to me or my wife. But all night, every night, she talks to her friends."

"Thanks, Kyle."

Lujack found himself on Melrose Boulevard going west to talk with Ginger's best friend. As usual, Kyle Thurgood had surprised him. Lujack was glad he didn't have to make book on the homicide detective's next move. Maybe that's why Thurgood was the department's best detective. He was always two steps ahead of the good guys as well as the bad guys.

The Zodiac was not the newest or the hippest of

LA's thousand-some nightclubs, but Lujack had it from a trendy source that the Zodiac was coming into its own. Now that Princess Stephanie had left Vertigo and the Stock Exchange had fallen on hard times, it seemed the place to be for the people who wanted to be there was the Zodiac.

The sign was barely visible. A purple neon horoscope on a black backdrop. Lujack's trendy friend, a record executive who loved young LA girls as much as he did the New York Mets, had given Lujack the address or he would have missed it . . . except for the line of people waiting to get in. Over the years, Lujack had heard many stories about LA's club scene, but he'd never understood the allure of driving across town to pay outrageous cover charges to dance the night away in a dark room full of strange, sweaty people where the drinks were either too weak or too expensive and usually both. Even when he'd been working Hollywood vice and didn't have to pay the cover charge or the drink tab, he hadn't liked the clubs.

After spending fifteen minutes looking for a parking place, Lujack was in no mood to wait in line. Walking past every make of punk in Southern California, from the cover boys and girls of *Surf Nazi Living* to the Calvin Kleined mothers and daughters of Rodeo Drive, Lujack found himself face to face with a large black man standing in front of the door. It wasn't the man's six-foot-five, 275-pound frame that bothered Lujack but his slow, dangerous eyes. The guy reminded him of Deacon Jones just before the opposition quarterback lost consciousness.

"My name's Lujack. I'm here to see Molly."

"My name is Aristotle and I'm here to see you wait in line."

"Would it help if I told you Freddie Nunn recommended me?" Lujack said, dropping the record producer's name.

"Not much."

"How about if I told you I know karate?"

"Less."

Lujack reluctantly reached in his pocket. "How about Grover Cleveland?"

"How about Ben Franklin?"

Lujack peeled off another fifty, swearing to himself that Tommy Chin's blood lust had gotten out of hand.

"Have a good time now, Lujack," Aristotle said, opening the door with a flourish and pocketing a hundred dollars of Lujack's money.

He quickly realized that getting into the Zodiac was only half the battle. Lujack followed a narrow, maze-like dark hallway in the direction of the music. On the walls were various murals of the twelve signs of the Zodiac. Lujack wondered if there was any added significance to the macabre marking above and below the sign.

The club opened into a bar which was packed with humanity. To the right, back toward the street, was a large area for dancing. A nameless punk band was playing a nameless punk song on the stage. The room's only saving grace was its bad acoustics. He could actually hear himself think.

"What's your sign?" a tall brunette asked as he elbowed his way up to the bar. She was wearing a black T-shirt that read, "I Was with Prince in Helsinki." On second look Lujack saw it was a dress. A very short dress.

"You're not serious."

"What do you mean?"

"I mean you're not serious. About my sign."

"Everyone should be serious about their sign, even if it's Cancer."

"How did you know I was a Cancer?"

The brunette laughed. "I like Cancers. My name's Janis. I'm a model."

Lujack didn't have to be told.

"My name's Lujack. I'm a . . ."

Lujack remembered why he didn't like meeting people. Even beautiful twenty-year-old girls, especially beautiful twenty-year-old girls.

"Bookie."

Lujack felt someone come up behind him. He turned and saw an Armani shoulder that belonged to Chase Field, president and founder of the Chase Field Agency. Chase was in his early forties, older than Lujack, but doing everything he could to look twenty-nine, from the capped teeth to the Body by Jake. The only problem was, no matter how hip the cut of the coat and how white the caps, Chase Field still had the hungry eyes of the Jewish boy who grew up in the alleys of Tangier and sold his first wolf clock before he was ten.

"What are you doing here, Chase? A little talent scouting?"

"Most of the talent here has already been signed. Right, Janis?" Field said with a lecherous smile. Chase Field's reputation with his models was legendary. Blondes were supposed to be his specialty.

"What's a bookie, Chase?" Janis asked.

"A guy who lays odds, not broads," Fields said, pleased with his conceit.

"Don't tell me, Chase. You're channeling with Ogden Nash." Lujack smiled halfheartedly.

"Oh, can you channel?" Janis wanted to know.

"Only with my remote control button, doll."

"What brings you down in this neighborhood? I thought you spent most of your nights out at the Riviera hustling the BMW crowd."

"If I'm too old for this place, what's that make you, Chase?"

"You're only as old as you feel, Lujack. And I've never felt better."

"I'll be sure and tell Tommy."

"Horrible. What happened to his niece," Field said as if he'd been waiting for the right time. "Ginger was a special girl."

"Ginger was one of my best friends," Janis said solemnly.

Lujack remembered Ginger talking about Molly and Janis, her two friends who got just as crazy as she did but who didn't get dead.

"You must know Molly Blair."

"She's meeting me here tonight."

"I thought she worked here."

"Molly's back with the agency," Field said. "We've given her a new look."

"What do you mean, a new look?"

"I mean that," Chase said, nodding toward the mouth of the maze.

Lujack didn't recognize her. The transformation was complete. He remembered her the night of Ginger's murder. The frightened girl who thought he'd killed her best friend. The girl with the cadaverous complexion of a punk rocker who'd traded her golden tan and boyfriend's Corvette for white power. Now Lujack was seeing a third Molly. A very chic, very sophisticated Molly with her blond hair piled on her head and her long, lithe body wrapped in a black, shoulderless Versace tunic.

"It came to me last week. I was trying to find the

right girl for the *Vanity* spread on Grace. You know, 'Grace Is Alive'? 'Did Rainier Kill Her for Diana'? It's the cover of the year. Then I looked at Molly."

"She looks awesome. Like a real rich bitch," Janis said, paying her friend the ultimate compliment.

Molly made her way over to where they were standing. She didn't recognize Lujack until it was too late.

"Hi, Molly."

"What are you doing here?"

"I came by to see you."

"I've told the cops everything I know."

"What's going on, Lujack? They got the bastard who did it," Field protested. "The girl's been through hell."

"Ginger went through hell, Chase. Not Molly."

"What do you want to know?" Molly asked. Lujack liked the girl for asking.

"Do you mind if we talk in private?"

"We can go in Henry's office," Molly said, motioning Lujack toward the end of the bar.

"Henry's office sounds fine."

Molly moved past him. He could smell her perfume. She rubbed her breast gently against Field as she passed him. Lujack wondered if Field had slept with her. He wondered what Molly had had to do to make Field put out the kind of money her new look so obviously cost.

"You don't have to say anything to him, Molly. Mr. Lujack is no longer with the police department. Not by a long shot."

"It's all right, Chase, I can take care of myself."

Field wasn't so sure and grabbed Lujack's arm as he went by.

"What are you doing, Jimmy? I have a right to know. Ginger was one of my girls."

"You'll be the first to know, Chase, when I figure it out myself."

Molly knocked twice. An Oriental man opened the door. He was wearing a buttoned-down white shirt and western-style string tie. Lujack made a mental note to try and find the three string ties his grandfather had left him. Maybe he could sell them to a chic Melrose store and make a fortune.

"Henry, can I use your office for a minute?" Molly asked.

Henry looked at Lujack and grunted. "What for? You not work here now."

"We want to talk . . . in private."

Henry tapped his nose and smiled. He thought he knew what Molly had in mind. Molly encouraged that thought. One thing you could always count on with Orientals, they accepted most vices, especially round eyes' vices. Lujack wasn't sure, but judging from Henry's broad features and large frame, almost six feet, he thought Henry was Korean. Koreans, even more than Japanese and Chinese, knew all about vice. For centuries they had been providing their more powerful neighbors with everything from prostitutes to murderers.

Henry smiled again as he let Lujack and Molly into the little office. It was then Lujack noticed that the tip of the little finger on Henry's left hand was missing. Henry noticed Lujack's noticing. The Korean was still smiling but not in a joking manner. No ex-LAPD vice cop had to be told about the custom of *yubitsume* by which members of the Yakuza (Japanese organized crime) severed the top joint of their little fingers in contrition for certain violations of their criminal code of honor. The severed finger was then presented to the *oyubun* (godfather). If he accepted the digit, the transgressor was forgiven. Lujack had heard stories about the Yakuza's growing influence in Koreatown but was surprised to see one of its members managing a chic LA nightclub.

"What do you know about Henry?" Lujack asked after the Korean had left them alone.

"I think he's Japanese or Korean. His last name is Park."

"That's Korean."

"At least he speaks English. The one before couldn't."

"Which one before?"

"Micky Kim."

"This Micky, was he also missing the end of his little finger?"

"Yeah, he was. One of the bartenders said it meant they were in the Mafia."

"I thought Mark Lyman owned this place."

"He does, but I think he has partners."

"These partners, they wouldn't happen to be of the Oriental persuasion, would they?"

"I never met them. Ginger told me . . ."

"Ginger told you what?" Lujack said, trying to be patient.

"Ginger told me she met this nice Oriental man at one of Mark's parties who told her he owned the Zodiac. He told her nobody was supposed to know."

"Do you remember if Ginger told you a name?"

Molly bit her lip. She looked fifteen. "I don't think she did. You know how they all sound alike," she said apologetically. "Is that what you wanted to talk to me about?"

"No. Not exactly."

Molly reached into her bag and pulled out a plastic cigarette lighter. Lujack politely took the lighter and waited for Molly to pull out a cigarette. Instead she laughed.

"What's so funny?"

"I don't smoke," she said. Taking the lighter out of his hand, she began to twist the bottom which came off. She held up a vial full of white powder. "I snort."

"Never seen that one before."

Molly put some of the cocaine on the back of her hand and snorted it up her nostril.

"Want some?"

"You know that can stunt your growth."

"I'm big enough."

"Nobody's big enough."

Molly put the false bottom back in the lighter. "You didn't come all the way down here to lecture me, did you?"

"I came down here to ask you some questions. About Ginger. Lieutenant Thurgood tells me you weren't all that forthcoming."

"He didn't want to talk to me. He wanted me to help convict Dave."

"By not telling the police anything, you're doing a pretty good job of exactly that."

"Ginger was my best friend. Dave was in love with her. He'd do anything for her," she said forcefully. Lujack didn't know if she cared or if it was the coke kicking in but he had a hunch.

"Did she love him?"

"No. Not in the way he wanted."

"So why couldn't he have done it?"

"I just told you because he loved her," the girl insisted. "No one who loved a person could ever . . ." she shuddered.

Lujack didn't think she was acting, but the more he heard the less he liked about Ginger Louie's life and death.

"Who did she love in that way, Molly?"

"How should I know? I was working that night,

remember? She came in with Dave. I don't know who she was with before or who she was with after."

Lujack nodded. "I thought you wanted to help Mason."

"I do."

"The police lab found a trace of semen on Ginger's pubic hair. If they could match it with Mason's gene print, they would have."

Lujack waited for Molly to figure it out.

"That afternoon she got dressed up. She said she was meeting someone. When I asked her if I knew him she said she couldn't tell me."

"Had she ever not told you about anyone before?"

"Ginger always liked to be mysterious. She said it was in her inscrutable nature. But I usually found out who she was seeing, even if I had to read it in the *Enquirer.*"

"Maybe this guy was famous. Did she date movie types?"

"Ginger's a model. She dated lots of famous guys. This is LA, you know."

"What about Dave Mason? He told me he knew Mick Jagger and Chevy Chase."

Molly laughed. "Dave is a drug dealer. He's turned on half the town, but he doesn't know anybody."

"Did you ever hear Ginger mention the name Dolph Killian?"

Molly started slightly. There was more than a hint of uneasiness underneath her cool. "Ginger used to go out with him. But not after she went to Betty's."

"Do you know why Ginger stopped seeing him?"

"Yeah, I know why. He was an agro creep."

"Meaning?"

"Meaning he used to like to get rough. One night Ginger came home with blood all over her. She said

Killian got drunk and started swearing at her, calling her a gook, hitting her."

"Did you tell the cops about this?"

Molly shook her head. Lujack felt he might finally be getting somewhere. Although it wasn't a place he wanted to go.

"How long ago was this? It's important."

"Three, four months ago. It was just after I started here. I was taking off my makeup. Ginger came into my room. She bled all over the carpet."

Molly took out her lighter. The memory of Ginger bleeding on the carpet combined with her last memory of Ginger's head propped up on a pillow called for another toot. Lujack couldn't stand to see such a beautiful girl shove white poison up her nose.

"You know, that stuff ages you worse than the sun."

She stopped unscrewing the cap.

"It's true. A doctor I know, plastic surgeon, told me the alkaline in the cocaine takes the natural moisture out of the skin. Keep doing that and pretty soon you can stop modeling perfume ads and start doing dog food commercials."

Molly screwed the cap back on the bottle. Lujack realized he might be onto something. Nancy and Betty had it all wrong. "Just say no" would never work. "Just say old," there's an idea.

"If Mason is innocent, I'll get him out."

"Sure you will, Lujack," Molly said, opening Henry's door, letting in the din of the Zodiac's iniquity.

# Chapter Six

## *Pick up Sticks*

Mu shu pork dripped between Lujack's wooden utensils. He was determined to make Tommy pick up his tab with Aristotle, but after his third helping of pork he began to wonder if Tommy didn't have a hidden agenda.

"My stomach feels like the inside of the *Hindenburg* about to dock on the Jersey shore."

"Even Germans know when to stop eating."

"You promised you'd stop using MSG."

"There's no MSG. Ask Wing Fu."

Lujack was in no mood to deal with Wing. The last time he had accused Wing of a culinary transgression, the old Chinaman had thrown a vegetable knife at him. Luckily, Wing could chop a lot better than he could throw.

"Forget it," Lujack said, laying his chop sticks down in surrender. "What's happening with the Dodgers?"

"They're winning four to zip in the fifth. Gibson hit another home run."

"Who needs Guererro?"

"We do. Everybody's betting Hershiser. We didn't get one play on the Cards."

"I hate baseball," Lujack said.

"You hate everything when you're hung over."

"I'm not hung over. I told you, I stopped drinking."

"When? This morning?"

"No, last night . . . about eleven-thirty."

Tommy didn't laugh.

"I had a little talk with Molly Blair last night after I saw Kyle."

"And?"

"Did you know the place she and Ginger used to hang out is run by some Korean hoods?"

"Yakuza?"

"I didn't ask the guy if he used to be a butcher, but he was missing the tip of his little finger."

Tommy frowned. Lujack knew the only Oriental criminals Tommy approved of were his cousins and his associates in the Hong Kong triads.

"Koreatown is bigger now than Chinatown and Japantown combined. Lots of room for Yakuza to grow."

"It's hard to figure Mark Lyman in business with the Yakuza. Molly told me Ginger may have met some of his partners."

"You think there's a connection?"

"Can't say. Molly also told me Dolph Killian roughed up Ginger a few months back."

Tommy frowned again. "Do the police know?"

"The less the police know about people like Dolph Killian, the longer they keep their jobs," Lujack said. "The cops are waiting for a break. For Mason to crack. Kyle doesn't think a guy can have a headless body lying in his bed without knowing something about it."

Tommy didn't respond to the gallows humor. "Let's go see Killian," he said abruptly.

"I'll go see Killian. You mind the store. Where's Jackie?" Lujack asked, suddenly noting that Tommy's wife wasn't at her usual position behind the cash register.

"Liz called this morning. She's been having trouble at work. Jackie went over to talk to her."

Tommy looked tired. Ginger's death had put a dark shadow over all the Chin family and Lujack was only now realizing the depth and power of its presence. In the very formal world of Chinese life and death, the living were at the mercy of the uneasy dead, and there was little easy about the way Ginger had died.

"Any word from Ray?"

"Ray Louie isn't fit to be a human being, much less a husband or father."

"Tell Liz not to worry. We'll find out what happened."

"The worst thing is that she really doesn't want to know."

"Yeah," Lujack said. He knew the feeling.

Tommy picked up the half-eaten plate of mu shu pork and carried it back to the kitchen.

"Tell Wing I loved it," Lujack yelled after him.

"Dolph Killian is the kind of guy who makes men like Richard Secord look patriotic and men like Gordon Liddy seem sane," Morris Breen said in his Beverly Hills barrister know-it-all voice. Breen had been Lujack's sometime lawyer and full-time client since the Good Book opened. "He was decommissioned from the Navy during the Carter presidency for his peripheral involvement in the sale of Navy jet fighters to the Korean Air Force. What the Koreans wanted with fighter planes designed for aircraft carriers when they don't have any aircraft carriers, I don't know. I assume Carter didn't either.

"But war heroes like Dolph always land on their feet. He set up a military think tank just in time for the Reagan-Bush shopping spree. If Ronald Reagan never met an arms deal he couldn't make, Dolph Killian never met a weapons system he couldn't defend, provided he was being given a big enough kickback by the defense contractor involved."

"You're telling me Killian is a crook?"

"I'm telling you Killian is a success story," Mo Breen said, and Lujack thought he could detect a note of warning in his voice.

"Why is it everyone in town is afraid of Dolph Killian?"

"Who's everyone?"

"Mark Lyman for one. A friend of Ginger Louie for another."

"I thought you were checking out Dolph as a customer."

"Dolph doesn't sound anything like a betting man."

"You didn't hear anything from me, Jimmy boy, not even the part about Dolph having friends in very high places, the kinda places you don't see from the pews."

"What's this pew crap, Mo, you're Jewish."

"Religion don't mean shit with guys like Dolph Killian, Jimmy."

"You mean the guy's with the CIA?" Lujack asked, starting to make sense of his unusually cryptic lawyer.

"I mean if you mess with Killian, you can get hit from almost anywhere."

Lujack mulled over his recent off-the-record conversation with the attorney as he approached the five-story glass headquarters of Global Resources in Hawthorne. Killian's company was one of many military-industrial consulting firms in the south bay area of Los Angeles. The companies sprouted up like so many stalagmites around the giant aerospace corporations—Rockwell, TRW, Northrup Hughes—that dominated the landscape between the 405 Freeway and the ocean. Lujack knew enough about the defense-consulting, think-tank business to know that, like all business, it was who you knew as much as what you knew. No one ever accused the Pentagon or the nation's defense contractors of being equal opportunity employers.

He parked the Mustang in the visitors' lot and walked past the wrought-iron globe that was perched in front of the building. Two F14 Tomcats were suspended in the air, one over the Pacific and one over the Atlantic. Lujack reminded himself to sleep safer tonight knowing Dolph Killian's sculpted jets were watching over him.

A man in his early thirties wearing a custom-made security uniform sat inside a large square enclosure in the lobby. Lujack knew the man had checked a metal-detecting monitor when he walked through the door.

"I left my Uzi in the trunk," Lujack cracked.

The man smiled but he wasn't happy. Lujack guessed he'd heard that one before. His chapped lips and stained teeth along with his cold gray eyes told Lujack this man was no stranger to long nights sleeping with AK-47's.

"Name's Lujack, I'm here to see Mr. Killian."

The man checked a list and put a laminated ID card on top of the Formica ledge. "Please pin that to your jacket pocket, Mr. Lujack. Mr. Killian's office is on the fifth floor."

"Sure you don't want my voice print?"

"That won't be necessary, sir," the man said, emphasizing the *sir* the way a career top sergeant would address a second lieutenant. Except that Lujack knew the kind of army this guy had served in didn't have such a structured chain of command.

The elevator doors opened and Lujack found himself facing a pretty blonde sitting at a high-tech desk. Everything about Global Resources reeked of technological advance. Behind the girl was a picture of the USS *Kennedy,* all seventy thousand tons of her. Sitting on her decks were enough Navy Tomcats to take over most countries in the world before dinner.

"Impressive, isn't she?" came a booming voice over Lujack's left shoulder.

Lujack turned and faced a man as large as himself, with a fleshy face and thinning brown hair. He put Killian's age at fifty, a hard fifty judging from the broken blood vessels that dotted his large nose. The suit was tailor-made, but Dolph Killian needed more than a two-thousand-dollar suit to look like Cary Grant.

"She should be—for the money she cost."

Killian's blue eyes did a quick take, judging Lujack's intent. "You're not one of those liberal assholes that think Gorbachev should be the godfather of their next child, are ya, Mr. Lujack?"

"I leave politics to the pros, Mr. Killian," Lujack said evenly.

Killian stuck out his meaty hand as a reward. Lujack took it. The former Navy pilot shook hands like a pit bull.

"That's good advice, Mr. Lujack, I wish more people followed it," Killian said, smiling. "Come on into my office."

Lujack followed Killian down the corridor through a pair of large wooden doors. The corner office was everything expected of a Los Angeles millionaire, from the view of the Pacific Ocean to a picture showing Killian shaking hands with the president.

Another picture showed Killian on the back of a boat, *Santana,* holding a fishing rod. Next to him was Senator Peter Rudlow, ranking member of the Armed Services Committee and evidently a close friend of Killian's.

"After you called I did some checking on you, Mr. Lujack," Killian said, sitting down behind his desk. Lujack took a chair opposite. He wondered what kind of plane was flying over Killian's desk. It looked like an artist's rendition of the new stealth bomber. What better way to convince customers that you had the right connections.

"It seems you have had a unique career. A college man who becomes a cop, a cop who becomes a bookie, a bookie who is a sometime private eye."

"You have good sources, Mr. Killian."

"So do you, Mr. Lujack. Not that many people knew I was a friend of Ginger Louie."

Lujack was even more impressed. He hadn't told Killian of the matter he wanted to discuss, only that it involved a mutual friend.

"Not even that many people at the Marina Shores?"

Lujack wasn't about to give up Mark Lyman, not that he owed Lyman anything. Lyman had never been a big depositor at the favor bank.

"Ginger is, was, the cousin of a friend of mine, Tommy Chin."

"The Chin Up is the best Chinese restaurant in Los Angeles . . . for the money."

"I'll be sure and tell Tommy."

"Ginger was a very beautiful girl. A perfect mixture of East and West. Skin like porcelain, as they used to say in the movies."

"I know, I introduced her to Chase Field," Lujack interjected before Killian started jacking off.

"She could have been a great model, another Iman or Paulina, except she didn't have any brains."

"Since when does it take brains to be a model?"

"If you knew her, Lujack, you knew what her problem was. She couldn't say no, to anything or anybody."

Lujack wondered if Killian had been jealous. Jealousy might make a man send his mistress to the guillotine.

"But it was all right that she said yes to you."

Again Killian sized him up. "I'm too old and too rich for lectures, Mr. Lujack. The only reason I'm talking to you is because people who I respect, respect you. But don't push your luck. Ginger Louie was a gorgeous girl, she was also great in bed, for a girl her age, but the bottom line is she lived like a whore and she died like a whore."

"Remind me not to invite you to deliver my eulogy, Mr. Killian."

"I call 'em like I see 'em. So far it's worked."

"Then you don't mind me asking you where you were the night Ginger was decapitated."

"You should read the papers, Lujack. The cops have Ginger's murderer in jail."

"So—you won't mind telling me where you were on the night of August sixth?"

Killian smiled. "I haven't seen Ginger since she went to the desert to clean up."

"But you did know she went out there."

"Hell, I offered to pay for her treatment. Betty and Jerry are old friends."

"Of course . . . Did the other regulars at the Marina Shores offer to pitch in too? Senator Rudlow, Larry Brownell . . . ?"

"You just wore out your welcome, mister," Killian

said, getting up from his desk. Lujack had pressed the right button.

"Are you going to beat me up the way you beat up Ginger, Dolph?"

Killian stopped halfway around the desk. Another button. "Did Mark tell you that?"

"Mark didn't tell me anything. It was a lucky guess. You just look like the kind of guy who would beat up girls."

"You don't know when to stop, do you, Lujack?"

Lujack heard the door open behind him. The security guard from the lobby, plus a much larger black security guard with a Beretta 9mm strapped to his waist, came into Killian's office.

"Looking for the men's room, boys?" Lujack asked.

"Take him to the roof and throw him off," Killian said bluntly.

The black guard made a grab for Lujack.

"Wait a minute," Lujack said, stepping back.

The guard pulled out the Beretta and aimed it at Lujack's chest.

"I've heard of not being able to take a joke . . ."

"We'll see how loud you laugh when your face hits the pavement at seventy miles per hour," Killian cackled. Lujack knew a sadist when he heard one. He wondered how many times Ginger had heard that sound.

The guard with the cold gray eyes looked at Lujack. He seemed to be enjoying the situation. He wasn't armed. Men like him didn't need guns to kill. Lujack didn't really believe they'd throw him off the roof. After all, this was El Segundo, not El Salvador.

"You better follow me," cold eyes said.

"That's all right, I'll see myself out."

Lujack walked toward the door. If the two men

followed him, there was going to be trouble. He wasn't going off a five-story building without company.

"Let him go," Killian ordered as Lujack approached the door. "I don't think Mr. Lujack will be giving us any more trouble."

Lujack didn't think it was the time or the place to debate the future of their relationship and stepped into the elevator.

# Chapter Seven

## *Billy Goes to Heaven?*

It was almost eight P.M. and the scores were starting to come in from the East Coast night games. The Dodgers won again. Another shutout for Hershiser. Maybe Lujack had been wrong about the kid from Lima, Ohio. There was no way he was going to break Drysdale's record, but you had to hand it to the guy. He was on a roll. Twenty-six scoreless innings. The good thing about it was that most of the Good Book's regulars didn't bet baseball very big. The bad thing was that all of them bet the goddamn Dodgers.

Susie Katz, the Good Book's sixty-plus-year-old "phone man," had gone home after the start of the games on the West Coast. The action was in and it was Lujack's job to prepare the lines for the next day and get ready for the start of football season the coming weekend. With the demise of Vegas kingpin Frank Nimmo, Lujack now dealt directly with the best oddsmaker in the business, Susie Katz's son, Irv. Irv had been an up-and-comer when he was setting the lines for Nimmo's Sports Book. Now that he had gone into business for himself he was quickly becoming a legend. Being practically a member of the family, Lujack got the opening lines from Irv before any other bookie in the county—for those early-bird players who couldn't wait for the Tuesday-morning paper.

Lujack had been looking forward to football season until Ginger Louie's murder had intruded on his preparations. He had been planning to install a new system this season, a mini computer that posted all line changes to both Susie and Tommy. If, for instance, the action was heavy on the Bears-Packers game with the Bears favored by four and still drawing all the money, Lujack, no matter where he was, could move the line to Bears minus four and a half or five. He also could change the over-unders. All Susie or Tommy had to do was punch up the game on their pocket-sized computers. Of course, getting Tommy to use a computer was like getting Ronald Reagan to use a hearing aid. Lujack explained that Tommy didn't have to keep the bets on the computer—he could still keep them in his head—only the odds. If you could be busted for quoting odds they'd have to close down every newspaper and TV station in the country.

There was a knock on the door. The knock startled Lujack. Susie was gone, and Tommy never knocked. Anyone else on the second floor shouldn't be there. It had been two days since Lujack's run-in with Dolph Killian, and he had been, if not exactly jumpy, more guarded than usual.

"Who is it?" Lujack asked, his hand sliding into the drawer and resting on his .38.

"Lionel," came the voice.

"Come in, Lionel," Lujack said, pulling his hand out of the drawer.

Lionel Chin entered the room. In the last year he'd grown out of his Ninja blood-lust stage and was now consumed by another kind of lust. Lionel had discarded his black Ninja outfits for the baggy contempo casual outfits of the Kirk Cameron set. Lionel was now very much into girls.

"What brings you up this way, Lionel?"

"I got off early tonight," Lionel said. Like the rest of the Chin clan, he worked in the restaurant as a busboy four nights a week.

"A friend of mine is having a party up in Cheviot Hills and Billy and I need some wheels."

"And you want to take the Mustang?"

"You know I can drive it."

"I also know you're fifteen."

"I'll be sixteen next week. I got an A in Driver's Ed. You said yourself I can handle the monster better than anyone."

Lujack hesitated. Lujack liked Lionel referring to the Mustang as the monster.

"Please, Mr. Lujack. Just for an hour or so. I already told somebody I'd be there."

"Somebody. You mean some girl."

"I told her I was the only one who knew how to drive the monster."

Lujack was wavering.

"Billy's sixteen, he even has insurance."

"That's reassuring."

Lujack pulled the keys out of his jacket pocket. Lionel smiled.

"Did you tell your father?"

"He said if you were stupid enough, I mean, he said if it was all right with you, it was all right with him."

Lujack threw Lionel the keys.

"Thanks, man. We'll have it back by ten."

"That's two hours."

"We might get lucky."

"God forbid," Lujack said, but Lionel was already

out the door. Lujack heard Tommy's chuckle on the intercom.

"You didn't put up much of a fight." Tommy laughed.

"You know I've always been a pushover for young lust."

"I hope his mother doesn't find out."

"I thought Chinese husbands were supposed to be the boss."

"You've been watching too many Bruce Lee movies."

Lujack was still smiling when a loud blast shook the building. His first reaction was EARTHQUAKE! But then, a native Southern Californian knows an earthquake doesn't explode, it consumes like a subway out of hell.

It was when he heard Tommy shouting that the horrible realization hit him. The explosion was a bomb. A car bomb!

"Lionel!" Tommy bellowed.

Lujack ran downstairs. He grabbed the fire extinguisher from the wall and ran through the dining room. The Chin Up diners were standing up, looking in the direction of the door.

"Call an ambulance," Lujack yelled to Pete Colima, who had left his usual bar stool.

Tommy and the waiters were already outside looking with horror at the burning car. Tommy was trying to open the door and pull out his son, except the door wouldn't open. Lujack smashed out what was left of the window with the bottom of the fire extinguisher. Lionel was slumped over the steering wheel. Lujack didn't know when the gas tank was going to blow, all he knew was he had to get the boy out.

"Start spraying," he ordered Winston Chin, throwing him the extinguisher.

Lujack tried the inside door handle. It was hot, but he managed to hold it long enough to get the door open. He pulled Lionel out by grabbing under his arms. The whole right side of his body was smoking. He couldn't even see Billy. The smoke was too dense. All that registered was the smell of burning flesh.

He laid Lionel down on the sidewalk. Tommy smothered his son's right side with towels and yelled for an ambulance. The boy was moaning, half in shock, half in pain. Lujack was going back to the Mustang when the gas tank blew. He and Winston were thrown back on the pavement. The last thing he remembered was putting his hand up to block the fire extinguisher.

Lujack came out of it slowly, fitfully, trying to escape a bad dream. He was back in the police academy, about to take his last exam, when the instructor came in and took the test away, explaining Lujack's father couldn't afford the tuition. "Tuition is for college," Lujack screamed, "you get paid to be a cop." The instructor laughed: "Not if you're an honest cop, you don't."

"You don't look too bad, Jimmy, your Polish helmet saved you again."

Lujack looked into the fleshy mug of Lieutenant Kyle Thurgood. He wasn't sure if the dream was over or not. Then he caught a whiff of the Mustang and saw the covered body next to the smoldering car.

"How's Lionel?"

"He's gonna be okay. Tommy went with him in the ambulance to Brautman."

"Is that Billy?"

"What's left of him. I hear you were pretty close yourself."

"Billy was the one with the insurance."

"I don't think the policy will do him much good now."

"Bastard."

"Any bastard in particular?"

"What?" Lujack asked, having forgotten where he was, then remembering. "No. Just the bastard who did it."

There was no reason to give him Killian's name. Not before Lujack had a chance to do some personal investigating.

"Pritchard, our bomb man, thinks the charge was placed under the tire. The left front."

"That's an old terrorist trick."

"This wasn't meant for those poor kids. Someone was trying to give you a message, Jimmy. A very clear message. You don't have any idea who that might be? You've been making your payouts?"

"The Good Book always makes its payouts."

"How about your girlfriends?"

"Get real."

A uniform came over. "Lieutenant, the deputy chief wants to talk with you."

Thurgood grimaced. "I'll be right back, Jimmy," Thurgood said. "Don't go anywhere."

He watched Thurgood amble in the direction of the nearest police radio. Two representatives of the coroner's office picked up the plastic-covered bag and loaded the body of Bill Cridmore into the van. Lujack hadn't been able to remember Billy's name until then. He hadn't been able to remember the face either. Now he could see the wary, pale face of Lionel's friend. Tommy had told Lujack he was glad Lionel's best friend wasn't a Chinese-American, he was just sorry that it had to be Billy. Lujack remembered silently agreeing. Billy's sulking manner didn't win him a lot of popularity contests.

Lujack made a move to get off the pavement. The usual things didn't happen. Nothing was broken, but his equilibrium was more memory than reality. He carefully balanced himself on one knee, then mastered two. He wanted to get to the hospital. He wanted to see Tommy, to check on Lionel. He looked at the remains of his prized Mustang. The monster was dead. So was Billy.

A medic who had been talking to Thurgood came over to Lujack. He didn't want to take an ambulance to the hospital, but, he thought, at least it's a ride.

Tommy and Jackie were sitting silently in the waiting room outside the burn ward. Lujack could feel Tommy's frustration and Jackie's sorrow. First Ginger, now Lionel. It wasn't shaping up as a very good year for the Chin family. Lujack wasn't positive but he thought it was either the year of the dragon or the year of the snake. It must be the snake.

Tommy looked up as Lujack approached. Jackie pointedly turned away and began sobbing quietly. He didn't expect Jackie to make it easy on him.

"I'm sorry, Jackie," Lujack began. "I had no idea . . ."

"Bullshit!" she said under her breath. Lujack couldn't remember hearing Jackie ever say such a word.

"It's not his fault, Jackie. I could have given him a ride. I knew he was going to ask Jimmy," Tommy said.

"Always too busy with everyone, but never time with your son," Jackie said, not letting a chance pass.

"How is he?"

"Most of the burns are on his right arm and leg. Second and third degree," Tommy said. "But the doctor doesn't think they'll have to operate. The important thing is keeping the skin free from infection."

"That's always important with burns," Lujack said, remembering how very little he knew about burns, although he unfortunately had been around more than one human fire.

"Who did this, Jimmy? Who did it?" Tommy asked him in an even voice.

"I don't know, Tommy, but I'll find out."

"We'll find out together."

"I know how you feel, Tommy, but the bomb was meant for me. Your family needs you."

"My family needs me to protect their honor and to protect their lives. What happened to Lionel, the other boy's death . . . these things are related to the low regard in which the Chin family is held."

Jackie Chin nodded her head in agreement. Lujack didn't see any point in challenging their irrational rationale. The Chinese were great ones for blaming things on themselves. Lujack figured better themselves than him.

A young doctor came out of the burn ward. Both Chins stood up.

"You can go in now, but don't stay too long. We've given him something to make him sleep."

"Doctor, will there be any scars?" Jackie asked.

"We won't know, Mrs. Chin, until the scabs form. We will work against any contractures, but there is no way of knowing right now. Nature must take its course."

"What is this, *Wild Kingdom?* There's got to be something you can do!" Lujack said, venting the frustration that had been building up in him.

The doctor looked at Lujack as he would a rude waiter.

"My name's Lujack. It was my car."

The doctor nodded, as if he expected as much. Lujack didn't like doctors. They reminded him of Todd Barnes. But then doctors never liked him either.

"You can go in now," the doctor said, then added, looking at Lujack, "but don't stay too long."

Tommy picked up Lujack the next morning. Tommy had a Thunderbird that Lujack was borrowing. His insurance company had not been happy to hear about the explosion. Lujack had been in no mood to console them on their loss. In fact, he had almost told his agent where to stick the policy when the guy wondered aloud if indeed the explosion were actually covered by the company. Lujack explained that the boys weren't driving the car, they were just sitting in it. Lujack knew it was going to get ugly before he got any money, but he was going to get Billy Cridmore's family something, no matter how many lies he had to tell the goddamn insurance company.

Tommy didn't say much on the way to Marina Shores. Their plan was simple enough. Killian worked out every morning at the Shores, then drove to work. The only time to get him alone was on his morning jog. Both Lujack and Tommy were in jogging suits to add to their cover. Tommy still didn't look the part. He was too short, too round, and too Chinese.

"All he talked about was that he was in the same room Michael Jackson had," Tommy said after a while.

"I'm sure he's still in shock."

"He didn't even ask about Billy."

"He'll have plenty of time to mourn Billy. Does he remember much?"

"Only getting into the car, turning on the key, and the explosion."

"It sounds like it was hooked to the ignition. Thurgood said the bomb guys said it was under one of the wheels."

"What else does Thurgood think?"

"He thinks it was an unhappy customer. I didn't tell him about Dolph."

"It wasn't an unhappy customer," Tommy said harshly.

"No," Lujack said. "It was someone who didn't want me asking questions about Ginger."

Tommy parked the T-bird next to the Crows Nest Bar. It had cost Lujack a favor to get Killian's daily route. Two tickets to the Dodger game on Sunday. The Expos were in town. Lujack had long felt Canadians shouldn't be allowed to play baseball. Just as he felt hockey should not be played in Los Angeles. Now that Gretsky was in LA he'd been losing that argument more and more. This winter he knew he might even have to start booking games. In a celebrity-oriented town like LA, the sizzle was always more attractive than the steak.

"Shit," Lujack said, watching two men come puffing toward him. "There's someone with Killian."

"Bodyguard maybe?"

"Worse than that. A senator."

"What do we do now?"

"Start running."

Lujack and Tommy got out of the car and began running down the Promenade in the direction of the two men. Rudlow was taller than Dolph and in better shape. He had the pampered body of a man used to his own private workouts in the Senate gym. He was in his mid-forties and had the white-bread good looks of a successful '80s politician. What he was doing with Killian on the Marina at eight o'clock in the morning

Lujack could only guess. With the current public mood about politicians and defense consultants, an early-morning jog was preferable to a long, boozy lunch at the Beverly Wilshire.

Killian didn't recognize Lujack until almost ten yards separated the two sets of joggers. He could read the defense consultant's lips. "Shit," Killian said.

"How ya doin', Dolph?"

"What are you doing here, Lujack?" Dolph asked as Tommy and Lujack came up on either side of him, Lujack jogging between Killian and Senator Rudlow.

"Tommy and I love to jog along the water in the morning, don't we, Tommy?"

Tommy nodded. Lujack could see from Tommy's condition that he would be lucky to make it to the Ancient Pelican at the end of the quay.

"What's going on, Dolph?" Rudlow asked.

"Don't worry, Senator, this doesn't involve you. Unless you know anyone who plants car bombs for a living," Lujack said politely.

Dolph stopped jogging and faced Lujack. He looked like a red balloon about to burst. Rudlow and Tommy also stopped.

"What's the matter, Dolph? Your blood pressure always give you trouble when you get away from your bodyguards?"

"Who is this asshole?" Rudlow demanded.

"Shut up and keep running, Pete," Lujack said with the familiarity only a nonvoter could have.

"Let me take care of this, Senator. I'll catch up with you," Killian suggested.

Rudlow gave Lujack and Tommy a hard stare.

"I don't know what these people want, Dolph, but they can't intimidate a United States senator."

"We're not here to debate club rules, we're here to talk about the murder of a young girl and an innocent young boy. Ginger Louie and Billy Cridmore. You remember Ginger, don't you, Senator?"

Rudlow's handsome face did a quick freeze. Lujack thought he could see the hairs of Rudlow's graying temples cringe. The senator shot a look in Dolph's direction that threatened in only the way a ranking member of the Armed Services Committee could threaten a defense consultant.

"I heard about what happened last night, Lujack. I didn't have anything to do with it," Killian said in a bored tone.

"What happened last night?" Rudlow asked, directing the question to Killian.

"Someone planted a bomb under Lujack's car. Some punk was killed," the defense consultant said. "Another was hurt."

"My son! My son was in that car, you dumb shit!" Tommy grabbed at Killian, but the old Navy fighter pilot was more than a match for Tommy and threw him to the pavement on the edge of the water.

Killian's hand was raised to deliver a karate chop, when Lujack caught the Navy hero with a Nike in the Adam's apple. Killian fell back gasping for air. Rudlow took a look at Lujack and decided to yield the floor to the ex-cop from Hollywood. Tommy got in a good kick at Killian's rib cage before Lujack grabbed him.

"You're dead. You're both dead men," Killian yelled at them.

Rudlow seemed embarrassed, as if Killian had spilled soup on his shirt front at a state dinner.

"Excuse me, Senator," came a voice from the direction of the highway.

Lujack turned and saw Mark Lyman walking toward them. With him was Debbi Arnold of Channel 7 News and her camerawoman. Lujack wondered how much of the melee the blonde had seen . . . or filmed. All he knew was that the girl in the sweatshirt and industrial-length ponytail was grinding away at Dolph Killian lying on the sidewalk.

"What the fuck is going on here? Tell her to turn that goddamn camera off before I shove it down her throat!" Killian screamed.

"Please, Debbi, I think it would be better if your assistant stopped shooting," Lyman suggested.

"Keep it running, Nance," the roving reporter ordered. Debbi was looking camera-ready at this early hour in a purple shirt and short black skirt.

"I'm sorry, Senator, Debbi said she wanted to get your reaction . . ." Lyman broke off.

"Senator, I wanted to get your reaction to the president's latest warning to the Japanese prime minister on the trade deficit. I didn't know we'd find you in a street fight."

Dolph Killian was on his feet heading in the direction of the camera girl.

"Cool it, Dolph! Cool it!" Rudlow demanded.

Killian stopped abruptly as if he finally could see the pictures on the evening news.

"This is hardly a street fight. Just two joggers who ran into one another on a morning run," Rudlow said smoothly. "I'm afraid my friend Mr. Killian got carried away."

"Dolph Killian of Global Resources?"

"The very same," Killian said, suddenly sounding like Chuck Yeager.

"Dolph and I were having what you might call a business workout, I'm afraid we weren't looking where we were going and Dolph ran into this gentleman."

Rudlow nodded toward Tommy.

"I've heard of freeway shootings but never jogging punchouts," Debbi said.

Everyone laughed but Tommy. Lujack made the brilliant decision that retreat was the better part of surrender. Righteous bookies were just behind child molesters and savings and loan executives in the current public eye. Even senators and defense consultants ranked higher.

"If it were another time we'd challenge them to an EKG but we're both late for work," Lujack said with an easy smile. "Come on, Tommy, five more miles."

Tommy scowled at Killian, then Debbi, and finally at Lujack. Just when Lujack saw tomorrow's headline, "Bookies Attack Senator and War Hero," Mr. Chin smiled inscrutably at the camera and began running toward the Ancient Pelican.

The last words Lujack heard were from Mark Lyman, faithful Good Book customer of the last six years.

"It's a tragedy, Debbi, who they let out on the street."

He followed Tommy five hundred meters to the restaurant. When Tommy reached the black chain that hung between the two pilings that were the restaurant's entrance, he almost collapsed.

Both men sat on the chain. Lujack looked back at the press conference. Pete Rudlow and Debbi Arnold were locked in meaningful dialogue concerning the future of U.S.-Japanese trade.

"You never stop surprising me, Mr. Chin," Lujack said while Tommy caught his breath.

"And you never surprise me, Mr. Lujack," Tommy said, looking at him in a way that made Lujack both proud and uncomfortable.

"I would have killed him, Jimmy," Tommy said. "He would have beat me up but I would have killed him."

"You're a lot of things, Tommy. But you're not a killer."

Tommy looked back at the group on the sidewalk in front of the cameras, then out toward the water. He was hurt, offended. "All men are killers, Jimmy, when they have to be."

"Every animal will kill to protect itself or its young, but there are very few animals who are killers, born or self-made."

"Like you," Tommy said.

"Like me," Lujack said.

Tommy laughed.

"What's so funny?"

"This chain, it's plastic. In the Chin Up everything is authentic."

Lujack felt the chain with his hands. It was plastic. It was also sturdy and could easily hold his weight. He had stopped asking questions once he'd determined it could hold them both.

# Chapter Eight

## *Lay Them out Straight!*

Lionel Chin came home from the hospital two days later. The same day Dave Mason was murdered in the recreation room of the county jail. Deputies found Mason with his throat cut, his blood smeared on the wall.

Thurgood met Lujack later that afternoon at Barney's Beanery in West Hollywood and showed him a picture of the rec-room wall. Barney's was an artists' hangout, the last nongay bar in West Hollywood. It even had a sign on the wall to prove it: "No Credit for Aids."

"The marks on the wall . . . like Mason's house."

"Similar. Milch is checking it. The strokes were made by a brush. At Mason's they were made by hand."

"Any hands in particular?"

"Two Korean kids were found with blood on their shirts and pants. A witness put them in the rec room shortly before Mason was found. We haven't found the weapon."

"What do they say?"

"Nothing so far."

Lujack started counting. Eight. Nine. Three. He remembered roughly the same number of marks on Mason's wall. Eight. Nine. Three. He wanted to talk to Tommy.

Lujack pushed past a buxom blonde lining up a four ball in the side pocket. There was no way she was going to make it, but he didn't seem to care as long as she kept bent over. He moved a glass of stale beer off the top of the phone and dialed Tommy's home number. He hoped Jackie wouldn't answer. She didn't.

"The numbers eight, nine, and three. What do they mean?" Lujack blurted.

Tommy didn't hesitate. "Yakuza."

"Yakuza?"

"They are the Japanese numbers eight, nine, and three. *Ya-ku-za.* They are the worst score in *hanafuda,* a Japanese card game."

"The number of marks at Mason's house and in the cell where he was murdered. They're the same. Eight, nine, and three."

Tommy didn't say anything.

"I told you about the Zodiac. The place is crawling with Yakuza. Molly told me there was an Oriental man at one of the Marina parties. He said he was a part owner of the Zodiac."

"Yoshida," Tommy said.

"What's a billionaire Japanese banker doing mixed up with the mob?"

"In Japan the politicians, the corporations, and the mob, they are very close."

Lujack doubted they were that close. "How's Lionel?"

"He says he's sorry about your car."

"Tell him I'm not. The thing cost more to insure than to drive."

"There is going to be a service tomorrow for Billy."

"I'll be there," Lujack said and placed the stale beer back where he found it.

The blonde was still shooting when he came back. This time she was bending over the two ball. The way she was aiming she'd be lucky to hit the cue. Her partner and her two opponents didn't seem to care.

"Don't bruise those," Lujack said, walking past.

Thurgood was fumbling for his lighter when Lujack got back to the table.

"Where'd you go?"

"I called Tommy. The marks, the number of scratches on the wall, their arrangement. First, eight; second, nine; third, three.

Thurgood restudied the picture. "So what?"

"So it's the Yakuza. The numbers mean Yakuza. Did you happen to notice if the two Koreans were missing the last digits of their little fingers? Or if they had strange tattoos covering their bodies?"

"I know all about the Yakuza," Thurgood said, lighting up a Marlboro. "These guys weren't Yakuza."

"Why not?"

"Because they didn't have tattoos and they had all their fingers."

"If you knew anything about the Yakuza, you'd know not all of them have tattoos and only a small number commit *yubitsime.*"

"Could be a frame. Why advertise the fact you kill people? Especially when you're from out of town."

"I ran into a guy, Henry Park, at the Zodiac the other night. He's Yakuza. Mark Lyman owns the Zodiac, along with a few other secret partners."

"Oh no you don't. Senator Rudlow and Dolph Killian have already let Chief Bane know how pleased they are with your 'investigation.' You're not going to be bothering any more members of the Marina Shores, not if you want to keep living west of Lakewood Boulevard."

"You know smoking is bad for your lungs?"

"And hanging around with you is bad for my career. If the chief didn't love your ass for chopping down Frank Nimmo and Ernie B., you'd be on the next train to Tijuana."

"Ever hear of a guy named Kazuo Yoshida?"

"Jesus H. Christ."

"You've heard of him."

"The guy only runs the biggest bank in California. I'm afraid to ask why you brought him up."

"He spends a lot of time at the Marina Shores. He likes young girls. Tommy says he's got ties to the Yakuza."

Thurgood was shaking his head. "No, no, no. You're not going to drag a respected Japanese business man into this thing."

"I saw him on Lawrence Brownell's yacht with two party girls. Molly Blair told me she met an Oriental guy at one of Lyman's parties who said he owned the Zodiac."

"Was it Yoshida?"

"She wasn't sure. I'll dig up a picture."

"What if she IDs him. You gonna run into him jogging? Why don't you go after Brownell while you're at it? He's only the president's best friend."

"Tommy got carried away. You can't blame him."

"The guy assaults a U.S. senator and you can't blame him."

"Nobody touched Rudlow. It was Killian he went after."

"Two bookies mug naval hero."

"Your girlfriend, Debbi Arnold, has the whole thing on tape. Killian is crazy. He was threatening to kill Tommy. He almost did kill his kid."

"You don't know if Killian had anything to do with the bombing and you don't know that Ginger was involved with anyone at the Shores."

"The next thing you'll be telling me is the car bomb was an accident, Dave Mason committed suicide, and you don't owe me that hundred bucks."

"That reminds me. One of your friends from the neighborhood. Davey . . ."

"Rosenbloom."

"Yeah, that's him. He said he saw a guy hanging around your car the other evening. Said the guy looked funny. Your friend Davey figured he was going to boost it."

"Davey Rosenbloom can't see across the street."

"He said he thought the guy was Oriental. The guy drove away on a motorcycle."

"If I were you, I'd bring in the Asian Task Force. If it is Yakuza maybe they can help."

"I'll call Rick Matsuda tonight. His contacts are the best in the department."

Lujack knew Rick Matsuda. There was little love lost between them. He also knew that because Matsuda was Japanese-American, Nisei, second generation, as he remembered, Matsuda would be of little use in the Korean community, which is where the police should be looking.

Lujack pulled out a typewritten letter. "I need you to sign this."

"What is it?"

"It's your official statement. For my insurance company. The bastards won't pay for Lionel's hospitalization unless you say the car didn't move."

"The car didn't move."

"Kyle, I wouldn't ask you to sign something that wasn't true. You want another beer?"

The lieutenant gave Lujack a strange look as he signed the statement.

"What are you up to, Jimmy?"

"Nothing," Lujack said, pocketing the statement.

Lujack met with Mo Breen in Breen's Beverly Hills office. Lujack wanted to make sure his claim was air-tight. There were a few items he hadn't filled Thurgood in on. One was the fact that the Pacific Rim Auto, in the person of Miles Overland, had informed him that Pacific Rim would not pay out any claims when an unlicensed driver was operating a policy holder's vehicle.

"Of course I lied to him," Lujack said.

Breen was smiling. He had on a turquoise shirt and maroon tie. Mo was going with the new Melrose Avenue ultra-hip look, but he was still the Beverly Hills High debating team captain whose greatest asset was that he knew where the Gabor sisters buried their *real* jewels, and more than one of their husbands.

"I told him that the kids wanted to see what it felt like to be behind the wheel. I gave them the keys so they could listen to the radio."

Mo studied the statements from Thurgood and from Tommy as well as Lujack's own. Lujack didn't like lying about the dead—or the living—but he sure as hell wasn't going to pay out fifty thousand dollars in hospital bills and new car payments because of some insurance loophole.

"They might want to talk to Lionel."

"Lionel's a good kid. He'll say the right thing."

"Of course, there's the matter of damages to the Cridmore family. That could get very messy. You could be put on the stand. So could Lionel. Perjury is a serious offense."

"So is murder. The bastard who should be paying the Cridmore family is the guy who put the bomb in the car . . . and the guy who ordered it done."

"Are there any leads?"

"A couple. Thurgood is taking his sweet time."

"I hear you had a little run-in with Dolph yesterday."

"You have big ears."

"I told you to be careful around him."

"He's crazy."

"I'm sure Larry Brownell's competitors don't think he's so crazy."

"Come again."

"Let's just say that Killian's firm has a special relationship with Brownell Industries. A relationship that might lead someone who knows the defense game to think that Dolph wasn't just jogging with Pete Rudlow the other morning, he was lobbying Pete Rudlow on the new long-range bomber Brownell is developing."

"Tommy and I walked into it, eh?"

"Let's put it this way, Jimmy. It would have been better for a lot of people if that little jog had been kept a secret. Luckily a reporter like Debbi Arnold is too stupid to see the connection."

"But your source did."

"My source works for Brownell. He said the old man was livid that they had been seen together."

"I thought Brownell and the president were bosom buddies. What's he need Rudlow for?"

"Rudlow's the ranking minority member on the Armed Services Committee. In this country you have to pay off both parties to get a project like the B-3 off the ground. Literally and financially."

"This B-3, it's pretty hot?"

"My source says it maneuvers like an F-16, has the range of a B-1, and costs more than the Stealth."

"I'm beginning to think that Marina Shores is more than a social club."

"Once you get rich and powerful men down to the water, you have to give them something to play with. Like your friend Ginger. Once they're relaxed, then they can do business. Kind of like the Bohemian Grove except it has models instead of trees."

"Maybe Ginger heard something she shouldn't have."

"And someone makes it look like a drug killing," Breen said, following Lujack's scenario.

"Except it wasn't a drug killing or a satanic cult."

"You're sure about that?"

"Mason was found dead in his cell this morning. The markings were similar to those at his house. We think it might be Yakuza."

"Yakuza. Here? What the hell is going on?"

"That's what I'd like to know. Do me a favor, will ya, Mo? See what you can find out about the Zodiac Club. Mark Lyman says he owns it, but I think he's a front."

"I know a few people on Melrose. I guess I could ask a few questions if we came to certain other arrangements."

"Like?"

"Like you give me odds on Hershiser's next outing. Like five to one on a shutout."

"You're out of your mind. He's the hottest pitcher in the majors. Twenty-six scoreless innings."

"That's why I should be getting five to one."

Lujack hesitated. "Three to one. No better."

"I'll take it for five yards." Mo smiled.

"Since when did you become a high roller?"

"I believe, Jimmy. I believe in Orel and Tommy and Peter."

"What about Steve Garvey?"

"Steve never should have left the Dodger Blue."

"And he never should have let his first wife hire you as her attorney," Lujack said on his way out.

Lujack didn't see any need to tell his lawyer about Kazuo Yoshida, but the more he thought about Ginger's whereabouts on the night of August 6 the more he was convinced that the girl who left the Zodiac Club with Dave Mason visited one of her boyfriends at the Marina Shores. Lujack didn't know if it were Mark Lyman, Chase Field, Dolph Killian, or even Larry Brownell or Yoshida himself, but she saw something. She heard something that night that got her killed. Lujack believed that. That was the assumption he was working on, no matter whose toes got stepped on.

He picked up his rental car that night just after visiting Miles Overland, who was in no hurry to help Lujack "adjust" his claim, but did agree to certain provisions after he read Thurgood's statement.

"Of course, the underwriter is going to have to see the complete police report," Miles said with polite understatement.

"Of course," Lujack said. "By then I'll have an estimate on the funeral expenses. Maybe you'd like to come to the funeral to make sure the boy is dead."

"That won't be necessary," Miles responded smoothly.

After that Lujack couldn't resist picking out a vintage Jensen convertible from his old pal, Sports DeLane. Sports had been renting exotic sports cars in Beverly Hills since the days of real movie stars. Supposedly he was the second black man ever to make a million dollars in Beverly Hills, the first being Al

Jolson. Sports said he never did believe Jolson ever made any million dollars.

"I'll give you the Ferrari for two fifty a day. I hear you've been doing some private eye work around town, now you can be just like Magnum."

"I was thinking more in the David Niven mold. How much is that Jensen convertible?"

"For you, Jimmy, one fifty a day, plus mileage."

"How much is it for some bacon salesman from Des Moines?"

"One fifty a day. Plus mileage."

"Thanks."

"No bacon salesman takes all my money on the basketball playoffs like you do."

"Yeah, but I'm better for your cholesterol."

"My cholesterol is past caring," Sports said with a hearty laugh. He weighed two fifty if he weighed one pound. "The phone, that's extra, but I'll throw it in for free, you give me some decent odds on Orel Friday night."

"What do you mean, decent? The game's seven to five. It's been that way all week."

"I'm talking shutout."

"You too."

"The man is invincible."

"No pitcher is invincible. Not Koufax, not Gibson, not Denny McLaine. I'll give you three to one."

"I'll take it for a thousand." Sports smiled, then added, "You know you have to charge the calls to your own phone."

"What I know is your buddy Orel is going into the toilet Friday against the Expos."

Lujack pulled out onto Wilshire Boulevard with practiced nonchalance. He never had a car phone before, the ultimate LA weapon. He knew better than to talk business, but he had to call somebody and

Suzie was the only person he knew would be home. It took him three or four tries to get through. He kept getting a recording about the mobile system being busy, but after he found the automatic redial button, he couldn't be denied.

"East-West," came the raspy voice.

"Susie, it's me. I'm using my new car phone."

"I'm very happy for you, Jimmy."

"I had to call someone, so I'm calling you."

"It's your five spot."

"Five spot?"

"Those car phones aren't cheap, honey. Irv calls me on his all the time. He says we should get a fax machine for the office so he can write me notes from his car fax. It would be cheaper in the long run."

"Cheaper for who?"

"You got a message from Chase. He says he has to talk to you. He didn't sound too good. Like his daily double winner flunked the drug test."

"Where is he?"

"He'll be at the Zodiac at nine o'clock. He said something about Dave Mason not being guilty. What time is it now? Oh-oh, time for the first pitch of the West Coast games, I'm gone."

"Thanks, Susie. You better lock up. Tommy won't be coming in tonight."

"I know, he called. I talked to Lionel. He's pretty shook up."

"I would be too."

Lujack tried one more number. There was no answer. He wanted to tell Molly about her friend before she heard about it on the news. He was probably too late. If Chase Fields knew, Molly would know soon enough.

* * *

There was no such thing as a slow night in the LA club scene. Not if you're happening. And judging from the line in front of the Zodiac that stretched to the corner, the Zodiac was happening.

"I heard Slash will be here tonight," a refugee from Venice Boulevard said to his friend seriously. Lujack actually knew who Slash was. A chain-smoking, booze-swilling guitar player. Lujack was glad in such holier-than-thou times that the kids still had someone to look up to.

Lujack walked to the front of the line. He hoped he wouldn't have to play presidents with Aristotle. Luckily, Aristotle felt the same way.

"Good evening, Mr. Lujack."

"Whatever you say, Aristotle."

"Mr. Field is expecting you."

Lujack nodded and walked past a row of disappointed would-be patrons. He negotiated the dark, winding maze of walls toward the bar. It took a while for his eyes to adjust and he guided himself by hand as much as by sight. The walls felt cold and clammy. As he had done the first time, he followed the music.

When he finally made it to the bar he felt an excitement that was missing from his first visit. The feeling that anything could happen in this sweaty, crowded club. Was it because of the Yakuza? Was it because of the club's ties to Ginger's death? Or was it because he knew the man who watched him from the far end of the bar, Mr. Henry Park, was a member of the world's largest and most dangerous criminal society.

"Hey, Cancer," came a voice from behind him.

"Janis, fancy meetin' you here."

Janis was coming off the dance floor. She was wearing one of those off-the-shoulder numbers that remind you just how sexy a woman's shoulders can be. The guy who had been dancing with her disappeared into the crowd. Lujack didn't get a good look at him, but he felt the man's eyes on him. He was Korean.

"I'm looking for Chase. You seen him?"

Janis looked around. "He was here about twenty minutes ago. I saw him talking to Henry at the end of the bar."

"How's Molly?" Lujack asked.

"She's getting fat. Put on two pounds last week."

Lujack couldn't imagine Molly being fat if she gained twenty pounds. "Is she here tonight?"

"She's in New York. *Vogue* and *Elle* are fighting over her."

"That should make Chase happy."

"Chase is always happy." She smiled, then remembered. "Except tonight he didn't look too happy."

"Then Molly didn't hear about Dave," Lujack asked.

"Dave Mason? What about him?"

"He was murdered."

Janis hesitated, as if she'd forgotten something else. Maybe her lipstick. "Murder. That's pretty heavy."

"It doesn't get much heavier. Even for models."

"Molly always liked him. I never did," she said defensively. Lujack had a theory about beautiful women. They remained childlike because their beauty never forced them to grow up. He wondered if the thought were original.

Lujack saw that the Korean kid who had been dancing with Janis was talking to Henry at the end of the bar. Both were looking in his direction.

"That kid you were dancing with, you know him?"

"He hangs out here. Friend of Henry's. I think they're related. Cousins."

Lujack doubted Janis could pick the kid out of a lineup, much less give Lujack any pertinent information.

"I take it you're not going steady?"

"You're not very friendly tonight, Lujack. You should learn to relax. I know a masseuse who could really help you."

"The last massage I got didn't work out," Lujack said. "Excuse me, honey, I've got to see a man about a murder."

Lujack took another look around the bar and a cursory look at the dance floor. The Zodiac Club didn't lend itself to surveillance.

Lujack sauntered back toward Henry and his cousin. Henry bowed politely. The boy who had been dancing with Janis looked to be in his early twenties and was missing the end of his little finger. The cousin was wearing black. Evidently he hadn't enough time, or money, to go shopping.

"You Molly's friend," Henry said in passable English.

"I'm looking for Chase. You know, the guy with the white teeth, big schnooze, likes blondes."

"Not here tonight."

"Wrong. Aristotle and Janis both said they saw him."

"I've been in the office. Maybe he come in," Henry lied.

"He come in all right, but as far as I can judge, he not go out."

"Try dance floor?"

"Chase isn't the dancing type. Mind if I take a walk back to your office?"

Henry stood up. So did his cousin. Both seemed determined Lujack wasn't going to be nosing around the back of the club.

Whatever Chase Field wanted to tell him about Dave Mason, it had to be important. It wasn't like Chase to volunteer information for the good of humanity, but Lujack wasn't sure if a karate match with two Korean hoods was the best policy. He was wishing he'd brought along his trusty .38 when a screaming girl came running out of the maze.

"There's a man in there! There's a man in there!" she yelled, and for a moment the club members smiled as if she'd mixed a batch of bad acid in her hair spray.

"He's dead. I swear he's dead." So saying, the girl screamed again as she realized her right hand was covered with blood.

Henry and his cousin ran to the end of the maze. Lujack followed. He felt his way along behind the two men. Once into the dark passage, Henry and his cousin spoke in Korean. Lujack had the feeling he was in a bad Japanese horror movie. Oriental voices, fluorescent markings. Suddenly the voices grew more excited.

Lujack saw Henry hold his flashlight to the wall. In the Carravagioesque lighting he could see the lifeless face of Chase Field. He was hanging on the wall like a piece of slaughterhouse art.

"You better call the police, Henry. Ask for Detective Thurgood."

Henry gave instructions to his cousin in Korean. The boy went back the way he came in. Henry and Lujack were left in the hall.

"I guess Chase was here after all."

"Looks like he had trouble leaving," Henry said.

"Are there any other ways in and out of here?"

Before Henry answered, Lujack heard voices coming down the hall.

"This is tubular," said one of the voices.

The kids stopped when they saw Henry's light and the three faces looking at them. Two sets of live eyes, one dead set.

"What happened to that dude?"

Suddenly the lights went on, revealing Chase Field hanging on the wall. He was supported by a rope tied to the air-conditioning vent. From the blood on his pearl silk shirt, it looked as if he had been stabbed in the heart right under his gold name necklace. On the wall next to the body were markings made with Chase's blood. Rows of lines. Eight, nine, and three. Lujack thought Henry reacted to the markings.

One of the surfers lost his dinner. The two left as soon as they were able. Lujack didn't see any immediate entrance to the hall, but he noticed the walls were made of plywood, easy to move back and forth, especially for anyone who knew his way around.

"Eight, nine, and three," Lujack said, pointing to the wall. "Those numbers mean anything to you, Henry?"

"I see no numbers," Henry said warily.

"Sure you do. Those numbers say the Yakuza killed Chase Field. You know anything about that, Henry?"

The Korean's brown eyes fixed on him with calculated calm. Lujack didn't know if Henry was going to shoot him or confess. He suspected the former.

"You don't know anything," he said.

"I know three people have been murdered."

"You don't know who you are dealing with."

"This is America, Henry. The Triads and the Yakuza have no power here."

Henry nodded to the body on the wall. "Tell that to him," Henry said softly.

Lujack had the impression that Henry was more frightened than ironic.

# Chapter Nine

## *A Stitch in Time . . . Saves None*

There is a certain rhythm to evil. Most people, luckily, never get the opportunity to hear it or feel it. Lujack could feel the beat this warm Southern California day as he stood in the Mt. Sinai Memorial Chapel at Forest Lawn. He had felt it for a while. The sharp, awkward pounding. He could also feel the strain. Very few men could walk or run to such a discordant beat.

It was his second funeral in as many days. Yesterday Billy Cridmore had been laid to rest in St. Alban's Catholic Church in Culver City. It was possibly the worst experience of Lujack's recent life, that and reading about Orel Hershiser's shutout in the paper that morning. He had shaken hands with Billy's parents, muttered condolences for a boy he barely knew and for whose death he felt somewhat responsible. The Cridmores had been as uncomfortable as Lujack.

Every gorgeous model in Los Angeles was sitting in Mt. Sinai chapel, listening to Mark Lyman pay homage to his good and dear friend. Lujack noticed that none of the other Marina Shores fraternity members were in the crowd, although there were more than a few Hollywood types in attendance, mostly male producers and agents. Chase Field was a man who had dispensed many favors in his lifetime.

"I never even knew he was Jewish," Molly said as they walked out to Lujack's car. He had planned on enjoying his Jensen, but now every time he looked at it he was reminded of what Tommy had told him about Sports DeLane, that he was about to be cut off. Even Orel's streak couldn't help him.

"I always thought he was a Virgo," Janis said, smiling, appearing at their side. Both girls were in short black dresses. It occurred to Lujack he had never seen either one of them in the daytime, much less in mourning. They were even more stunning in natural light. He wished the same could be said for him. He'd spent the night with his fingers wrapped around the neck of Johnnie Walker. That can make for some disquieting rhythms of its own.

"Janis, do you need a ride, or have you just heard about my new car?"

"What new car? Not that bitchin' Interceptor?"

"Watch the brand names, dear. It's bad for good conversation."

"What's gotten into him?" Janis asked Molly.

"He's been that way ever since he picked me up at the airport last night."

Janis gave Lujack an approving look, assuming he'd spent the night with her nineteen-year-old friend. Lujack wasn't about to tell her it was a twelve-year-old bottle of scotch. For her part Molly didn't seem to care, which Lujack could understand under the circumstances. After all, her roommate, her friend, and now her boss had all been killed in the last two weeks.

"You are going to see him buried, aren't you?" Janis asked with a touch of anticipation.

"Wouldn't miss it," Lujack said, watching the long-legged girls climb into his car.

They were a bit cramped for the drive up the hill to the plot, but Lujack enjoyed the smell. He could think of worse ways to go to funerals.

"Who do you think is going to take over?" Molly asked her friend.

"I heard it might be Mario."

"I hope not," Molly said with disgust. "He's a pig."

"I know he tried to hit on you when you did that Mexican shoot."

"What about Jacob? He's kinda cute."

"You know he's married," Janis said.

"So what?" Molly smiled. "He always lets us fudge on our expenses."

Overhearing their grief, Lujack began to understand what Thurgood had been trying to tell him about teenage girls.

"I heard that Mark Lyman has final approval," Janis said as they got closer to the grave. The crowd had already gathered by the gravesite. There was another burial taking place a little way down the hill. Lujack had trouble finding a parking space due to the glut of mourners.

"Why does Mark have final approval?" Lujack asked.

"I guess Mark was some kind of silent partner," Molly said with a model's grasp of business.

"More parties at the Marina," Janis sighed, accepting the new rules.

Molly pulled the cigarette lighter out of her purse. She unscrewed the bottom. The new rules seemed like the old rules, Lujack guessed. She did a hit of coke and pushed the vial to Janis. Two of the prettiest girls in the world dragged God knows what up to their brains. Maybe it was easier than dragging God knows what back to their beds.

"So much for my health tips."

Molly smiled plaintively at him. He felt closer to her than he ever had to Ginger. He wasn't sure why.

"Let's park here, Lujack. I don't want to miss the part where they throw dirt on the coffin."

They were getting out of the car when Lujack's phone rang.

"You girls go ahead."

Molly hesitated but Janis dragged her along. Lujack picked up the car phone. From his vantage point on the north side of Forest Lawn he could see the shimmering sheets of smog and heat rise from the San Fernando Valley floor.

"You owe me fifteen hundred bucks," the voice said.

"I hate the Dodgers. And I especially hate Orel Hershiser."

"Jimmy, you're a bookie. You shouldn't get emotionally involved with the local teams."

"Tell that to Lane Randolph."

Mo Breen chuckled on the other end. "Are you sitting down?" Breen asked him.

"What do you think? This is a car phone."

"They're portable."

"I don't think Chase Field would enjoy me talking over his final descent."

"Knowing Chase, where he's going there are lots of young girls . . . naughty young girls." Breen chuckled again. "Is Mark Lyman there?"

"He gave the eulogy. All about how he and Chase were such good friends and, before their respective divorces, such good family men. It was very nice."

"Just doing his job."

"Meaning?"

"Meaning I found out who Mark's partner is in the Zodiac Club. I also found out whose money is behind the Marina Shores."

"I give up."

"Your friendly Pacific National Bank."

"Yoshida."

"None other than."

"The yellow peril is growing more perilous by the minute." Lujack began hastily arranging the last pieces of the bizarre puzzle that began with Ginger Louie's death.

"That's why you haven't heard this from me. First Dolph Killian, then Larry Brownell, now Yoshida. You can pick 'em."

"Tell me about it," Lujack said as he watched Debbi Arnold get out of the Corvette that had pulled up behind him. She was wearing black too. The dress fit her like a sexy glove. Lujack noticed all her joints were in the right places. Channel 7 was the arbiter of bad taste in television news but he couldn't believe they'd actually go to the gravesite for a story.

"Do me a favor, Jimmy. Do you mind sending me a messenger with the fifteen hundred . . . today?"

"What's the matter, Mo, don't you trust me?"

"It's not you I'm worried about, Jimmy. It's your new friends," Breen said, hanging up.

Lujack wasn't sure if Mo had been joking or not. Lujack didn't use messengers often, but he did have a service he trusted. The Flying Bernstein Brothers never asked too many questions; after all, Chin Up was a cash business.

"We keep running into each other in the strangest places," Lujack said, getting out of the car in front of the reporter.

It took her a second to place him. In that second he noticed she was prettier than the first time they'd met. She wasn't glossy. She almost looked human. Maybe that's what TV did to people. It took a few meetings to get beyond the sheen.

"Mr. Lujack, right?"

"You did your homework."

"Mark Lyman and Dolph Killian did it for me. They said you were a cop who became a bookie and the only reason you're not in jail is because you have something on the police chief."

"With friends like Mark Lyman, who needs enemies like Dolph Killian?"

Debbi Arnold laughed. Lujack was liking her more all the time.

"Do you?"

"Do I what?"

"Have something on the police chief?"

"Not that I know of," Lujack said easily. "Can I walk you up?"

She took his arm. He liked the way she felt. Like a woman. Lujack bet she didn't do drugs.

"Chase Field was one of my first friends in LA," she said as they walked up the hill toward the crowd of mourners. "I was an eighteen-year-old girl from Beaverton, Oregon. Chase got me my first job modeling for The Broadway. In those days his name was Feldman and the only gold he wore was in his teeth."

"You both came a long way."

"I guess we did."

She stopped short of the crowd, not wanting to disrupt the rabbi's singing. Lujack remembered the way she'd pushed the microphone in Liz Louie's face after Ginger's funeral. Just doing her job, as they say in television land.

"How did you know him?" Debbi asked.

"Business."

Her blue eyes twinkled. "Maybe we could have a drink sometime and reminisce," she suggested.

"I'd like that very much," he said and watched her meld into the crowd.

Like everything else he knew about the Jewish religion, the burials were straightforward. Not a lot of rigamarole about the hereafter like the Catholics. Lujack remembered his father telling him the Jews were different from Catholics. They could go to heaven, but it wouldn't be until Judgment Day. Until then the good Jews, like the good Hindus and good Muslims, would stay in a place called Limbo. Lujack considered Limbo to be something like detention and, of course, when compared to the alternative—hell—detention didn't seem so bad. It was when his second-grade teacher, Sister Redemption, told him that Judgment Day might not come for hundreds or even thousands of years that he started thinking it might not be so hot to be a Jew or a Hindu or a Muslim, or any religion other than Catholic. But it also got him started thinking. Maybe the deck was stacked. It was that kind of thinking that got him kicked out of St. Stevens's in the fourth grade.

Chase Field's casket was lowered into the ground. Lujack told Molly she would have to find another ride home because he had some business to take care of. She didn't seem distressed, and Molly and Janis went off with a guy wearing sunglasses that cost more than Lujack's suit.

Lujack waited for Lyman at the parking lot near the chapel. When the hearse brought Lyman back to his car, Lujack was standing in front of the Mercedes.

"Nice speech, Mark."

"What do you want, Lujack?"

"I want to talk."

"I just buried my best friend and you want to talk."

Another hearse pulled up and disgorged one of Chase's ex-wives and a cute little girl Lujack took to be the modeling agent's daughter.

"Give me a few minutes. I'll meet you at the train museum in Griffith Park," Lyman said as he looked around the parking lot. "Make sure you're not followed."

Lujack waited next to the miniature train that drove around the museum. Traintown had always been one of his favorite parts of growing up in Los Angeles, that and the Hollywood Stars, SC football, Disneyland, and, of course, Malibu. There weren't many bookies who could say they'd ridden the Matterhorn with Annette Funicello and surfed with Mickey Dora.

Lyman was alone when he drove up. He again looked behind him before getting out of the car. The owner of the Marina Shores was scared. Lujack could see it in the way his tan forehead pressed down on his tinted eyebrows. Lyman rolled his window down and beckoned Lujack to come over.

"Take it easy, Mark. There's no one behind you. I can see all the way back to Chase's grave."

"Chase was killed because he talked to you."

"Chase was killed because he didn't talk to me or the police when he had the chance."

"Five minutes, Lujack, that's all I've got."

"I thought you were a smooth operator, Mark. How did you let yourself get hooked up with the Japanese mob?"

"I don't know what you're talking about," Lyman said, looking back up the hill.

"I'm talking about the Pacific National Bank, Mr.

Kazuo Yoshida, and the funny-looking guys with tattoos and missing pinkies who run your nightclub."

Lyman sighed. He put his head forward on the padded steering wheel. Lujack had known Lyman a long time. This wasn't the Mark Lyman he knew.

"Let it go, Lujack. You can't do anything. The police can't do anything."

"Four people have been murdered. The police can do something about that. That's what they're paid for."

Lyman gave a stilted laugh. "People like Brownell and Killian and Yoshida, they don't answer to the police. They answer to presidents and prime ministers, if there's enough money in it for them."

"You think one of them killed Ginger?"

"Like I told you when you came down with Tommy. I don't know who killed her. I don't care who killed her. She was a tramp."

"But you know Killian is capable of something as sick as Ginger's murder and you know Brownell and Yoshida would go to great lengths to keep Dolph out of jail."

"Do I know that?"

"What's the tie-in between Killian and the others besides hanging out in your playpen?"

"Why should I tell you?"

"Because if you don't I'm going to the police and tell them you're an accessory after the fact and then I'm going to the papers and tell them who your silent partners are. And I'm not just talking about the Zodiac. I'm talking about the Chase Field Agency *and* the Marina Shores."

Lyman looked at him. Lujack looked back. Lyman was in no mood to play chicken.

"I've known Dolph since the seventies," he began slowly. "He was one of my first investors. He and a coupla other Navy pilots set up a consulting firm by the airport. They were always after me to put together a development in the Marina for guys who love to party but can't afford their own yachts."

"And don't like to clean up their own messes," Lujack added, imagining the kind of parties Dolph Killian and his friends would have.

"I guess you could say Dolph gave me the idea for Marina Shores. Dolph knew Larry Brownell through business. Larry was impressed with the parties Chase and I put on."

"I bet the old geezer was."

"Before I knew it Brownell was the cosigner on the loan I got for the expansion. The bank was Pacific National. I didn't even know who Yoshida was until three years ago. Larry asked me out on his yacht. He said he wanted to introduce me to the man who owned my development. I thought he was kidding."

Again the desperate laugh.

"Yoshida and Brownell had quietly bought out most of my original investors. Before I realized it, I was a subsidiary of the rising sun."

"What about the Zodiac?"

"Yoshida occasionally likes to go out. So do his clients. He likes discretion."

"So he bought a nightclub and brought the Yakuza in to run it," Lujack said, continuing Lyman's scenario. "Meanwhile you and Chase provided the girls as an interest payment to the new owners of the Field Agency. You start out as a developer and end up a pimp for a Japanese banker."

"That's one way of putting it."

"But then one of your associates, probably Dolph Killian, got carried away with Ginger," Lujack said, knowing in the back of his mind that Ginger's death was not so much the answer as the catalyst of the mystery. "Field must have known who the murderer was, or did he just want his agency back? Does that bother you, Mark? That one of your new partners killed your best friend?"

"Chase knew where the money was coming from. He wanted to expand, go into film production. I told him there was no turning back," Lyman said, then looked at Lujack. "Let it drop, Jimmy. That way, no one else will be killed. No more of your friends, no more of mine."

Lujack thought to himself how few friends he had. None of the victims, not Ginger, not Field, were who he would call friends. Lyman was right about one thing, though. It wasn't going to be easy getting those responsible. The case had all the earmarks of a high-stakes cover-up. A cover-up where arrogant men killed witnesses the way drug dealers killed competitors. A rich Japanese banker and a huge defense contractor covering up the indulgences of a valued defense analyst or an important senator. But still, there was something else he wasn't seeing.

"You can't treat the death of a man like Chase Field like another drive-by shooting in Watts."

"Don't worry, Lujack. They'll make it look official."

"You don't have much faith in your country's law enforcement, Mark."

"You, of all people, should talk."

"I may earn my money illegally, but I don't betray my country when I do it."

Lyman winced. Lujack had hit a nerve.

"How much yen did you cost them, Mark?"

"Whatever you think you know, Lujack, take my advice. Forget you know it. Besides, it's not the

Japanese you should worry about. It's the Americans."

"I'm not good at forgetting, Mark. Never have been."

"Then I'll visit you up on the hill with Chase," Lyman said, starting his car. "Good-bye, Lujack. Tell Tommy it's nothing personal but I can't afford to be a Good Book player anymore."

Lyman nodded as if he really didn't expect to see him again. As if one or maybe both of them would soon be dead. Lyman knew enough about men like Dolph Killian and Lawrence Brownell to be that afraid. He had just buried his best friend, but there was no sadness in Lyman, only fear. As for Lujack, he didn't scare that easy.

Kyle Thurgood was waiting for him at the Okie Dog stand on Santa Monica Boulevard. Kyle, for all his silk ties and seven-hundred-dollar suits, would much rather hunker down with a foot-long Okie Dog and a sack full of greasy Okie fries than poke at a warm duck salad at Joss. He was midway through his dog when Lujack showed up. A group of Hollywood lowlifes were making a drug deal at a picnic table next to Thurgood. The lieutenant was oblivious.

"How was the funeral?" he asked, between bites.

"Lots of beautiful girls, a few tears. Mark Lyman and a few rent-a-rabbis said what a great guy he was."

"Did anyone say why he was murdered?"

"That's your job."

"Right."

"What do the Yaks who killed Mason say?"

"They say they were watching 'MTV Dance Party.' You know, downtown Julie Brown," Thurgood said, polishing off his last inch of Okie dog. "Mason comes into the rec room and changes the channel. Doesn't even ask them. Just goes up and changes the channel. He wanted to watch one of the soaps. They're not sure which one. They barely speak English."

"They killed him because he wanted to watch a soap opera?"

"I can think of worse reasons," Thurgood said. "That was when he pulled the knife. I guess Mason was really into this soap. You know drug dealers, they sit around and watch a lot of TV."

"Where did Mason get a shiv?"

"Where does anyone get anything in a city jail? Anyhow, they fought and Mason ended up with his throat cut. According to the Koreans' lawyer it was self-defense."

"They have a lawyer?"

"They have a damn good lawyer. Dave Levine. Matsuda tells me Levine represents a lot of the Korean kids."

"Who pays him?"

Thurgood smiled. "According to Matsuda, Levine bills the vice-president of the Pacific National Bank. A Korean national named George Kim."

"A Korean Yakuza working in a Japanese bank. Now what do you think about my Yoshida theory?"

"What Yoshida theory is that?"

"We know the Korean Yakuza have close ties with the Japanese crime families. We know that Yoshida knew Ginger. We also know that he probably knows, or can guess, which of his deranged American associates killed her. He uses his Korean Yakuza soldiers to cover up the murder by moving the body, framing Mason, then killing him and Field when the frame began to come apart."

"Provided I accept the first three or four jumps in

your illogic, why would a man like Yoshida, who is supposed to be one of the richest men in California, if not the world, care about anyone at the Marina Shores killing a girl like Ginger?"

"I'm not sure, although my guess is it has to do with a defense contract Killian and Brownell are working on. Some kind of technology transfer, possibly having to do with the new B-3 bomber."

Thurgood shoved a handful of fries into his mouth. "You're saying this is some sort of spy shit?"

"I'm saying four people are dead under very strange circumstances and that there's got to be more to it than a party girl ending up in two different beds."

"Lujack, I'm a homicide detective, not a spook. You worry about the balance of global power, I'll try to nail the creep who cut up Ginger and Field."

"You really think it's one man who's responsible? What about Mason and the bomb under my car?"

"Okay, creeps, does that make you happier?"

"Not really."

Thurgood nodded in the direction of the Jensen. A pale-faced girl in a black miniskirt was walking around it. She looked more like a mongrel than a teenage girl.

"How's your new car running?"

"Sports is giving me an option to buy," Lujack said, in no mood to talk about cars. Thurgood was being awfully casual about the case. Cases. Lujack wondered why.

"Do you think he has a brother named Micky?"

"Who? What?"

"George Kim, the banker. The former manager of the Zodiac, his name is Micky Kim."

"Kim in Korea is like Smith here," Thurgood said, again looking in the direction of the girl who was now leaning on the Jensen. "I think that girl likes you,

Jimmy. She's trying to polish your door handle with her snatch."

"Probably just putting some C-4 under the latch."

Thurgood did a double take. The girl stuck her tongue out and walked away. Both men laughed.

"I knew I could get your attention sooner or later," Lujack said. "You don't seem too anxious to push on this one."

Thurgood sighed. He corralled his last french fry.

"There's a good chance Matsuda and the Asian Task Force are going to end up with the whole thing, so you're right, I'm not pushing."

"What are you talking about?"

"I'm talking about a memo I got from your friend Chief Bane this morning. It seems Matsuda and his friends in the department see a chance for some publicity. There are nearly a million Asian-Americans and Asian nationals in Southern California and most of them have never heard of the LAPD's crack Asian Task Force. The mayor smells votes on this one."

"But homicide is homicide."

"Not anymore it isn't, Jimmy. Not in LA. Not since the Crips and the Bloods started killing each other at a rate of one every other day. Not since the drive-by shooters started killing more innocent people than drunken drivers. Homicide is the Gang Task Force, the Asian Task Force, anyone who has the time to pick the bodies up off the street," Thurgood said, smoothing his expensive tie over his expansive stomach.

"Kyle, a girl was murdered. Then she was decapitated and her head or her body was moved to another location. There was no blood outside of either bedroom. No screams. No witnesses. No sign of the hideousness of the crime. Only some kind of Oriental graffiti. It's like it happened in a movie or a hospital."

"That's not a bad idea. The hospital. It could explain the sterility of the crime scene," Thurgood noted.

"But what about the mind of the person who did it?" Lujack yelled.

"I told you, Jimmy, homicide isn't what it used to be. That's why the Feds came up with the Occult Task Force."

"The Occult Task Force. What's that?"

Thurgood looked at him, not joking, "It's the latest excuse for a society that's gagging on its own violence. The devil makes us do it."

# Chapter Ten

## *She Did It Again*

Lujack got the invitation three days before the actual wedding. It was the least she could do. He called her to accept and she sounded pleased.

"I'm glad you're coming," she said over the phone.

"I didn't know it was going to be so soon."

"Todd didn't want to wait."

"Yeah, that Todd's an impetuous son of a gun."

"Be nice, Jimmy."

"I'll try."

Silence.

"Saturday afternoon. I was going to the SC home opener against Washington. I even had a date," Lujack heard himself saying for no apparent reason.

"Why don't you bring her to the wedding?"

"Maybe I will."

"Do you know how to get to Todd's?"

He knew exactly how to get to Todd's. She'd been living with Barnes for the past few months. She was never home when he called. No matter what hour. He had even gone to see her a few times, but she hadn't been there. Her car had been parked in the driveway of Barnes's Pasadena home.

"He's on Highland above Foothill."

"I think I can find it."

"There won't be a lot of people there. Some friends from the clinic. Todd's kids."

"Maybe I can talk to his ex-wife after the ceremony."

"You're the only ex-spouse who'll be attending. Because we're such good friends," she said.

"These kids. How old are they?"

"Milton is thirteen. Jessica is eleven."

"He named his kid Milton?"

"It was Todd's father's name," she said defensively.

"Do you get along with them? The kids?"

"They live mostly with their mother, but, yes, I think we get along pretty well. You'd have to ask them."

They both hesitated. Lujack could feel them both hesitating.

"We're going to try and have children. Maybe not right away," she laughed, "but I'm not getting any younger."

"No. I mean, you look great. That's great," he said, wanting to hang up. "I know how much it would mean to you."

"I'll see you then, Jimmy. With your date."

"Saturday, right," he repeated. "We got married on Friday."

"No, Jimmy, we got married on Thursday. You always worked Friday nights."

"The eagle flies on Friday. So do the cops."

"That's what you said when we got married."

"I did? Guess I haven't changed much."

"No, not much," she said and hung up. He asked

himself if it would have made any difference if he had changed. He doubted it.

Lujack was still thinking about the conversation when he walked down to San Vincente Boulevard to pick up his new business cards. The cards were an idea he'd had the night before after hearing about "Bones" Crenshaw being busted in his Toluca Lake home. If the cops were going after stand-up bookies like Bones and it was only the first week of the football season, Lujack figured it was time to beef up his cover. The only problem was he wasn't sure where the printer's shop was located in the mini mall. He wasn't even sure if he was in the right mall. That was one of the problems with this neighborhood he lived in, too many malls.

The longer he lived in Brentwood the more he thought Tommy was right. He should buy a boat and move to the marina. It was bad enough that Brentwood was full of aspiring young filmmakers with wide ties and low-slung cars whose alarm systems cost more than their transmissions. Add to that the yogurt stores and health clubs and mini malls, plus the gridlock developers had predicted but had called "casual traffic." Not to mention the last notice he'd received from his landlord, saying that because of the new security system that had to be installed after the rash of summer burglaries, Lujack's rent was being raised to $1,900 a month. There was something downright immoral about having to pay almost $2,000 a month rent for a one-bedroom apartment in the middle of an overcrowded yuppie crime zone. If he bought a sailboat or an old Hatteras, he could at least be on the water. Maybe his former friend Mark Lyman could get him into a slip at the Shores.

"Gail McCrell, Creative Genius," the sign read in front of the white low-tech awning.

He'd found the right mini mall. There weren't a whole lot of printers like Gail. She had wild red hair and freckles and a voice that sounded like it belonged on the back of a package of filterless cigarettes. She was a welcome respite from the other entrepreneurs in the area. She insulted her customers instead of insulating them.

"Lujack, you want fast service," she said, looking up from her drafting table. This day she was wearing a T-shirt she had designed herself. On it was a picture of a guy who looked like a cross between Jesus Christ and Jerry Garcia. He was smoking a joint. "We light up your life—Humboldt County, Ca.," the lettering read.

"Nice T-shirt."

"It's my Debbie Boone model."

"I'm sure it'll go over big at her next concert."

"Your cards are ready. I couldn't squeeze all of your ego on one side of a card so I just put your name."

She handed him the box of business cards he'd ordered.

"James Lujack, Personal Consultant," he read.

"What exactly is a personal consultant, Lujack? Is that sort of like a guy who'll mind your business while still minding his own?"

"That's not a bad description," Lujack said. "Maybe I should put it on the card."

"Not without a royalty you won't," she said. "Which brings me to your bill. Five hundred business cards. That's $21.75 or a night in your favorite motel."

Lujack wasn't seriously considering the second option when a man in a lightweight parka and Levis walked into the store behind him. There wasn't a lot of room to maneuver in Gail's ten feet of storefront. When he noticed two other familiar faces outside, one on each side of the doorway, he knew there was no use trying anything. The two men outside worked for Dolph Killian. The last time he'd seen them they were about to throw him off a building.

The man in the parka looked to be of the same mercenary ilk. He was stocky, muscular, with a military haircut graying at the temples. He smiled and pushed a metal object in the small of Lujack's back.

"Got a minute, Mr. Lujack?"

"That depends."

The gun barrel jammed harder into his back. With his free hand the man frisked Lujack. He didn't have to. Lujack hadn't thought of bringing his .38 to the printer's.

"No, it doesn't."

"You're right, it doesn't."

"What's going on, Lujack? This guy's got his hand down your pants."

"Shut up, Red, or I'll blow your fucking head off," the man in the parka said in a businesslike voice, pulling a Beretta out of his pocket. "Maybe you'd like this down your pants, eh, honey?"

Gail, for the first time in her life, was speechless.

"Let's get out of here, Colonel," the black man said from the doorway.

"Lujack, you're not going anywhere 'til I get paid," Gail said forcefully.

Lujack pulled out a twenty. Gail was just brave enough and crazy enough to get herself, and possibly him, killed. He placed the bill on the counter.

"I owe you a buck seventy-five," Lujack said, trying to tell her with eyes to back off, for God's sake. "You know I'm good for it."

Gail took the money. "You better be."

"This is a private matter, lady. Don't do anything stupid," the colonel said, grabbing Lujack's arm and dragging him outside where the merc with the cold eyes had pulled up a Jaguar sedan. The gun was back in the parka but still snug against Lujack's side.

"You've been watching too many late movies, Colonel. I'm not a lady," Gail yelled as they sped off.

"Mouthy bitch, we shoulda shot her," the driver said as they headed down San Vincente toward the freeway.

"You do the driving, I'll do the shooting," the colonel said crankily.

Gail was right, the whole thing had the feel of an old movie.

"I didn't know Dolph and I were still talking," Lujack said to no one in particular.

"You're not going to see Dolph Killian," the colonel said, and the way he said it Lujack almost wished he were.

By the time they reached the marina and drove through the private Marina Shores gate down to the Yacht Club, Lujack had figured out where they were headed and who he was being summoned to see.

Dolph's mercenaries waited in the car while the colonel walked Lujack up the portable stairs to the covered ramp connecting Los Angeles to the gleaming white yacht. Lujack remembered a client telling him that to really appreciate a world-class yacht you have to smell it. The only thing Lujack could smell was the brackish water of the Marina Channel, but that didn't lessen his appreciation for the six-million-dollar yacht he was about to board.

"I hope there isn't any symbolism in this," Lujack said as he walked across the water onto the deck of the *Southern Cross.*

The colonel gave him another push. So much for gangplank jokes.

"Nice boat," Lujack observed to the white-haired man standing behind the railing.

"Yacht, Mr. Lujack," corrected Lawrence Brownell.

"Right. Nice yacht," Lujack answered.

"It's a beauty. I bought it from an Australian but he wouldn't recognize her now. I've made her mine from the port lights to the engine room. Would you like a tour?"

"Is that why the colonel and I rushed over here? For a tour of your boat . . . yacht?"

Brownell ignored the question and walked into the spacious salon. Lujack and the colonel followed. The interior of the *Southern Cross* was every bit as modern and spectacular as the exterior. Like the sleek white lines of the outside, the salon of the *Southern Cross* was elegant and uncluttered in a tasteful, high-tech style. It was like walking into the showroom of an interior designer. Far more elegant than the living rooms of some of Lujack's richest clients. But then Larry Brownell wasn't a millionaire. According to the latest issue of *Forbes* magazine, Brownell was a billionaire. Lujack tried to envision a thousand million dollars. That was a lot of point spreads on a lot of games.

"You're quite right, Mr. Lujack. The tour can wait. What we have to talk about can't."

Brownell held out a hand, motioning Lujack to sit down. He was wearing a business suit and it was obvious he had come from his office in the ultramodern Brownell Industries Plaza for their little chat. There would be no cruising today.

"Just what is it that we have to talk about, Mr. Brownell?"

"Politics, Mr. Lujack," the industrialist said, still standing. "You can leave us now, Martin," he told the colonel.

"Are you sure, Mr. Brownell?"

Brownell nodded. The colonel walked outside.

"What kind of politics, Mr. Brownell?"

"Real politics, Mr. Lujack. The kind that makes the world go round. The kind that your misguided investigation into Ginger Louie's death has involved you."

"Four people are dead, Mr. Brownell. That's pretty real too."

"I'm talking about the future of the world's political structure, Mr. Lujack. The possible future of this planet."

"I'm sorry if my investigation has inconvenienced your worldview, Mr. Brownell, not to mention the future of the planet. But to me politics means the U.S. Constitution. The rule of law. It doesn't mean the success of a multinational corporation."

"Dolph told me you were a crusader," Brownell said with some bemusement.

"Did Dolph also tell you that he raped and murdered Ginger Louie?"

"I've known Dolph Killian for thirty years. He's a lot of things. A great pilot. The best Navy pilot in the Pacific for my money. He's a brilliant weapons analyst and a good friend. He likes his booze and his women, but he isn't a rapist or a murderer."

"Chase Field seemed to think different."

Brownell leaned forward. Lujack was fishing but he didn't know if Brownell knew it. The billionaire's eyes locked on him the way the vectors of one of the missile systems he built would lock on a target.

"Chase Field is dead, Mr. Lujack. That's why I had you brought here today. It's time for the killing to stop, before serious damage is done."

"Are we talking real politics again?"

"You don't seem to understand, Mr. Lujack. I'm trying to help you. I don't control what's happening. I don't know who killed that girl or Mr. Field. What I do know is that it is in both our interests to stop the forces that have been put in motion."

"Is that a threat or a proposition?"

"I don't make threats, Mr. Lujack."

"I'm still listening."

"From what I've learned the police now believe the Korean Yakuza are responsible for the murders," Brownell said diplomatically.

"All three crime scenes had Yakuza markings. There was an Oriental youth seen near my car before the explosion. The two boys who killed Dave Mason are known Yakuza members. You might say the Yakuza are somehow involved," Lujack said, guessing Brownell's sources in the department were probably better than his so there was no reason to beat around the usual bush.

"You know, of course, the Yakuza are different from crime families in America. Both in Japan and in Korea."

"Oh."

"There are thousands of members. The Japanese Yamaguchi-gumi has over ten thousand members and is over three hundred years old. Their syndicates have levels of management—like corporations. They control thousands of businesses from prostitution and gambling to insurance and moviemaking."

"I thought the Japanese had laws against racketeering."

"In Japan the ruling Liberal Democratic Party and the Yakuza go back many years. There are some who believe if it weren't for the alliance between Japan's politicians and Japan's criminals, the country would be communist today," Brownell said, gauging Lujack's reaction. "Have you ever heard of a man named Yoshio Kodama?"

Lujack said he hadn't.

"Kodama was released from the Sugamo prison in 1948. He used his Yakuza booty to finance the Liberal Party. He later became the link between the Liberal Democratic Party, U.S. Intelligence, and the Yakuza syndicates. It was Kodama who was instrumental in stopping the breakup of the Japanese combines like Mitsui and Mitsubishi in the late 'forties and early 'fifties. He was also behind the Yakuza attacks on the Japanese Communist Party. In my opinion Kodama is the man most responsible for Japan's success over the past forty years. It has been said men like Nakasone and Tanaka owe their careers to the man."

"What's this guy have to do with Ginger Louie?"

Brownell smiled. "Everything and nothing," he said. "Kodama is dead now. But there are other men in Japan, powerful men who share Kodama's devotion to Japanese society."

"You mean there are other right-wing gangsters with political connections. Men who might be embarrassed if they were linked to murders in the U.S."

"That isn't how I would put it, Mr. Lujack, but your description isn't entirely inaccurate."

"Men like Kazuo Yoshida," Lujack said, dotting the *i*.

"Kazuo is a banker, not a gangster."

"But he wouldn't be too happy about any publicity linking him to the cover-up of Ginger's murder. Say if a certain vice-president in his bank, a Korean gentleman by the name of George Kim, were known to be paying the legal fees of the two men charged with the killing of Dave Mason."

"That's a stretch, Mr. Lujack, but again, not entirely inaccurate," Brownell conceded, and Lujack thought they were finally getting down to the payoff.

"If information such as you just volunteered were to be given to an irresponsible media . . . we both know how the press can ruin reputations."

Lujack looked past Brownell to a white sloop tacking out to the channel. He knew how the press could ruin reputations. "Berserk Cop Beats Suspect," the headline had run in one of the Los Angeles papers. The only phone call he had got the next day was from his mother. She hadn't believed it. Lujack tried to explain that, like most headlines, it was only partly true. Anna had been in the kitchen pretending not to listen. She'd never asked him about it. Five days later she left him.

"Five hundred thousand dollars, Mr. Lujack. You can disperse it any way you see fit. To the victims' families, to your favorite charity, or to your favorite Swiss bank."

A half a million dollars got Lujack's mind back into the conversation. "Just the other day I was thinking about moving out of my apartment. A half a million bucks could make that move a lot more enjoyable. Maybe I could buy a little sailboat and move in near you."

Brownell smiled condescendingly. A bribe was one thing. A neighbor was quite another.

"There's only one problem," Lujack said, feeling more angry than righteous. "How could I be sure that the man who butchered Ginger and killed an innocent boy would see justice?"

"You can't be sure, Mr. Lujack. You have to let the police do their job. You said yourself this is a nation of laws. It is also a nation of law enforcement. No one appointed you as the arbiter of justice."

"You're right, nobody did. I just seem to fall into it."

Brownell's hands cupped over his knees. The hands were smooth and covered with brown spots. Lujack hadn't thought of Brownell as old until that moment. The man must have been in his late sixties, his life spent building up one of the biggest companies in the United States. A former number two man in the Defense Department. A friend of four presidents. And now he had to carry water for a Japanese banker. Yes, the world was changing. Real politics. Real yen.

"A million dollars. Would that soften your fall enough?"

One thing you had to say about billionaires. They knew how to negotiate.

"You mean make me not want to jump," Lujack said, and he stood up. "I promised myself a long time ago that I never wanted to get that comfortable."

Lujack's movement startled the industrialist. Lawrence Brownell wasn't used to having his conversations ended by someone else. "That's your answer then," he said, slowly getting to his feet. "You're going to continue making a pest of yourself."

"I'm going to find out what's going on, Mr. Brownell. If it embarrasses you and your Japanese friend, or costs you the contract on the B-3, that's the way the procurement crumbles."

Brownell grabbed Lujack's arm. It was like the old man had just stepped on a power line. The hand was viselike.

"Who told you about the B-3? That project is top secret."

"Don't worry, Mr. Brownell. I may be a lot of things but I'm not a traitor. I love this country as much as you and Dolph Killian."

Lujack didn't see Colonel Martin enter the salon but he heard the click of the safety on his Beretta being released.

"Is there a problem, Mr. Brownell?" the colonel asked.

"Yes. Mr. Lujack has become a problem. A national security problem."

"Don't worry, sir, I enjoy taking care of problems like Lujack."

Lujack guessed he shouldn't have said anything about the B-3, although he finally understood why there were so many bodies lying around. One of which might soon be his.

"I'm afraid we failed to reach an agreement. Dolph was right. Mr. Lujack is not the kind of man who can be reasoned with. Not even for the good of his own country."

"Since when does the good of our country include the murder of fellow Americans, Mr. Brownell?"

"Since the days of George Washington," the industrialist said. "But don't worry, Mr. Lujack, nothing will happen to you. At least nothing that can be traced to me. If I were you, though, I'd start going over my tax returns. From what I hear bookies need a lot of time to prepare for an audit."

"You know something, Mr. Brownell, you may be a billionaire but you're also a real asshole."

The butt of Colonel Martin's Beretta struck him on the skull, just above the nape of his neck.

When he came to, he was lying in his doorway. A cool cloth was being rubbed on the back of his head.

"You're a lot prettier than Kyle Thurgood."

"I hope so," Debbi Arnold said, continuing to wipe his brow.

Lujack made a move to get up. The back of his head throbbed. There were little white things running around behind his eyes.

"Take it easy. You've got a pretty good bump back

there," Debbi said, holding his arm. She smelled like perfume which was better than the rubber doormat he had just left.

He managed to sit up. When he did, he remembered Lawrence Brownell.

"I've been trying to reach you all day. I even called your partner, but he said he didn't know where you were either. You were three hours late for an appointment then."

Lujack remembered there was the sticky matter of collecting an overdue bill from Sports.

"I came by to leave you a note about Saturday and found you lying on the step. I don't know how long you've been here. You'd think one of the neighbors would have done something."

"I'm not too popular in the building ever since the wife of one of my customers threw a baseball through my front window."

He was on his feet now. A bit wobbly but able to take in all of Debbi Arnold. She was in a beige suit and her honey-blond hair was combed out on her shoulders.

"I take it her husband wasn't a very good bettor."

"You take it right. Old Glen couldn't pick a winner at a fox hunt."

"So—tell me what happened."

"I'm not sure. Although I think I might have some tax problems this year." Lujack gently touched his head. The bump seemed to be growing. "What about you? What is your note going to say about Saturday?"

"I have to work. A special report on teen pregnancy. I am going to be interviewing an abortionist who supposedly had a sex change. He was a woman, now he's a man, but worst of all, he's an abortionist."

"The miracles of science. Sounds like a candidate for Geraldo."

"Don't laugh," she said, and he didn't. "Maybe I could meet you at the reception later? You never told me who's getting married."

She waited for an answer. When he didn't give one, she had another question. "Are you all right?"

"Yeah. I'm fine. That would be nice if you could meet me. Did I give you the address?"

"Yeah. I've got it in the car."

She looked at him and smiled. It was an amused smile, but there was affection, he thought, and maybe something more. He thought maybe she wanted to sleep with him. That was okay too.

"I thought I was in a tough business," she said. "The guy who beat you up. It was over money, wasn't it?"

"You could say that, yeah. It was over a lot of money."

# — Chapter Eleven —

## *Anna wore white—Lujack wore black*

It was an elegant if unpretentious wedding. Anna wore a silk brocade dress that glistened under the Southern California sun. Barnes was in a morning coat with a black-and-gray tie and pearl-colored cummerbund. He could have been going to Ascot if he were a betting man. But as Anna had reminded Lujack more than once in the last few weeks, Todd was no betting man.

"You look radiant," Lujack told her in the receiving line. He wasn't lying. She wore her hair up like a princess, her cheeks were flushed, her eyes full of love. Lujack hated it.

"Thank you, James. I feel radiant."

She looked at him in a different way. He could feel it. It wasn't the same way she looked at him when she was with Marty. Or later, when she'd come back to the world. There was resolve in her expression, commitment. She was gone.

"That's a beautiful dress," he said, remembering the department store dress she'd worn when they got married. She had looked radiant that day too.

"Todd picked it out," she said demurely.

"Ah, Lujack. Glad you could come," Barnes said, forcefully shaking Lujack's hand.

Lujack noticed his shoes were some sort of patent leather. The guy was sick.

"Congratulations, Todd."

"Dr. and Mrs. Barnes. It has a nice ring to it, doesn't it, darling?" Barnes said, kissing his new wife.

Lujack thought briefly of mentioning the first Mrs. Barnes but realized he was in no position to bring up former wives. That didn't stop Barnes, however.

"You know, a lot of people would consider it in bad taste to invite an ex-spouse to a wedding. But I think it has a certain salutary effect. Completing the emotional circle. A sort of benediction. I invited my own ex, but she had a previous engagement."

"I hate to rain on your parade, Doc, but I never gave this ceremony my benediction. I came out of respect for Anna."

"Of course you did, and I'm glad you came," Barnes said, feeling a certain tension from his new wife communicate itself to him.

"Save me a dance," Lujack said to Anna.

"What about your date?" she said, holding firmly to her husband's arm and smiling at Lujack.

"I'm not even sure she's going to make it."

"Of course she will," Anna said, and Lujack took that as a compliment, if only because it came from a friend.

He moved off toward the patio, wondering why in the world he had come. A girl in black pants and a white shirt offered him a tray of champagne.

"Do you have any scotch?" he asked crankily.

"Try the bar," she said.

The bar was a table set up next to the pool. Some sort of jazz group was setting up on the patio. Barnes had a pretty nice house. Old, pseudo-Spanish, two stories. Lujack guessed it was worth nearly a million dollars in today's go-for-broke Southern California real estate market. Psychiatrists obviously made decent money. Lujack, of all people, should know. He'd paid the bastard enough money over the past five years.

"How about a scotch, partner?" Lujack asked the bar man.

"I hate champagne too," the bartender said, pouring Lujack a two-fingered shot.

He had the glass to his lips when he spotted Anna's father.

"Still like the hard stuff, eh, Jimmy?" Denny Dole said with a grade A smile on his face.

Lujack had always despised Denny. Anna said it was because of her father that she left home before she left high school. After meeting Denny, Lujack knew why. He was a lineman for the gas company. Anna said he used to think he was the world's greatest engineer, who, if he'd had a chance to go to college, could have been a millionaire. Instead, he was a bitter, self-pitying slob who alienated his wife and family. His wife had died while Anna was in the hospital. Lujack thought Denny had barely noticed.

"What are you doing here, Denny? I thought weddings were for family and friends."

"A father should give his daughter away," Denny said, although Lujack had failed to see him during the ceremony. "Damned if I didn't get caught in cross-town traffic coming over here, though. They had to go ahead without me."

Denny pushed his glass toward the bartender for a refill. Lujack almost felt sorry for the poor son of a bitch.

"Well, this sure beats that courthouse you got married in," Denny observed, casting an appreciative eye around the surroundings.

"Yeah, when I married Anna her father didn't have any money," Lujack answered, quickly getting over his pity.

"I told you I'd pay for a church wedding. It was Anna who didn't want a big wedding," Denny said, as usual casting the blame elsewhere.

"Right, Denny, nothing was ever too good for your daughter."

"You got no room to talk, Jimmy. I always said cops made bad husbands," he said, taking a gulp of the bubbly. "I never blamed her for leaving you."

"I never blamed her for leaving you either," Lujack said.

He felt himself beginning to lose what little composure he had left when he saw Debbi Arnold step through the sliding doors out onto the patio. She was wearing a royal blue suit and a fuchsia scarf. Lujack didn't mind that his head wasn't the only one that turned when she appeared.

"I'd love to chitchat, Denny, but I have to take care of my date."

"Jesus, that's Debbi Arnold of Channel Seven," Denny said, following Lujack's glance. "What's she doing here?"

"Watch," Lujack said, and he walked toward his date, leaving Denny to celebrate by himself.

The groom had already introduced himself by the time Lujack reached Debbi. Barnes was the kind of man who couldn't resist celebrity or celebrities. Lujack felt a twinge of the future watching Anna watch her new husband make a fool of himself.

"The piece you did on the mentally ill and the

homeless last month was truly groundbreaking," Barnes was saying.

"Thank you, Dr. Barnes," Debbi said politely. "I'd be very interested to read your book."

"I take it you two know each other," Lujack said.

"We met a few months ago at a mental health conference," Debbi said.

Barnes gave him a blank look, finding it inconceivable that Lujack could know someone like Debbi Arnold.

"How was your interview?"

"You were right." Debbi laughed. "He already talked to Geraldo."

"And you know each other?" Todd Barnes asked.

"She's Jimmy's date," Anna said. "I'm Anna Barnes, the bride."

"I might not be the best reporter in town but I figured that out." Debbi smiled, sticking out a hand. "Congratulations."

"Dear, we better get back to the receiving line," Anna said gently.

"Of course," Barnes said, still not quite believing. "I'm so glad you could come," he finished lamely and followed Anna back to the line.

"What a coincidence, you knowing Todd."

"Tell you the truth I don't remember ever meeting him."

"Todd has that impression on people."

"His wife seems nice."

"She is," Lujack said.

"A friend of yours?"

"An old friend. A very old friend. We were married for six years."

"I'd say that does make you old friends," Debbi said.

Lujack and Debbi stayed at the wedding until the cake was cut. Lujack noticed there was no best man to give a toast. Not surprising, knowing Todd. The closest thing to a scene came when Clem Williams, one of Todd's patients, tried to throw the good doctor in the pool. No one exactly said why Clem did what he did, but none of the other patients seemed too upset about the attempt. Lujack never got his dance with Anna but he left the wedding feeling good. Todd was a jerk, but he was a steady jerk.

Lujack followed Debbi back to her Bunker Hill condo. She dropped off her car and they took the 10 Freeway west toward the Chin Up. One of the stipulations of their PDA (predate agreement) was that Debbi got to see where Lujack "worked" and got to meet his partner. Lujack had tried to explain that Tommy had certain preconceptions about Debbi after she had stuck a microphone in his face at Ginger's funeral, but she said that was why she wanted to meet him, so she could apologize. Surprisingly, Tommy had agreed. Lujack couldn't figure his partner out lately. It was bad enough they were losing money on Orel Hershiser, but Tommy didn't seem to care. Tommy not caring about money, that was a scoop.

"Maybe he's still upset about his niece and his son. Can you blame him? Some very strange things have been happening to the guy," Debbi said.

"I know he's upset. Why do you think I got mixed up in this mess to begin with? Because Tommy was upset. His ancestors were unable to rest."

"I'm afraid there's something more sinister going on than restless ancestors," she said pointedly. "If the DA thinks we're going to swallow that story about the ax found in Chase Field's garage with Ginger's blood on it, he's dumber than Hamilton Burger."

Speaking of which, Lujack wasn't dumb enough to think that *his* good looks and sordid profession were the only reasons Debbi Arnold was hanging out with him. He hadn't told her about his run-in with Lawrence Brownell, other than what she saw after Brownell and Killian's goons had dropped him off on his own doorstep, but Debbi hadn't become one of LA's top TV reporters by not knowing a sexy story when she saw it. She had been making oblique references to the holes in the latest police scenario all afternoon.

Kyle Thurgood had briefed Lujack that morning. During a routine search of Field's Palm Springs condo the local cops had found an ax in the garage. The ax had traces of dried blood on it. A lab analysis came back with a match between Ginger's blood and that on the ax. It did seem a bit convenient. Like the body in Dave Mason's bed seemed convenient, in a surreal, almost too obvious way. Thurgood was now hinting that if the Asian Task Force could pick up a certain Korean Yakuza who used to work at the Zodiac, who had fought with Chase Field once in the parking lot and who was seen around the rear entrance to the club the night of Field's murder, the case would be as good as closed. "Who's the Yakuza?" Lujack had asked, already knowing the answer.

"Micky Kim," Thurgood had answered.

"Kim. Who told you about Kim in the first place?" Lujack had asked, already knowing the answer.

"I know, the Yoshida theory. Japanese banker covers up murder by American associate to protect . . . what was it? Some sort of missile contract?"

"The B-3 bomber."

"Right. The bomber no one has ever heard of."

Lujack wanted to know what was wrong with the

Yoshida theory and asked if the cops had checked out George Kim, the bank vice-president, to see if there was a connection. Thurgood said they had and there wasn't. The task force was treating it as a turf war between different Yakuza factions. Somehow Ginger, Dave Mason, Billy Cridmore, and Chase Field had gotten caught up in something that had nothing to do with them.

"What about the semen, Kyle?" Lujack had asked later.

"I'm sorry I ever told you about the fucking come," Kyle had said, shaking his head.

"I bet it's not Chase Field's."

"I'll bet we could find samples of Chase Field's jizz on half the models in this town."

"It doesn't match, does it?" Lujack had insisted.

"No, Jimmy, it doesn't fucking match, but it doesn't make any difference either."

"Why doesn't it make any difference?"

"Because Chief Bane says it doesn't. Because the DA says it doesn't. Because the mayor says it doesn't. This isn't a sex crime, Jimmy, it's a gang crime."

"Do you believe that, Kyle?"

"I believe it doesn't make much fucking difference what I believe. It's Matsuda and the Asia Task Force's case."

"Matsuda will never put it all together."

"No, he won't," Kyle had said precisely.

It was at this point in their conversation that Lujack had decided not to tell Thurgood about his visit with Brownell. Not because he didn't trust Kyle, but because Kyle had just told him not to trust the people Kyle worked for.

"There are a lot of people in this city who would like the Yakuza murders wrapped in a very neat, very inscrutable package and thrown in the city dump," Lujack said to Debbi, coming back to present company.

"Including my station manager. He says it's all right to sensationalize the Yakuza, but he doesn't want to offend the Korean and Japanese communities. I told him hired thugs don't go around cutting people up because they don't like the colors of a certain nightclub."

"What's your theory?" he asked as he came off the freeway at Robertson.

"I don't have one. That's why I'm with you."

"I thought it was my money and good looks."

"Those too," Debbi said, smiling a smile Lujack was not sure how to read.

Lujack followed Robertson north past Hamilton High. Each time he passed the old three-story school building, he was shocked by the latest edition of the LA teenager. A very hip black kid, replete with high-top orange basketball shoes and a purple tunic, chugged across the street in front of them. The boy was holding something that looked like a bag or a purse. Seeing the boy made Lujack think of Lionel. Tommy had said Lionel was going to be starting back to school next week.

"What makes me think there aren't any books in that boy's purse?"

"It's Saturday, give the kid a break. Only an ex-cop would be so cynical."

"I've heard reporters that didn't exactly believe in the Easter Bunny."

"Reporters believe in the truth. You should know that."

"I believe in the truth too. That's why I'm a bookie. The point spread never lies."

"You're a strange one, Lujack, but I knew you would be."

Lujack wondered what that comment meant but decided he would find out soon enough.

Tommy looked happy to see him, which surprised Lujack. Tommy seldom showed happiness. Then Lujack saw Lionel sitting with his mother in one of the booths. Lionel waved to Lujack. Jackie Chin scowled at Lujack. Lujack left Debbi with Tommy at the bar.

"How's it going, Lionel?" Lujack asked, noticing the bandages on Lionel's left hand.

"Sorry about the monster, Mr. Lujack."

"The monster's nothing. I'm sorry about Billy. Real sorry."

Lionel's eyes fell to the tablecloth. The bandages were all the evidence left of Lionel's close call. The bandages and the memories. Up until a month ago Lionel's only experiences with death had been the Kung Fu and Rambo movies and the hallways of Venice High. Now his cousin had been decapitated and his best friend burned alive in front of his eyes.

"I hear you're going back to school next week," Lujack said quickly.

"Is that really Debbi Arnold you're with?" Lionel asked.

"Yeah, you want to meet her?"

"My mom does."

Jackie Chin gave her son a dirty look. She didn't want to be in Lujack's debt for anything.

"Hey, Debbi, come over here. I have a friend who wants to meet you."

Debbi came over to the table with Tommy. They seemed to be hitting it off. He liked the ease with which Debbi fit in his world.

"This must be Lionel," she said with the smile all of Los Angeles loved.

"You're even prettier than on TV," Lionel said.

"Why, thank you, Lionel. You're looking pretty good yourself."

It was the first time Lujack had ever seen Lionel blush.

"Debbi, this is Jackie, she's Lionel's mother."

"Very nice to meet you. Please sit down and join us," Jackie said, smiling at Debbi and even Lujack.

For the first time since he could remember, Lujack had done something right. Jackie would be the envy of every Chinese-American lady west of La Brea, having dinner with Debbi Arnold, hearing stories about the interesting personalities of the nation's second largest television market.

Tommy, along with the irredoubtable Winston, served them the best Chinese meal Lujack had ever eaten at the Chin Up. Some of the items were things Lujack had never heard of, but they were delicious.

"Every dish is better than the last. They're all marvelous," Debbi pronounced.

"Tommy, you've turned this place into something out of *Gourmet* magazine," Lujack said when Tommy brought out the dessert. Fortune cookies.

"We're just keeping up with the times, Lujack. Wait 'til you see the new kitchen." Jackie beamed.

"New kitchen?" Lujack asked, having heard nothing about a new kitchen.

"New menu needs new kitchen," Tommy said a little defensively.

Although Lujack had no say in the running of the Chin Up, it was still the headquarters of the Good Book and he wasn't at all sure that turning the place into a chi-chi LA eatery à la Wolfgang Puck was the smartest idea. It was one thing to serve greasy Chinese food to low-rent lawyers and real estate brokers, it was something else to serve nouvelle Chinese to politicians and movie stars. Maybe he and Tommy were having the same kind of thoughts, going-straight kind of thoughts.

Lujack opened his fortune cookie.

"May all your wives die rich," he read to much laughter.

Lujack picked up a glass. "To rich wives and long lives," he said, looking at Jackie, then Debbi, and finally looking past both of them to Anna. He couldn't see her too clearly, there was a certain film on the lenses, a film of time and loss and love, but there was one thing he knew, she was rich.

"Are you married, Debbi?" Lionel asked.

"Not yet, but from the sound of Lujack's fortune I may be in the market."

"You could do worse," Lionel said.

"Thanks, Lionel," Lujack said.

Tommy motioned Lujack over to the bar.

"Excuse me, ladies. I'm sure Lionel will keep you entertained."

Lionel smiled. He was definitely smitten with Debbi.

Lujack joined Tommy at the bar. Tommy had an ice water waiting. He kept better track of Lujack's alcohol consumption than Lujack did. It was a good thing Lujack had stopped smoking and didn't do drugs or the Good Book would never have been born.

"Both SC and UCLA didn't cover," Tommy said with a smile.

"How much did we win?"

"Fifteen and change."

"Not bad for a day's work. Now you can start tearing out the old kitchen."

"I was going to tell you. Jackie's been talking about

it for a while. After what happened with Lionel, it's better that I let her be the boss for a while."

"No sweat. I just thought it might be something more, like maybe you wanted to close down. Go legit."

"Legit?" Tommy asked. "I just made fifteen thousand dollars in one afternoon taking bets with you. To make that much here I'd have to sell six months' worth of lunches."

"I want you to know. If you ever feel like closing up, all you've got to do is say it. Our luck won't last forever, buddy."

"What's the matter with you, Jimmy? This TV girl got you going soft?" Tommy said, then guessed a better reason. "It's Sports, isn't it?"

"How much is he down this week?"

"Another eight. That includes the three he won on Hershiser."

"So that's about forty grand total."

"It's been two months, Jimmy."

"Yeah, I know. I'll go talk to him. I need the oil changed in the car anyway."

"The man has to make good money, renting cars for three hundred dollars a day."

"He told me he was getting killed on his insurance rates."

"Who isn't?"

"Yeah, but you don't lease a hundred and twenty cars."

The worst thing about being a bookie was collecting. Lujack had never had to rough anyone up, but there were other pressures. Just showing up didn't exactly make you Mr. Popular. He'd had more than one ugly scene. He didn't want to have one with Sports. He and the fat man went back. Also he liked his new car.

"Don't worry, Tommy. I'll work something out."

"That's what you said last week."

"I was indisposed last week, remember?" Lujack said, pointing to his head. "I was getting beat up by Ginger's boyfriend's goons."

"I forgot to tell you," Tommy said casually. "Liz called me last night. She wants us to drop the inquiry."

"What!"

"She said after what happened to Lionel and the others, including Mr. Field, she doesn't want any more people dying because of her daughter."

"No one is dying because of Ginger. The girl was murdered," Lujack said, his voice rising.

A few heads turned at the dining tables, including those of Jackie and Debbi. Both Lujack and Tommy smiled reassuringly in their direction.

"What's going on, Tommy?" Lujack said through his teeth.

"Nothing is going on. She just wants the police to handle it," Tommy said, adding, "I think she got a call from her husband. He's moved to San Francisco. I think he wants her to come up and see him."

"What about Ginger's soul and the evil spirits?"

"The living sometimes take precedence over the dead, even with the Chinese."

"You're sure it's not any dead presidents who are talking to Liz or her estranged husband?"

"Dead presidents?"

"You know, McKinley, Grant . . . the kind they put on big bills."

Tommy shook his head from side to side.

"There are some very rich men who don't want us to keep stirring this pot, old friend."

Lujack had told Tommy about his visit from Brownell's and Killian's goons, but he hadn't mentioned the million dollars. Now he was wondering if Brownell had made a deal elsewhere. He also hadn't told Tommy about Brownell's threat. The IRS is scary enough when you do pay your taxes.

"What are you saying, Jimmy? You think my sister would sell the soul of her own child?"

"I think Ray Louie would," Lujack said.

Tommy pulled his glasses off his forehead and balanced them awkwardly on his nose. He often did this when he was flustered, fiddled with his glasses. There was something Tommy wasn't telling him. Lujack hoped it didn't have anything to do with the new kitchen Jackie was putting in. Lujack knew that Tommy was a rich man who made his investments work. He trusted him with every dollar they earned. It was Tommy who managed the Good Book's quarter-million-dollar reserve fund. Tommy liked and respected money, he was a natural. That was what bothered Lujack.

"This has been a hard time for Liz. Let me talk to her," Tommy said finally. "But I can't promise anything. She's sick of the whole thing."

Lujack left it at that. He didn't want to force Liz or Tommy to be further involved with the horror of the past month if they didn't want to be. So a man had killed Liz's daughter and almost killed Tommy's son.

"Who do you like tomorrow? Marlins or the Cowboys?" a regular asked Lujack on his way to the john.

"Who cares who I like?" Lujack said, and that was pretty much how he felt.

"I like the Chins very much, especially Lionel," Debbi said as they drove home. "Jackie reminds me of a Chinese doll with very sharp teeth."

"You got that right."

"The food was fantastic. I think it's a great idea to

change the menu. Do the yuppie thing. You're not going to lose the old customers, and think of all the new faces. I'll bring my friends down there. It's the perfect mix of Shanghai and . . ."

"And Chinoix," Lujack said.

"Something tells me you don't like our city's elite diners."

"All I need is for people like Nancy Reagan and Betsy Bloomingdale to start lunching at the Chin Up. Maybe Susie can join them for a shooter after their meal and they can talk about the sixth race at Aqueduct."

"At least they might know some nice girls." Debbi laughed.

"Like Vicki Morgan." Lujack smiled.

After dinner Lujack had taken Debbi up to the phone room. Susie had stayed late to talk to her son in Las Vegas. He and Debbi had walked in as Susie was telling Irv that no matter how clean prostitutes in Nevada were, he should settle down and find a nice girl. Lujack nearly fell back through the door. Susie looked up from the phone totally nonplussed, then she saw Debbi and told her son she'd have to call him back. "It looks like we're being featured on 'Eye on LA.'"

"I must admit your office is pretty interesting. Have you ever thought of setting up cameras and filming it as a sitcom? Kind of like 'Cheers' with betting?"

"The cops and the IRS would love that."

"What were you and Tommy talking about at the bar? It looked serious," she asked as they neared the smattering of highrises that made up "downtown."

Lujack couldn't get excited about downtown LA, even with the new metro rail that was expected to be in service any decade.

"Whatever happened to the Century Freeway? Remember they bought up all those houses in the 'sixties so they could build this super freeway across South Central LA?"

"I take it you don't want to tell me what you and Tommy were arguing about?"

"You take it right," Lujack said, thinking he'd rather think about the Century Freeway.

He walked her into the lobby of her condo tower. She hadn't said much since he cut her off. In fact, neither had spoken in the last ten minutes.

The doorman opened the double glass doors. "Good evening, Miss Arnold."

"Good evening, Whitley," she said.

The man gave Lujack an off-balance look, as if he wasn't supposed to be there. Lujack wondered who was.

"I don't blame you for being pissed."

"That's all right. It wasn't any of my business."

"Thanks for coming to the wedding."

"I enjoyed it. I had a great day."

Their shoes echoed on the clean granite floor.

"I'd like to see you again, if you want," he said, feeling her slip away. He didn't want to lose two women in the same day.

"I want."

She pushed the elevator button.

"Twenty-one, that's my lucky number," he said, feeling more confident.

"Not tonight it isn't," she said, and kissed him on the lips.

Before he could recover she had disappeared into the elevator. He watched the numbers tick off as she ascended. The light stopped at twenty-one.

He walked back toward the doorman and his waiting car. The car reminded him of Sports and the overdue bill. Sports reminded him of Tommy and his dark suspicions about the long ermine arms of Larry Brownell. When he thought about it all there wasn't much to look forward to, except that walking toward the door he wasn't sure that he didn't give a little skip. Lujack was no expert but he knew enough about kisses to know the difference between the first and the last. The one he had just received wasn't the last.

# Chapter Twelve

## *Into the Bay We Delve*

Officially it was winding down. The police were still looking for Micky Kim, but interest in the "Yakuza murders" was growing stale. The scenario as put out by the DA's office involved modeling magnate Chase Field, some of his party-girl models, a splinter group of coke-snorting Korean Yakuza, and a fringe Hollywood drug dealer, all of whom hung around the Zodiac Club and had gotten a little out of hand one night. A lot out of hand. There had been no mention of the Marina Shores.

According to Deputy DA Toomey, the murders were another example of the tragic price Los Angeles paid for drugs (Dave Mason's business) and gangs (the Yakuza). There was also no mention of the fact that Ginger's body was drug-free, as was Chase Field's, or the fact that the last Yakuza killing in California prior to last month had been in 1981 or that none of the suspects or victims had a DNA structure that matched the semen found on Ginger's body. Nagging little facts that the DA, the mayor, Kyle Thurgood, and Tommy Chin chose to ignore.

Sports, as usual, was on the phone when Lujack pulled into the lot. It was evening, and the pale light of a summer night reflected off the polished hoods of cars parked on Sports's lot on Santa Monica, just past Doheny.

Lujack had first heard the stories about Sports DeLane's big bucks when he was still a cop. He and Marty had pulled over more than one of Sports's customers while cruising Hollywood in the old days. In those days if you didn't get your Rolls Royce convertible from Sports you might as well take the bus. But nowadays people could lease their cars for the same amount of money, in some cases even less, than renting one from Sports. And anyone who wanted to make a good impression in Hollywood drove a Honda. Lujack didn't have to chip away the paint on the red and white sign announcing "Sports for Imports" to know that Beverly Hills's second black millionaire wasn't what he used to be.

"Hey, Lujack, how's your new baby running?"

"I think it's low on oil. You know these English cars, Sports. The indicators never work."

"You honkies always driving by the lights, even when you got a cloud of smoke coming out of your exhaust bigger than most semis."

"You've been blowing a little smoke of your own, old friend."

Sports nodded. "It's up past the limit, ain't it?"

"Try fifty yards as of last night. The only reason we haven't pulled the plug is because of that big deal you're supposed to be signing with Avis."

"Sports can carry the mail, you know that, Jimmy."

"I remember in the city finals against Birmingham

you did," Lujack said. "Made the nicest catch I ever saw. Pushed off to do it, but my daddy never liked to call much in the end zone."

"Your daddy was a great ref. He always watched the ball, not the jersey."

"Not with me, Sports. It was always the sidelines."

"No one ever got hurt with quick feet."

"Don't tell that to Darryl Stingley."

"Give me to the end of the week, Jimmy, the papers should be final by then."

"There aren't any papers, buddy. I talked to a friend with Avis this afternoon. The only equity you got in this place is the sign. The cars are loaned and the land is rented."

Sports tried looking across the street. There wasn't much to see if you didn't like bus stops and Mexican maids. "You been a busy boy," he said, moving uneasily away from the light on the cars.

"We have to cut you off and we have to have our money."

"You'll get your money, Jimmy. I pay my debts."

"When, Sports?"

"When I can, Lujack," he shouted. "What are you gonna do, break my legs, motherfucker?"

Lujack busted Sports in the mouth before he realized why he did it. The big man went down like a collapsed air bag.

Sports rubbed his jaw and looked at Lujack. He decided it was smarter to stay down. "Guess I was wrong about you, Jimmy. You're just like all the other assholes shakin' people down."

"And you're just like all the other assholes who play with other people's money. See you next week, Sports."

Lujack started the Jensen with a roar. He was a mile down Santa Monica Boulevard in front of the new

Beverly Hills City Hall before he had cooled off enough to think straight. He had never laid a hand on a customer before—not in six years of working with Tommy at the Good Book, not in six years of making collections. They had picked their clients carefully, judging their temperament and ability to pay, just so they wouldn't spend most of their time chasing after deadbeats and welchers. Sports had fit their profile nicely—he was rich, he was an old friend, he was a man who paid his debts until the automobile insurance rates of California had put his back to the wall. Should Lujack have paid more attention, should he babysit his clients? He didn't think so. A man was responsible for his actions. No one had forced Sports to bet. Sports would have collected if he'd won. He'd collected before.

But then why did Lujack feel so shitty?

Sports had pissed him off. Sports had insulted him. Sports had hit a nerve. Lujack tried to hide the nerve but it was there, just below the skin. His own doubts about his profession. Maybe that was why he struck out, because he was frustrated and unsure and Sports just happened to be there. Something was happening to him. He was losing control. He was losing focus. Sports had been in the wrong place at the wrong time, and he shouldn't have called Lujack a motherfucker.

The car phone gave an electronic gurgle before his rumination could run its course.

"Jimmy, it's me."

"What's the matter, Deb?" he asked, sensing an unusual edge in her usually confident voice.

"Can you meet me in front of the station in half an hour? It's important."

"What is it?"

"I can't tell you over the phone. Just be out in front at eight o'clock."

"Sure, babe," he said and swung the Jensen down Santa Monica, heading east.

Although Debbi didn't say it, Lujack guessed her frantic manner had to do with the Yakuza story. Over the last week she had been rattling cages in city hall and the DA's office. Thus far, nothing had shaken loose. From the sound of her voice, something was about to. Lujack had to hand it to her. When push came to shove, Debbi was not afraid to push back, but he also knew the people behind the so-called Yakuza murders did more than push.

The ABC studios were on Prospect and Sunset. She was in her Corvette at the gas station across the street. She got out of the car when he pulled in. She looked upset and a little pissed off.

"You look like someone just died."

"Someone did," she said.

He wanted to kiss her, but they'd only gone out twice and she didn't look to be in a romantic mood. Although she did look awfully good.

"I was talking to a friend of mine today. Kelly Green, do you know her?"

One of Debbi's least endearing qualities was that she expected everyone she knew to know everyone else she knew.

"Should I?"

"She works for our sister station in San Francisco," Debbi said, taking a deep breath. She didn't seem to notice that she was breathing carbon monoxide from a busy LA street corner. "I was talking to her this morning about the Yakuza story. You know, seeing if there was a tie-in. A lot of times an Asian crime story like the Chinese tongs or Korean hookers or whatever will hit more than one Pacific Coast city.

"And?"

"And she said she didn't know of any increased Yakuza activity in the Bay Area, Japanese or Korean. I mean, she said they were there, running gambling games, importing prostitutes—'yellow slaves,' she called them—but there had been no killings, no turf wars, no drug wars."

"So?"

"So that's when I told her about Ginger. She said she hadn't heard about it because she'd been in Maine visiting her parents last month. When I told her about the head and the body being in different places, she said that was odd. Six months ago the body of a girl had been found in the bay, on the rocks near Fort Point. The girl was young, in her late teens or early twenties, but a positive ID had been impossible because the girl didn't have a head."

"What do you mean, she didn't have a head?"

"I mean her head had been cut off like Ginger's," she said with an understandable edge in her voice. Women didn't enjoy talking about violence, especially against other women. Lujack didn't blame them.

"You're sure?"

"Of course I'm sure. I asked my station manager to send me up there tomorrow to see if there's any connection."

"That's a long shot, isn't it? There being a connection?"

"I don't think so."

"Why not?"

"Because the girl was Chinese-American."

It was then Lujack began to get excited. "If she didn't have a head and she'd been in the water, how could they know?"

"Kelly said there were certain body characteristics

that told the coroner she was Oriental. Skin color, body hair, bone structure, but it was the bracelet that was the key."

"Bracelet?"

"With a medallion from the Wong Family Society."

"Were they missing someone in their family, these Wongs?"

"Not in San Francisco, or so they said, but there are many Wong Family Societies, you know that."

"Just like there are many Chin Family Societies. One for every town in California with a population over ten thousand people. At least that's what Tommy says. What do the SFPD think?"

"To them she's just another Jane Doe."

"Or Jane Wong."

"I told my station manager I thought it might be worth pursuing, maybe even running a piece—two decapitated girls, both Chinese-American. Maybe the family of the missing girl might come forward, maybe we could pry loose a lead."

"And he said forget it, we have our killer."

"That's what he said."

"I know a guy who works for the SFPD. Maybe I could give him a call."

"I was thinking of something better."

"What's that?"

"We could fly up to San Francisco together, this weekend."

"You're right, that is better."

"We could mix business with pleasure."

"I'm not sure where this business might lead, Debbi. If the two murders are connected, the people who get connected aren't going to be very happy."

"Good," she said firmly.

"One more thing. The girl in the bay . . . was there any evidence of sexual abuse?"

Before she answered, a car honked as it drove by.

"Lookin' good, Deb," a man yelled.

Debbi winced, hearing the cat call. Lujack guessed it wasn't always easy being pretty and famous.

"I don't know, Jimmy. Kelly didn't say anything."

"Let me make a few calls. When do you want to go?"

"I have to do a nightside report on the Dodgers, but I could get away tomorrow."

"Since when did you become a sports reporter?"

"Since Orel Hershiser started throwing shutouts and the Dodgers started thinking World Series. I'm doing a remote from the parking lot. You want to come? I get to sit in the press box until the eighth inning."

"I pay out enough money every time Orel pitches without having to watch the bastard in person."

"But if he gets two more shutouts he'll break Drysdale's record."

"He'll never get Double D's record. No way."

"What kind of odds will you give me?"

"Sorry, Debbi, house rules. I never date my customers."

"Honor among bookies."

"Something like that," Lujack said, wondering if Sports DeLane would think he was so chivalrous.

Debbi left him for Orel. Lujack drove back to his apartment. Tonight there would be no stop at the Chin Up. He was in no mood to discuss business with Tommy. The truth was, with the exception of the Dodgers and the problem with Sports, business wasn't too bad. The local college football teams were winning but they weren't covering the spread. One thing about USC and UCLA—they never really learned how to run up the score like some of their southern rivals.

Even the Rams were making them money, thank God for Joe Montana, the LA bookies' dream.

The real reason he didn't want to go by the restaurant wasn't business, it was because he was mad at Tommy. He'd never completely bought Tommy's story about his sister's wanting them to drop their investigation into Ginger's murder. He wasn't about to call up Liz and confirm it, he cared about his relationship with Tommy too much to do that, but still he had these lingering doubts that didn't seem to be going away.

Jackie's redecorating was one thing, what was more disturbing was Tommy's manner the last few days. He didn't want to look Lujack in the eye. Every time Lujack had come into the restaurant Tommy had been doing busy work behind the bar. Instant busy work. Even Susie said Tommy was acting strange. He'd actually started eating Chinese food, forgoing his beloved hamburgers and fries. He remembered their conversation on the quay after Tommy had attacked Dolph Killian. Tommy said he would have killed Killian, but Lujack knew better. Killian would have killed Tommy. Still he'd expected Tommy to keep turning the heat up until Killian cracked. Instead Tommy had become less and less interested. Why? Was Tommy afraid for himself and his family? Killian's men were the real thing. Or had Tommy succumbed to more subtle stimulants? A threatened IRS audit? A good old-fashioned sack of money? Or was Lujack making shadows from lines?

Gail McCrell was still working when he stopped by the print shop. She looked up from her drafting board when he came in. She was in jeans and a T-shirt. Today's model was tame by her standards: "Gutenberg fixed his own machines." She waited a second, then smiled.

"A buck seventy-five, right?"

"Plus interest."

"Right," he said and put the money on the counter.

Gail reached under the counter and pulled out his business cards.

"You were in a hurry last time and left these here."

"Thanks for not calling the cops."

"I did call 'em," she said indignantly, "but when I told them who the man being kidnapped was, the guy on the other end laughed and said you could take care of yourself."

Lujack almost believed it.

"James Lujack, Private Consultant. I'm not sure I'd like to be in your line of work. Too many ex-Marines with beady little eyes chasing after you."

"Sometimes I get to chase them."

Gail shook her head. "Goodnight, Lujack."

"Goodnight, Gail," he said and walked out.

When he got home there was a baritone message from Sports: "Lujack, this is Sports. I'll get your twenty grand next week. Maybe we can work something out for the Jensen, the owner is a friend of mine. Oh yeah, one other thing, you're not a motherfucker."

There was also a message from Molly. Her voice sounded out of sync. Like all her synapses weren't hitting. She was either drunk or high or both. "Hi, Lujack, what are you doing? . . . Not much I guess . . . Janis and I wanted to know if you could come over and play . . . (an amused giggle) . . . bye."

The phone went dead. Lujack thought it was like one of those crank calls he got from kids in the neighborhood. Molly wasn't much older. As sophisticated as she looked on the cover of *Vanity Fair,* the next Grace Kelly, basically she still was a little girl.

He called his friend Tom Clancy of the SFPD. Tom was a homicide detective and would know everything there was to know about an unsolved murder in the Bay Area. He and Tom had boxed against each other in the Police Olympics back when both of them had legs with working joints. Unfortunately, the homicide desk told Lujack that Clancy wasn't scheduled to come in until the next night. Lujack left his name and said he was going to be in town and would be in touch. When the desk sergeant asked where Lujack was going to be staying, Lujack laughed. "I wish I knew," he said.

Lujack opened his refrigerator and pulled out what he thought was a piece of cheese. He was too tired to go out and too lazy to cook, but the Monterey Jack had taken on a life of its own. So much for cheese and crackers. He found a can of chili and thanked the Lord that cans were never out of season.

He had just managed to wrestle the contents into his favorite (only) pan when there was a knock on the door. It was after ten, and he wasn't expecting anyone, so he took his .38 out of the desk drawer and walked toward the door.

When he opened it he was pleasantly surprised. Debbi Arnold stood before him with an overnight bag and a traveling case. For the first time since he had met her she wasn't wearing makeup, just a cotton pullover top and shorts, perfect for the seventy-plus Los Angeles night. She looked like a blond beauty queen who just got off the bus, except her luggage was designer and her hair freshly coiffed.

"They sent me home for a sports reporter."

"So you thought we should get an early start."

"Something like that."

"I'm not sure we can get a flight this late."

"Can I come in?"

"Yeah, sure."

He picked up her bag and walked her into the living room, doing his best to kick the various sports pages and tennis shoes under the couch.

"I didn't know you played tennis," she said brightly.

"I used to play a lot, over at Riviera."

"Why did you quit?"

"Ever since the Japanese bought the place I keep thinking I'm in an operating room, not a country club. The courts are too clean, the towels are starched, the ashtrays are spotless, even the soap in the shower looks like it's been pasteurized. The place is too damn orderly."

"I can see why that would bother you," she said, looking around the living room.

"Don't get me wrong. I don't have anything against the Japanese. Hell, the club manager, Kenji, is a great guy. We still get drunk together."

"Do you ever ask him about the Yakuza?"

"I haven't seen Kenji since all this started, but from my limited experience with the Japanese, they don't like talking about the war or the Yakuza. Just as Americans don't like talking about Hiroshima and Manzanar."

Debbi's nose scrunched up as if she'd inhaled something unpleasant.

Lujack hoped it wasn't his sweat socks. Then he caught a whiff. "The chili!"

"Is that what it is?"

Lujack rushed into the kitchen. The chili was smoking. Lujack grabbed a hot pad, threw the pan into the sink, and began running hot water over it. Debbi followed him into the smoke-filled kitchen.

"Don't worry. I disconnected the smoke alarm," he told her.

"That makes me feel a lot safer."

Lujack started to clean the pan, but the sponge and dish soap didn't seem to be making much progress.

"I think it would be better if you let it soak?" Debbi suggested.

"Maybe you're right," Lujack said, happy to leave the pan in the sink for as long as it would take to clean itself.

"No, no," Debbi said, grabbing the pan. "Here, let's clean it right now. Do you have any SOS?"

"I usually have some for the cleaning lady. She leaves me a list. It would be under here."

Lujack reached under the sink and found himself facing a maze of cleansing products. "I seem to have one of everything in the household section down here," he said, not sure what SOS was. He remembered something about pads, but he couldn't put a box to them.

"Men," Debbi said and bent down to join him. She found the orange box marked SOS immediately. Lujack liked the way she smelled next to him, a woman's smell among the disinfectants. Then she was gone.

By the time he pulled himself back above the sink, she was hard at work. The pan came clean almost immediately.

He liked her feminine efficiency. There had been an ad campaign for her when she first started working in the LA market: "The girl next door brings you the news from all across the city."

"What's so funny?"

"You really are the girl next door," he said and took the pan from her, wrapping it in a dish towel.

She blushed.

Lujack very much wanted to kiss her. He very much wanted to sleep with her. But he knew her well enough to know that he couldn't read her. Most women who show up on your doorstep late at night with their suitcases, well, you could assume certain things. With Debbi, she was so intense, so driven, there was a good chance she really did want to leave for San Francisco that night.

Before he could talk himself out of it, *she* kissed *him.* Once he got his arms around her, he knew they wouldn't be going to San Francisco that night.

It had been a while since Lujack had his arms around a woman. Longer still since he'd kissed a woman and felt his heart pounding like it was. This girl turned him on, there was no denying that, but there was something more. The way he felt when he closed his eyes and pushed his mouth against hers. He didn't want it to happen, the way his luck with women was running, but he wasn't sure he could stop it.

"You might not be able to cook, but you sure can kiss," she said, taking a breath.

He picked her up, carrying her into the bedroom. This was no time for talking.

Lujack put her down on the bed. It wasn't made, but she didn't mind. For the girl next door, she didn't waste any time crawling out of her clothes. She wriggled out of the cotton top as he grabbed her breasts. There was an extrasensory thrill touching her. He had seen her on television, he had wanted her from afar, and now he knew what it must have been like the first time John Warner got his hands on Liz Taylor's tits.

"What are you smiling about?" she asked him in a soft voice, and he licked her stomach muscles, cupping her breasts in his hands, wanting to touch and hold as much of her as he could.

"I always wanted to sleep with a movie star," he said, and they both laughed. He began pulling down her shorts. No matter how many times it happens, there's something about the first time you pull down a woman's pants.

When next she pulled down his, he figured from the way she looked at him what was good for the gander was good for the goose.

Their bodies mixed and mingled like sexual magic for the next couple of hours. She was more relaxed in bed than she was out of it, and he didn't know why he was surprised. He had the feeling there was a whole other being stored up inside of Debbi Arnold action news reporter. Maybe it was Debbi Arnold wife or Debbi Arnold mother or simply Debbi Arnold woman.

When she finally fell asleep with her head on his chest, her blond hair resting soft on his chest hairs, he couldn't help thinking about how wrong he'd been about her. How people were so formidable until you met them, then they were just people. But then it was never that easy. Life proved that every day. So did death.

# Chapter Thirteen

### *These Rhymes Can Get Old When You Have a Girlfriend*

"Do you think I'm stupid?" Debbi asked him as they buckled themselves in their seats for the commuter flight to San Francisco.

"Only when you ask questions like that," Lujack answered.

"No, really."

"First, *stupid* is a very subjective word. Second, no."

"A lot of men think I'm stupid because they don't like me. I threaten them."

"How come we're having this conversation?"

"Because I hate to fly. Will you hold my hand?"

Lujack took Debbi's hand and thought to himself maybe rhymes were easier than he figured.

No matter how long he lived in Southern California, he always felt a hint of betrayal when he went to San Francisco. The city was like "the other woman," beautiful, sophisticated, mysterious, romantic. Lujack remembered driving up north when he was a senior in high school to check out the Berkeley campus. He fell for the school the minute he saw it—the Campanile, the limestone buildings, the green hills, the trees, the clean air—but it wasn't until he'd driven onto the Bay Bridge and seen the classic outlines of "The City," Coit Tower, the Pyramid, the bridges, and the bay that he knew he was in love. The place did that to you, more than any other city he'd ever been to. New York, Paris, Rome. He'd take San Francisco.

Of course, he knew he could never live in San Francisco. The people were too smug, too self-satisfied, too provincial. The fact that so many San Franciscans thought themselves culturally and intellectually superior to Angelenos Lujack could never understand. If they were so wonderful, why did they spend all their time talking about how horrible LA was?

Another reason he couldn't live in the Bay Area was Candlestick Park. No self-respecting bookie could do business in a city where the major sports franchises were relegated to playing in a windy refrigerator. What kind of city spends more money on its performing arts center than its ballpark?

He had wanted to stay at the Holiday Inn near the police station on 7th and Bryant, but Debbi had insisted they stay at the Fairmont. Lujack hadn't put up much of a fight. "What are you laughing about?" she asked him as he negotiated Bush Street to the top of Nob Hill.

"I'm thinking about the time my roommate and I hitchhiked across the bay and came into the city to see Carol Doda. We got carded at the Condor and ended up in the Tenderloin, at the bar I just drove past, the Green Light Club. There was this gorgeous girl sitting by herself in a booth. My roommate and I bought her a few drinks and were feeling like we had the city under control. The next thing I knew the blonde was giving my roommate a kiss and he started to feel her up. Suddenly he screamed, "Jimmy, she has a hard on!"

"Mr. San Francisco."

"It's a shame we're here on business. I could really show you a good time."

"What makes you think I don't know my way around? A girl doesn't get from Beaverton to Hollywood without seeing the sights along the way."

"I wanted to ask you about that."

"About what?"

"About why you never married."

"Who said I wasn't?"

"Nobody. You never . . ."

"I'm not. Almost, last year, to a director."

"What happened?"

"He made a movie."

"And?"

"And the movie had a beautiful leading lady. And why am I telling you all this?"

"Remember, I invited you to my wife's wedding."

"Maybe someday we'll go see one of his movies."

Lujack pulled the rental car under the portico of the Fairmont. They walked into the stately lobby. It had been some time since Lujack had stayed in a nice hotel. Let alone one that had its own TV series. It had been some time since Lujack had been with a woman like Debbi. He wondered if they were going to share the same room. After last night he had been thinking of little else besides being in bed again with her, but there was the professional side of her that he knew he had to respect. He wondered how the director had dealt with that side of her.

"Don't worry, Jimmy, I booked us into the same room."

"How did you know?" he said with a smile.

"The way you're biting your lip."

Debbi signed her name on the registration card. The bellman took their bags to the elevator. Lujack gave the guy a five spot and said he could handle it from there.

Lujack and Debbi rode up the elevator in silence.

"You don't like hotels, do you?" she said.

"I don't like waiting for people to open doors for me."

"You just barge right in."

"Something like that."

"They don't make 'em like you anymore, you know that," she said and kissed him.

Lujack wasn't sure if it was a compliment, but he'd take the kiss. The elevator stopped at a floor above theirs.

"I thought we were on nine," Debbi said.

"We are." Lujack waited and then pushed nine.

"What are you doing?"

"Being careful," he said, and she gave him a strange look. He had seen something he didn't like coming up the hill. A late-model Ford that had followed them from the airport. Maybe it was nothing, but it didn't take much to be careful.

"If someone were following us, all they'd have to do is bribe the man at the front desk."

"Who said anyone was following us?" Lujack said as he escorted Debbi to their room.

The first thing she did when they had moved in was jump on the bed. Lujack liked that about her.

The second thing she did was take off her dress. Lujack liked that about her too.

"Look at that view," she said, standing by the

window looking out at the Bay Bridge. All she had on was a pushup bra and a flimsy pair of no-line panties. "This sure is a magnificent city."

"Magnificent," Lujack said in agreement.

Lujack kept a watchful eye on the rearview mirror as they drove out California Street to Divisadero. There were no late-model Fords lurking behind him. It was one of those classic San Francisco late-August evenings, when the wind disappears and the fog forgets to roll in.

They met Tom Clancy at the St. Francis Yacht Club. Clancy had taken up sailing after his boxing gloves and scar tissue wore out, but Lujack didn't think that was why the detective wanted to meet him at the yacht club. The St. Francis was about two miles due east of the rocks where the girl's body had been found.

Clancy was waiting for them in the parking lot just past the Marina Green beach. He was a few years older than Lujack, maybe forty, and looked about as fit as most SF cops can ever look who work in a city full of bars and restaurants.

"The last of the Irish heavyweights," Lujack said, greeting his old friend.

"The Polish Palooka," Clancy said, with a hint of the brogue. "Now that you're a gangster I see you're getting all the good-looking girls."

"Debbi Arnold, meet Tom Clancy, San Francisco's finest."

"My pleasure, Miss Arnold."

"Debbi's the one who told me about the headless body."

"It's too late to sail out there now. Anyhow we got no breeze, but I've borrowed a friend's Fountain. We're going to take a little spin."

"What's a Fountain?"

"A Fountain is like a Cigarette or a Scarab but it's faster. Don Johnson wouldn't dare ride in one of them."

Debbi gave Lujack a "Do we have to?" look.

Ten minutes later they were riding toward the Golden Gate Bridge at fifty miles per hour hanging on to the padded dashboard for all they were worth. There was no sitting in a boat like the thirty-foot Fountain, you just bent your knees, let the salt water slap your face, and prayed.

"Are you all right?" Lujack yelled at Debbi over the roar of the huge Mercury engine and the thumping of the boat's hull on the water.

She just looked at him, one hand gripping the handle, the other holding her hair. Clancy smiled at his passengers. It obviously wasn't the first time he had taken two landlubbers for a little spin on the bay. Lujack didn't get seasick. He hoped the same could be said for Debbi.

Clancy brought the throttle down and the boat settled into the smooth waters of the bay between the majestic south tower of the Golden Gate Bridge and the old brick fortress of Fort Point. The boat idled easily in the water as Lujack looked up under the bridge. He could hear the clanging reverberations of traffic crossing the bridge. Below the bridge to the west stretched the mighty Pacific.

"Most days a little boat like this would be tossing like a rubber ducky out here, but this time of year the Gate turns gentle."

"What about the tides?"

"The tide is almost out. See how far down the water line is," Clancy said, pointing to the rocks buttressing the concrete wall below the old fort. The water swirled gently around the moss- and barnacle-covered rocks. Everywhere Lujack could smell the sea.

"That's where we found her. One of the fishermen phoned in. You know these local fishermen, they probably tried to catch her for an hour or two then figured they should do their civic duty."

"What do you mean 'we'? You mean the Coast Guard?"

"No, I mean we. The race committee. I was one of the judges out here on the west buoy. We usually put our weather buoy out here by the south tower during the big races. A call comes in on the radio that the Coast Guard was going to pick up what looked like a body on the rocks. The club commodore knows I'm a homicide cop so we cruised over here for a look. Sure enough, I had to go to work."

"What do you think happened?" Debbi asked.

"I think somebody raped her, then cut her head off, then dumped her body overboard."

"Overboard?" Lujack asked.

"You see how calm it is along here and then how strong the current is just out past the tower."

Lujack and Debbi looked out maybe three hundred yards and saw the heavy current moving from right to left under the bridge.

"That current is the millions of acres of snow pack from the Sacramento and San Joaquin rivers. It runs out at almost six knots. Where we found the girl, that's where they used to find the guys who tried to escape from Alcatraz. They'd get caught up in the current and spit out right here or else the next stop would be the Farralones."

"What are the Farralones?" Debbi asked.

"The meanest, ugliest islands you ever want to see. About twenty shark-infested miles straight out there," he said, pointing in the direction of the horizon.

"You dump a body in the bay from the San Francisco side, it rarely is going to get out in that current without somebody finding it first. Hell, they got wind surfers out here most every afternoon fighting the tankers for the right of way."

"So why couldn't somebody just dump her off the wall?" Lujack asked.

"Fort Point is a national park and the Presidio is an Army base. The roads down there are patrolled by federal marshals and MPs. If I had a headless body, that's the last place I'd dump it. You have to go by at least one check point no matter how you get down there."

"Maybe whoever did it threw her off the bridge," Debbi said, looking up as if another body might be coming her way.

Clancy gave Lujack a skeptical look as if to say, Who is this babe? Lujack raised his eyebrows in a "humor me" gesture.

"You're right, that wouldn't be too smart," Debbi said, picking up the men's sign language.

"Believe me, Miss Arnold, I do this for a living. Judging from the time the body was in the water, which the coroner estimated as eight to ten hours, and the way the body was caught in the rocks, the girl was either tossed into the bay at the previous low tide from an area near the yacht club or she was thrown off a boat. Since the yacht club was pretty busy that weekend with the races and low tide was around five the previous afternoon, I always thought she was just dumped in the water from somewhere right out there."

Debbi and Lujack looked back toward Alcatraz. The bay stretched miles and miles from Angel Island to Oakland and beyond.

"That's a lot of water."

"A Chinese girl with no identifying marks, she could have come from anywhere. Hell, the crew of one those big freighters could have picked her up in Hong Kong, used her as their personal whore, then dumped her overboard when they came into port."

"But you don't believe that?" Lujack asked, feeling the stillness of the bay and the horror of the girl's death. It was a beautiful, calm evening on the bay, but he felt anything but serene. Like the current running out to sea there was an undertow of evil. The rhythm.

"No, I don't believe that, although according to the coroner the girl was no virgin."

Lujack saw Clancy watching Debbi out of the corner of his eye. He guessed the detective knew who Debbi was and didn't think much of her motives.

"The medal she wore around her neck, from the Wong Family Society, it was very quaint. Like something a Catholic girl would wear in a Latin American country. No self-respecting sing-song girl would be wearing a medal like that. She was probably a nice first- or second-generation Chinese-American girl who came to Chinatown and got in with the wrong crowd."

"She was raped, then?"

"Yeah, she was raped, but the salt water and exposure ruined any chance of a sample. The only clues beside the medal were the scratch marks on her inner thigh."

"Scratch marks?" Lujack asked.

"Yeah, like a cat would make."

"Or a Yakuza," Lujack said, steadying himself as a swell came under the boat. "The family never came forward, did they, Tom?" he asked.

The detective shook his head. Clancy stared at the battered sea wall, above the place where the body had first been discovered. A fisherman was climbing around below on the silt-covered rocks trying to get closer to the fish. There were clusters of tourists in parking lots, gawking at the underside of the great orange bridge and the old fort which had guarded the gate before the bridge was built.

"It's in the cold file now, Jimmy, although I plan to ask some questions at next spring's Bankers Regatta."

"Bankers Regatta?" Lujack asked.

"Yeah, that was the regatta we had that weekend. It's one of the club's biggest. There were so damn many three-piece sailors around that weekend, I never got a chance to talk to a tenth of them. Maybe somebody saw something."

"These bankers, they come from all over the country?"

"Mostly California and the other western states."

"What about the Pacific National Bank? Were they in the race?"

Clancy smiled. "Pacific National is the defending champion."

A passing gull shrieked in Lujack's ear. "How many people race on a team? Could I get a list of the Pacific National team?"

"There's a skipper and six or seven crew in the one-ton class. I could get a copy at the office."

"You don't remember if a George Kim from Los Angeles was on the list. He's a vice-president."

"I don't remember the name, but these races attract all the mucky mucks. Hell, Yoshida himself was up here last spring."

"Kazuo Yoshida!" Debbi blurted. "He was a friend of Chase's. They knew each other from the Marina Shores."

"Yoshida is a mean little bastard," Clancy said. "I've seen the SOB curse out his captain in front of half the dock for not getting his spinnaker up fast enough, and that's after the guy won the race."

"We did a story on him last year. He's supposed to

be the richest man in California," Debbi said, smiling at Lujack. "He came to LA in the 'fifties. First he worked for the Bank of America. Eventually he left and formed his own bank with mostly Japanese-American investors. Then when the Japanese commercial banks started to boom in the early 'eighties, Yoshida went with them. His bank is bigger than the B of A now."

"You don't think Yoshida had anything to do with this girl?" Clancy asked Lujack.

"There are certain tie-ins," Lujack said, trying to visualize Yoshida and not Dolph Killian as the brutal killer of two young girls. It was a stretch. He wished Debbi wasn't so talkative.

"What kind of tie-in? Chase Field was the modeling agent who was killed last week in LA, wasn't he? And the model who was murdered, she was Chinese-American."

"You've been doing your homework, Tom."

"I don't like unsolved murders on my watch. Especially when they're under my goddamn nose."

"You'll have to give me a few days on this, Tom."

"A few days. Lujack, you're not even a cop anymore."

"That might be an advantage. The people we're talking about don't exactly do wonders for a policeman's career. If you have to cover your butt, give Kyle Thurgood a call. He'll tell you what kind of case I don't have."

Clancy smiled. "You're right, Jimmy. I'm not going to be bothering Yoshida and his banker friends on a multiple murder rap without the kind of evidence a rookie DA can convict on." Clancy looked at Debbi. "What about your friend here? Is she going to be giving us film at eleven?"

"My bosses like their jobs as much as yours do, Detective."

Clancy nodded, again looking at the rocks. "You really think the son of a bitch is involved, uh?"

"Do you know where he stayed during the races?"

"As a matter of fact, I do. He stayed on the *Southern Cross.*"

"He stayed on Brownell's boat?"

"Best-looking yacht on the Pacific Coast. I told you, Yoshida was a regular General Tojo up on the bridge with his slope sailors running all over the decks."

"Was Brownell with him?" Debbi asked.

"I don't think so. I'm sure he wasn't. Some of the old salts commented that it was strange Brownell would bring his boat up here just so Yoshida could play fleet admiral."

"Not that strange, not when the banker is also your best customer," Lujack said to himself, and now he began to see the picture a little clearer. The scrubbed floors of the *Southern Cross,* a pretty girl invited aboard for a drink. Maybe she was taken below-decks on a tour. The *Southern Cross* was out on the bay, no one could hear her scream.

Another swell came under the Fountain. Debbi grabbed Lujack's arm to keep her balance. She wasn't looking too good, and the sea was starting to build as an evening breeze picked up.

"Do you mind if we started moving again," Debbi asked. "We don't have to go as fast as we were, but this rocking motion is starting to get to me."

"Seen enough, Jimmy?" Clancy asked.

"I think so, Tom. Let's go get that Irish coffee."

The detective swung the boat hard right and pushed the throttle down. Debbi was thrown into Clancy then back to Lujack. Clancy laughed as they began heading back to the yacht club. Lujack thought they were going even faster on their way back and began to understand why Tom Clancy had gone through three wives.

"He might be a good homicide detective, but he's an overage bozo," Debbi was saying to anyone who would listen to her, who happened to be Lujack.

They were sitting in the Tosca Cafe on Broadway trying to recover from a mostly liquid dinner with Clancy at the Buena Vista Cafe. Lujack had managed to grab a steak sandwich at the BV, but Debbi was in no mood to eat.

"The guy's a cop. All cops are alike. I don't care if you're in Buffalo or LA or here."

"You're not like him."

"I'm not a cop anymore," Lujack said, thinking about the club that would have him as a member.

"You know I like these coffees," Debbi said loudly, holding up her cappuccino glass. Lujack had always loved the Tosca. It was his favorite San Francisco bar. They had opera on the jukebox, five-foot cappuccino machines at either end of the bar, and the kind of dark Italian atmosphere that no self-respecting drinker could resist. The proprietress, a pert number with a diamond ring bigger than most ice cubes, had once told Lujack she wasn't Italian herself but she knew a lot of them.

"Deb, I told you, even though they call it a cappuccino, it's really a brandy with chocolate milk."

"It's delicious whatever they call it," she said and giggled. Her eyes were irresistible when she laughed. The happy blue-green eyes of a blond debating champ from Beaverton High who had come a long way but not so far that she knew the difference between reading the news and making it.

"Don't you think we better be getting back to the hotel? We have a lot to do tomorrow," Lujack said.

"Of course we do. We have to go after Mr. Yosh . . . Mr. Yoshida."

"You say that like Daffy Duck."

She laughed and hiccuped. Lujack paid the check and helped Debbi toward the door.

"Don't you just love San Francisco, Jimmy," she said as they spilled out on the sidewalk.

No matter how warm the evening, the fog usually found its way back through the Gate, and this night it came in with a wet, cold vengeance. Debbi had no coat. Lujack put an arm around her.

"It's so romantic," she said, barely noticing the twenty-degree temperature drop.

Lujack saw the man who planned to kill him before the man had begun the actual deed. The man was waiting in the alcove of a forgotten nightclub down the Columbus Street hill from the Tosca. Lujack and Debbi had joked about the pictures of the Smothers Brothers and Phyllis Diller in the now-empty Purple Onion on their way to the bar. Now the joke was going to be on them.

Lujack had two choices: run or attack. Debbi was in no shape to run but she was a perfect cover. He steered her down the hill toward the shadows where the Oriental man had disappeared.

"Take it easy, babe, the street is slippery," Lujack said, holding her with one hand and reaching across his chest to slide out his .38 with his other hand. Neither Debbi nor the man in the alcove could see the gun, and Lujack kept it in his palm like a discus.

"That's right, the car's just a few more steps," he said, and then without warning he tripped her.

"Shit," she yelled and fell forward on the wet pavement.

Lujack used Debbi's diversion to raise his arm

toward the shadows. When the man stepped into the light, Lujack saw the man's gun, then the man's arm. Three short pops, the man had an automatic. Lujack was saved by the lamppost in front of him. He got off one shot into the doorway before Debbi started swearing. The Oriental man took off down the hill. Lujack looked momentarily at Debbi, who was just high enough to be mad, not scared.

"You bastard, you tripped me."

"I'll be back," he said and ran off down Columbus after his would-be killer.

The man was fast, but Lujack was wearing tennis shoes. The gunman slipped on the slick pavement when he reached Pacific Street. He tumbled off the curb into an oncoming lane of traffic. The driver of a yellow cab slammed on his brakes and began honking his horn.

The gunman waved his automatic in the cabbie's direction, and the honking abruptly ended. Lujack couldn't get a shot off in the busy intersection and dodged his way through the traffic in pursuit of the man, who had resumed his getaway down the hill. Halfway down the next block the man turned and shot. The shot was wild. The man was feeling the pressure.

As Lujack reached the next corner he saw the gunman run into the Clown Alley hamburger stand across the street. The place was well lit but full of people. The man moved jerkily through the line of Clown Alley customers, waving his gun wildly. The startled patrons ducked under tables and the fry cooks tried to slide under their burgers.

Lujack quickly crossed the street and entered the outside courtyard. He kept his .38 raised. All that separated him from the other man was a plate-glass window and about fifteen customers. Lujack knew better than to waste bullets shooting into large windows at bad angles.

The shooter was moving toward the rear door, looking more and more frantic and more and more trapped. Lujack guessed the man had followed him from LA and didn't know San Francisco. He could have run across the street into Chinatown. Lujack had no plan, but he wasn't going to start shooting in a restaurant full of people. He didn't think the door marked "employees only" would lead to an exit for the gunman. On the other hand, he didn't want to let him out of his sight.

A disabled man in a wheelchair with a 101 Airborne cap and long hair made Lujack's next move for him. Lujack had seen the long-haired man move his chair away from the table in the direction the gunman was backing up. Lujack knew the type. Vietnam vet, disabled, half loaded, more than half pissed off, and at least half crazy.

"Look where you're going, asshole," the vet yelled when the gunman bumped into him.

The man with the gun turned and pointed the weapon at the vet.

"Go ahead, shoot me, Charlie," the vet dared him. "But first let me finish my burger."

The vet proceeded to bite into the burger that had been sitting on his lap. As he did it, he looked straight into the gun barrel.

The reaction so frustrated the gunman, he forgot about Lujack. By the time he turned back, Lujack had him in his sights. Lujack shot twice, and the man fell back on the floor without firing another shot.

"Nice shooting." The vet smiled, wiping mayonnaise and ketchup from his chin. "You got him two in the head."

"It's over, folks. It's all over," Lujack said to no one in particular as most of the other customers ran out the door.

"If it's all over, mister, maybe you should put that gun away," a black lady in a clown hat and a clown shirt said from behind a row of now very well-done burgers.

Lujack put the .38 back in its holster. He made a mental note to himself that he might have to start looking for a magnum of a Browning high-power or stop getting into gun fights.

"You better call the cops," he said to the lady, but saw she'd already picked up the phone.

"Who is he?" the vet asked, poking at the lifeless body with the footpedal of his wheelchair as he would the body of a dead enemy soldier.

"I'm not sure," Lujack said, leaning over and examining the dead man's right hand. The top joint of the little finger was missing. He then opened the man's silk shirt, revealing a green and red body tattoo.

"That's some brand," the vet said.

"If I had to guess, I'd say his name was Micky Kim." Lujack continued, guessing the man's age at about twenty-five. Too young, thank God, to be Ray Louie. "Thanks for your help."

"My pleasure, buddy. Never did like gooks with guns. You a cop or something?"

"Or something," Lujack said. "Do you mind keeping an eye on this guy while I go check on my date?"

"No problem," the vet said as if he would be watching Lujack's luggage.

# Chapter Fourteen

## *The Old Parker Center Routine*

It wasn't easy convincing Debbi that he'd had to trip her or else Micky Kim would have killed them both. What made it harder was the fact that X-rays showed Debbi's sore shoulder was in fact a broken collarbone. Lujack insisted that she broke it while rolling away from the gunfire. Debbi insisted it happened when Lujack tripped her.

The argument lasted most of the way back to Los Angeles. It was playful, but there was an uncomfortable edge in Debbi's voice. Maybe it was fear. Maybe it was anger. Maybe a little of both.

Lujack knew he had been right about Micky Kim as soon as he saw the smile on Tom Clancy's face when the homicide detective showed up at San Francisco General.

"I leave you alone for a few hours and you kill a guy."

"Nice town you got here, Clancy."

"How's little Miss Eyewitness News?"

"She hurt her shoulder. They're X-raying it now."

"As long as she doesn't have to have a blood transfusion," the detective said uneasily.

"Did you get a name?"

"Like you said, the infamous Micky Kim, wanted in the murder of Chase Field in Los Angeles and for various other Yakuza-related activities in Honolulu and Vancouver. You might get a medal for wasting him."

"I'd rather get the man who sent him."

"Speaking of which, you're supposed to call a Lieutenant Matsuda in LA."

"Bad news travels fast."

Lujack hadn't been to Parker Center in many years. Seven years to be exact. A lifetime, a marriage, and a career ago. The Asian Task Force was on the fourth floor. Kyle Thurgood was waiting for Lujack in the hall.

"I see you dressed for the occasion," Thurgood said, noting Lujack's Notre Dame sweatshirt.

"I didn't have time to unpack."

"Your Uncle Johnny would be proud of you."

"He was my cousin, not my uncle."

"I hear the Irish have a good team this year."

"College football should never be played in August."

"That's funny coming from you, Jimmy." Thurgood smiled. "Speaking of the Irish, Matsuda's waiting."

Rick "Kamikaze" Matsuda stood up from his metal desk as Lujack and Thurgood walked in. He was an inch or two taller than Tommy and about ten pounds heavier. Those ten pounds were all muscle. He wore his glen-plaid coat open at the waist. His black hair was cut short, and dark eyes betrayed constant vigilance. Rick was a Nisei Joe Friday.

"Long time, Jimmy."

"Two blondes at the New Otani, about four Superbowls ago," Lujack said.

Matsuda frowned. Lujack noticed that Matsuda had a detailed map of LA's ever-growing Asian communities. Chinatown just north of downtown, Japantown between Parker Center and the Los Angeles River, Koreatown stretching from Western to La Brea, and Little Saigon running along the Orange County border. The lieutenant took his cue.

"There are over a million Asian-Americans in Southern California. Japanese, Chinese, Korean, Filipinos, Thais, Vietnamese, Cambodians, Laotians. More are coming in every day."

"I've noticed."

"It hasn't always been easy for Asians in this country, but great strides have been made over the past twenty years. Naturally, like all communities, there has been some crime. This task force has grown from six to twelve officers in the last five years."

"I'm impressed."

"I told you he was a fast study," Thurgood chimed in.

"What has happened these past few weeks—the involvement of the Korean Yakuza in the murder of a prominent non-Asian such as Chase Field and of course the unfortunate attack on you and Miss Arnold up in San Francisco"—Matsuda smiled here to underline his facetiousness—"it has been a great shock to the community leaders who have strived so hard to establish their hardworking and law-abiding image."

"Why do I think I'm going to be asked to do something for the good of the Asian-American community?"

"Can it, Jimmy," Thurgood said.

"We heard that Miss Arnold was thinking of pursuing the story about the girl they found in the bay. We heard that she was going to try and link it with a certain Japanese businessman."

"You hear a lot," Lujack said, looking at Thurgood.

"Thank your friend Clancy for that, Jimmy."

"You don't really think I can control what Debbi puts on the air, Kamikaze."

Matsuda flinched at the nickname, which he had picked up as a rookie when he'd had one too many tequila shooters and bowled himself, not the ball, down the alley of the Tarzana Lanes.

"Don't be cute, Lujack. You're the one who got her on this Yoshida kick. You're the one who can damn well get her off."

"I take it you don't share my suspicions."

"He's not the only one, Jimmy," a familiar voice said, coming into the room.

Lujack didn't have to be introduced. He and Police Chief Tom Bane went back a long way. Lujack had an uneasy feeling his arm was about to be twisted.

"Don't get up," the chief said, waving at his officers.

"Now I know what I'm doing in Parker Center on a Sunday."

"We thought it was easier to bring you here than for me to go to the Chin Up," the chief said, putting Lujack back where he wanted him. "So what do you have on Yoshida?" Bane asked.

"A hunch mostly," Lujack said. "Very circumstantial. He was in both cities when the girls were murdered. He likes young girls. One of the vice-presidents of his bank, George Kim, is in with the Yakuza. I think if you look deep enough you could connect Kim with the man I killed in San Francisco. They do have the same name."

"The DA would laugh you out of his office."

"Probably, but if two or three more headless girls start showing up, nobody will be laughing."

The chief turned to Thurgood. "Where was Yoshida the night Ginger Louie was murdered?"

"We don't know."

"Can you find out?"

"It won't be easy. He's surrounded by loyal body-guards. His place in Bel Air is like foreign country. Occasionally he goes nightclubbing in the city or down to the Marina."

Bane took a few thoughtful steps around Matsuda's office. The three men were silent.

Lujack had made his best case, but even he had to admit it was only a hunch.

"The mayor doesn't want Yoshida involved. He made that very clear. And it so happens the mayor is on the board of directors of the Pacific National Bank," said Bane.

"At about twenty grand a year," Thurgood added.

The chief scowled at Kyle. Remarks like that were why Thurgood would remain the department's smart-est lieutenant.

"OCID can't find anything on Yoshida or on Kim. They think Kim is related to one of the kids being held."

"The organized crime unit can't find its asshole with a shit detector," Matsuda observed.

"Did you tell Chief Bane about the bomber?" Lujack asked Thurgood.

"Yes, he told me," Bane said with a pained look. "That's when I found out about Killian."

"What about Killian?"

"He's a part-time government official," Bane said.

"You mean CIA?"

"I mean he works for the people who run the

government. People who don't appreciate private citizens poking around into top-secret projects. Top-secret projects that involve sensitive technology transfers to the friendly powers."

"And billions of dollars of contracts," Lujack said aloud, and he thought to himself: and hundreds of millions of dollars of profits.

"Do we understand each other, Jimmy?"

"I think so. You want me to forget I ever heard of Yoshida and Brownell and Killian, even if they like to kill young girls."

"If they killed anyone, Lujack, we'll get 'em," Chief Bane said, "but until we have proof I think you should talk to your friend over at Channel Seven."

"I'll do what I can, Chief."

"Do better than that."

Kyle walked him to his car.

"Nice going, Jimmy. I didn't think you'd get the chief involved."

"I wasn't planning to."

"The mayor doesn't like ex-cops stepping on his pension plan."

"The mayor's a crook."

"Who isn't?"

"See you around, Kyle."

"Wait a minute," Thurgood said. "I got two tickets outta Chaves tonight. Hershiser's pitching. One more game and he's got the record."

"No he isn't. I heard on the radio he's got a sore shoulder. He's going to miss his turn. Besides, I've got a date. Thanks anyway."

Thurgood smiled. "I have to read about it in the paper. You and your girlfriend on a little romantic weekend in the city. Then some cop buddy of yours calls me up in the middle of the night telling me you shot Kim. How come I don't hear anything from you, Jimmy?"

"You know I don't shoot and tell, Kyle."

"The old man's serious, Jimmy. Give it a rest."

"I'll try."

"Like the chief says, you'll do better than that," Thurgood said, and Lujack knew it was more than an order.

Lujack did have a date that night, but it wasn't with Debbi. It was with Kazuo Yoshida. Bad news certainly did travel fast. It also came from the strangest places. It was Tommy who told Lujack that Yoshida wanted to see him. The same Tommy who never met a Japanese he liked.

Lujack stopped at Debbi's before he went home. She was taking the next four days off. The station wanted her to get used to her cast, but Debbi seemed to think it had more to do with the story she was investigating than with the discomfort of her cast. He tried telling himself he wasn't going to warn her off the story, but he knew that was exactly what he was going to do. Why shouldn't he? If she kept digging into Ginger's death, she might lose more than her job.

Whitley, the Bunker Hill Towers doorman, opened the door with a friendly smile. He had obviously read yesterday's morning headlines: "Ex-cop Saves TV Anchor." There were pictures of Lujack and Debbi. Lujack was described as a "personal consultant." He had given the two crime reporters his new card. Even the LA *Times* had run versions of the same story. In the Metro section, of course. When he checked his messages there had been eleven calls from the media, most of them women wanting to know what a personal consultant did for a living. One of these days he might call some of them back.

"Interesting trip, Mr. Lujack," the man with the English accent said as Lujack walked past. "Is Miss Arnold in, Whitley?"

"I think so, Mr. Lujack," the doorman said. "Shall I ring you?"

The doorman picked up the phone before Lujack got to the elevator. Lujack knew enough about doormen to know that Debbi wasn't alone.

Lujack made a private bet to himself between the elevator and Debbi's door. If she answered within two seconds of his first knock, they were going to be married. If he had to knock twice and someone else answered, like a movie director who wore boots and had a short-trimmed beard and talked about having the same agent as John Huston, they still might get married. If she met him at the door and kissed him on the lips before she said anything, Connie Chung was in trouble.

He knocked twice and waited.

"The door's open," she yelled.

He walked in feeling relieved, like he'd dodged another fortune cookie.

She was sitting on the couch looking languorous but not relaxed. Her lovely legs were tucked under her on the pillows. The salmon-colored Chinztia gown showed enough thigh to keep your attention but not enough to touch. Her back was to City Hall, Union Station, and County General, but Lujack couldn't see the buildings when he walked toward her, he remembered them from the previous night.

The man sitting across from her stood up before Lujack got halfway across the room. Men like him could never be embarrassed or awkward or remotely at a disadvantage as long as less than ten percent of U.S. citizens weren't in prison and more than a third of the rest still voted.

"You know Pete Rudlow, don't you, Jimmy?" Debbi said impishly.

"I think we met at the last Marina 10K," Rudlow said, giving Lujack a sturdy grin.

"Neither of us finished."

"No thanks to this young lady," Rudlow said with a bow.

Lujack tried to remember if Rudlow was married. He saw a picture in his mind of Rudlow with an adoring wife and two little boys. The guy was shameless, Lujack had to give him that.

"How's the shoulder?" Lujack asked.

"Better," she said politely. He would rather she hit him than be polite. "We were just talking about you."

"Do you want me to go back outside?"

"I was telling Debbi—Miss Arnold—that she was lucky to be alive. The Yakuza rarely miss."

"You know a lot about the Yakuza, Senator?"

"More than you might think, Mr. Lujack. Although, of course, my sources are privileged."

"Senator Rudlow is after Yoshida too, Jimmy. He's been working with Dolph Killian."

Lujack looked around for a place to laugh.

"It's all rather strange the way this has come about, but Debbi's right. Dolph has been helping me try to stop a certain joint venture between our country and Japan. A venture that was brokered and partially financed by Mr. Yoshida."

"The B-3 bomber."

Rudlow gave a respectful nod. "Dolph said you were smarter than you looked."

"I thought Dolph was working for Brownell and Brownell was building the plane."

"Dolph does sometimes work for Larry, they're old friends from the Navy, but they've parted company on this one, although Larry didn't know it until the other day."

"I'm having a little trouble sorting my way through the double-crosses here."

"It's a matter of patriotism, Mr. Lujack. Dolph does a lot of work for my committee. He's one of the three or four best weapons analysts in the business. Over the past few years he's been growing more and more wary of the Japanese inroads in our markets. First radios and televisions, then cars, and now fighter planes. Dolph came to me about six months ago when he heard the president and the Pentagon were going ahead with a Japanese joint venture on the B-3. He was horrified and rightly saw it as a national security threat."

"As I remember, Dolph wasn't always so patriotic about selling the Pentagon's fighter planes."

"You do your homework."

"Privileged sources," Lujack said, then continued. "If this is such a national security threat, why is the president going along with it?"

"There are some in the Pentagon and on the Joint Chiefs who think we need the Japanese to control the Russians and the Chinese. Also, men like Larry Brownell and Kazuo Yoshida can be very persuasive. I think they have the president convinced we need the Japanese as much as they need us."

"But you're not."

"America needs no one. Never has and never will."

"Don't tell that to the bankers."

"That's what Yoshida and Brownell are hoping, that the president and Congress will bend to the power of the yen and in so doing give away our best deterrent to world war."

"The B-3."

"Right."

"So what do you want with Debbi?"

"I came over to persuade her to hold up on the Yoshida story."

"That's funny. So did I."

"We want to blow the lid off all of Yoshida's dealings: his ties with the Yakuza; his hidden interest in the Marina Shores, the Zodiac Club, and the Field Agency; his loans to hundreds of aerospace workers, defense contractors, politicians; and ultimately his relationship with Brownell. Dolph thinks Yoshida, the Pacific National, and Yoshida's friends in the Japanese government are the de facto owners of Brownell Industries. That is what Dolph and I were discussing the day you and your partner and Miss Arnold blew our cover."

"You make him sound like a master spy."

"He is. I don't think there is any greater threat to our country."

"And we can help bring him down," Debbi said excitedly. Lujack had to admit, it was a big story, bigger than a guy who murders girls for kicks.

"So why not do it now?"

"Yoshida is a U.S. citizen. Brownell is one of the most powerful men in the country. What I've told you cannot all be proven. Dolph was getting close to the quid pro quo of their relationship when Brownell figured out he was working with me. Now we have lost our access."

"Sounds like more politics to me."

"We have to be very careful we don't offend the Japanese government or the president or the other key senators on the Armed Services Committee."

"If what you say is true, maybe you should do a little offending."

"There's a committee vote next week on the B-3. If

the bomber gets out of committee, then we'll go public with what we have so far."

"We can wait that long, Jimmy."

"I can wait forever, Deb. Yoshida isn't drawing lines on my neck."

Debbi abruptly turned toward the window. Lujack knew he had said the wrong thing, but he was beginning not to care.

"Yoshida is a lot of things, Mr. Lujack, but I don't think he's a murderer."

"Dolph Killian's a lot of things, Senator, but I don't think he's the savior of the Western world. For that matter, neither are you."

"Jesus, Jimmy. Can't you see the senator's trying to help?" Debbi said with exasperation.

"I think I should be going," Rudlow said. "I've got the red eye back to Washington."

Debbi walked Rudlow to the door. When she came back Lujack was watching an Amtrak train wind its way out of the city along the Los Angeles River.

"So what happens now?" he asked, still looking at the train, catching glimpses of it between the skyscrapers.

"With us or with the story?"

"Both."

"I think we put them on hold."

"That seems to be the consensus," he said.

"Honor and duty, Mr. Lujack. Most Americans think of our culture as a creaky edifice of honor and duty," Kazuo Yoshida said as he and Lujack walked through the most beautiful gardens Lujack had ever seen. Everything about Yoshida's ten-acre Bel Air estate was symmetrical, classically Japanese. Lujack felt like he was in the Imperial Gardens, not the Santa Monica Mountains. Yoshida was not unlike his garden. A cultured, powerful force not totally at ease with his environment.

"Are they wrong?"

"Not wrong, but like most Western perceptions of Japanese, incomplete. Are you familiar with Bushido, Mr. Lujack?"

"The code of the samurai."

"Very good. In my country the samurai are gone, but the Yakuza remain. In this way they are the last custodians of our tradition."

Yoshida watched Lujack for a reaction, but Lujack gave him none.

"The Yakuza remain because of *giri* and *ninjo. Giri* is the sense of duty and obligation that westerners think they understand, but there is no English equivalent for *giri.* It is heavy like a sword, yet it is also light like a flower."

Yoshida picked a chrysanthemum from a nearby bush. He held it in his hand, fondling it, then suddenly he crushed the flower in his fist.

*"Giri* can be gratitude for an old kindness, it can be revenge for an old insult," the man said as they started up a little wooden footbridge. When they came to the apex Yoshida dropped the petals into the pond below. A curious Koi came to the surface, picked at the petals, then disappeared.

*"Ninjo* is the human heart, compassion, feeling. When the two, *giri* and *ninjo,* are combined, say in the *oyabun* or godfather of a Yakuza family, they create a formidable enemy, very formidable."

Lujack wasn't sure but he thought he had just been threatened by the head of the most powerful crime family in Japan.

"This *oyabun.* He could also be the head of a great corporation," Lujack said.

"In the corporate world, the old values are not sacred. Even in Japan. It is why our corporations will become corrupt and lazy like the corporations here," Yoshida said with some bitterness.

Lujack tried to guess the man's age. He guessed Yoshida to be in his early sixties, younger than Brownell. That would have made him just young enough not to have been killed in the war, but old enough to remember.

"But in Japan they aren't exclusive, the world of the Yakuza and the world of business, and the world of politics."

"In Japan nothing is exclusive of *giri* and *ninjo,*" Yoshida said, stopping to pick an errant branch off a bonsai tree. Japanese, like the English and other anal-retentive cultures, were all compulsive gardners.

"Like nothing is exclusive of Shinto," he said, pausing in front of a shrine to the native Japanese religion.

Yoshida made a cursory obeisance and kept walking along the path. Yoshida had a respectful formality about his manner that Lujack was impressed with. Everything about the man was impeccably proper, from his bifocals to his fingernails. After meeting Yoshida it was hard for Lujack to imagine him as Ginger's killer.

They were approaching a smaller house at the bottom of the garden. The main house was above them, up the hill. Lujack had driven through a gate to get on the property, but he hadn't noticed a lot of security. He had seen only three men on the property and none of them was missing a finger or had visible tattoos.

"Your friend Mr. Brownell tells me you and he share an admiration for Yoshio Kodama."

The Japanese man nodded approvingly. "Kodama was a great man. He once came here in the early 'seventies."

"I didn't know that."

"He met with President Nixon in San Clemente. I drove with him to the meeting. It was a great day for our countries."

"That was before Watergate and Lockheed," Lujack said.

Yoshida shook his head in acceptance. "Another way our country is becoming like yours. This love for scandals."

"Isn't that why you invited me here? To prevent a scandal?"

Yoshida ignored Lujack's question and pushed open the door of the little house. Like the rest of the grounds, the architecture was classically Japanese but, once inside, Lujack found himself facing a wall of computer screens and market boards. Three Oriental men in suits were sitting at desks talking on telephones, speaking what he assumed was Japanese in abrupt, excited tones. In the corner were a teleprinter and a fax machine.

"This is my personal trading center. When I'm not at the bank I use it to keep track of the markets. It is Monday morning in the East, and my associates are very busy. Hong Kong, Singapore, and, of course, Tokyo."

Lujack looked at the rows of screens. There must have been twenty different markets being tracked.

"One man is trading gold, another is trading dollars."

"They don't mind working on Sunday?"

"They like making money more. The man trading dollars, I think you may know him. His name is George Kim."

"He's Korean, isn't he?"

The man Yoshida described looked at Lujack. He was ten years older than the man Lujack had shot in San Francisco, but there was a definite resemblance. If they weren't brothers they were at least cousins, no matter what Rick Matsuda's Asian Task Force said.

"Japanese-Korean. He was born in Japan, but he is of Korean ancestry. There are a great many Koreans in Japan. They are our largest minority, as you say here. Americans think the Japanese and Koreans are enemies. That is like saying the whites and blacks here are enemies. It all depends on who you ask."

Lujack nodded in Kim's direction. The Pacific National vice-president nodded back, but it wasn't a friendly bow. Lujack noted Kim had all his fingers.

Kim addressed a question to Yoshida in Japanese. For all Lujack knew, they could be discussing the caliber of bullets to be used for Lujack's firing squad. Yoshida shot an answer back, then smiled at Lujack's puzzled look.

"Anything I should know about?"

"He wanted to know how far I wanted to let the Canadian dollar drop before selling my position. I told him another half-yen. That will only give a twenty-six-million-dollar profit, but the trade took less than six minutes to execute."

"I get the impression you have a good head for numbers."

"Your impression is correct."

Yoshida led him into a private room off the trading center. A table was set up on the floor. Yoshida removed his sandals and Lujack took off his Nikes. A geisha appeared when the two men were seated. She was very beautiful, and Lujack wondered if Yoshida had a family. He had seen no sign of one in the big house or here in the tea house.

"The tea ceremony is sacred in Japan and is very beautiful, but I thought for our purposes we should partake in an equally important Japanese tradition."

The geisha set a tray down on the table. On it were a pitcher and two cups. Next to the cups was a bucket full of ice. The geisha bowed and disappeared.

"In Japan today most important business is done while drinking," Yoshida said, carefully dropping three ice cubes into each cup.

"Your partner said you like scotch, Johnnie Walker Red," Yoshida said. He poured a healthy shot of what looked like scotch into Lujack's cup. He did the same thing for himself.

"To numbers, Mr. Lujack. They work for bankers as well as for bookies."

Lujack took a drink of scotch. His meeting with Yoshida had been very interesting and very strange. He could handle billionaires like Larry Brownell, they were just like everybody else but a little more arrogant, but Kazuo Yoshida, he was an enigma.

"My partner has a similar toast. He says the only people who can count higher than the Japanese are the Chinese. That's why there are so many of them."

Yoshida laughed. "Your partner is a typical Chinaman. He chooses quantity over quality. In Japan we have a saying. Let the Chinaman count your change, but never let him count your blessings."

"I was surprised when Tommy said you had called."

"Why is that?"

"Because he thinks you almost killed his son."

"And I did kill his cousin, or so you are telling the police."

"It is hard for me to understand what *giri* and *ninjo* have to do with molesting and beheading young women."

The Japanese man's eyes closed slightly. It was then

Lujack saw Yoshida as a snake, not a dragon. A very deadly snake.

"Maybe they have nothing to do with such actions, maybe it is what is called a figment of your imagination."

"Maybe, but I don't think so."

"Do you have a family, Mr. Lujack?"

"No, I don't. I mean, I had a wife but she left me."

"Could that be why you like to live so dangerously, because you have no family, nothing to lose?"

"I've thought about it once or twice."

"I have no family either, Mr. Lujack. I sometimes think that's why I have been free to achieve all this. Do you know the last four prime ministers of Japan have stayed in this guest house?"

"I can understand why."

"And your President Reagan, when he retires he will be my next-door neighbor. I helped pay for his house."

"And his wife will lunch at the Chin Up."

"Pardon me?"

"An in joke."

"Right now I am preparing a trip for Mr. Reagan after his presidency. He will be a spokesman for the Pacific National Bank and visit all the Pacific Rim nations."

"That sounds like an expensive pitchman."

"He is very expensive, but Mr. Reagan is worth such an expense. He has been a good friend for Japan."

"And he also wants you to have the B-3 bomber."

"It sounds like you have been talking to some of my friends at the Marina Shores. Senator Rudlow thinks that with the B-3 technology Japan will become a world-class military power."

"But you don't."

"The Japanese leaders have learned their lessons about military power. We are content to let the United States and the Soviets rule the world."

"Or go broke in the process."

Yoshida laughed and poured two more drinks. This time it was Lujack's turn to toast. "To the capture of Ginger Louie's murderer."

Yoshida's eyes again narrowed, but he drank. "You're a stubborn man, Mr. Lujack."

"So I've been told."

"How long are you going to be carrying on this dangerous game?"

"You give me a blood sample and we could end it right now," Lujack said evenly.

Yoshida looked hard at Lujack. For the first time he was off balance. "My blood?"

"The police lab found a speck of semen on Ginger's body. A man had been with her just prior to her death. It wasn't Dave Mason or Chase Field. If you would give me a blood sample, the police could run a test on it and determine its DNA type. If it doesn't match . . ."

"Ah yes, genetic fingerprinting," Yoshida said, nodding slowly. "I have read about it. Another wonder of science."

Both men said nothing.

"So, Mr. Yoshida, will you submit a sample of your blood to the police crime lab?"

"I don't know, Mr. Lujack. That seems rather un-American."

"I think you're right. It isn't very American at all, but it is a way for you to get rid of me."

"There are other ways too."

"Yes there are."

# Chapter Fifteen

## *Something Has Come Between*

Lujack knew they had to get it straight between them or there wasn't going be a partnership. Monday morning was as good a time as any. He and Tommy had been meeting on Monday mornings for five years. It was the first week of the pro football season and there was a lot of work to do. Tommy had given him a preliminary rundown on the opening weekend. The Good Book was up $21,000 on the pros, down $8,000 on the colleges, and up $4,000 on baseball. Tommy's preliminary estimates were usually within a centime of the final figures, so no one had anything to complain about. Except that if they didn't talk soon, there wasn't going to be any Good Book.

Lujack felt a hot streak coming now that Hershiser had missed his turn in the rotation. With any luck at all, Hershiser's elbow bruise wouldn't heal and he'd get shelled his next time out. Drysdale's record would be safe and Debbi Arnold would lose her bet. It didn't matter to Lujack that no money was involved. With

Debbi a man had to create his own angles. But that didn't have anything to do with Tommy.

"He's a numbers freak like you are, Tommy," Lujack said over a cup of the Chin Up's Rustoleum-strength coffee.

"Who's a numbers freak like me?"

"Your friend Yoshida."

"What are you talking about, 'my friend'?" Tommy frowned.

"He called you, not me. I've been trying to figure that out. Why not call my house or go through Lyman or even Brownell?"

"What are you trying to say, Jimmy?" Tommy asked, taking a cigarette out of his pocket. Tommy only smoked when he was nervous or angry.

"I'm not sure."

"You're right, you're not sure at all."

"I thought you hated Yoshida."

"What makes you think I don't?"

"The way you've been acting."

"A man calls me and says he wants to talk to you. I know you want to talk to him so I pass on the message."

"That's all you do, pass on the message?"

"What do you think, Jimmy?"

"Brownell offered me a million dollars. That's a lot of money."

Tommy took a drag on his cigarette. He wouldn't look at Lujack, instead he watched his wife's decorator measuring the far wall. The decorator looked like he was framing a picture that wasn't there. Lujack was surprised to see that the decorator was an old Chinese man. He would have expected a Melrose Avenue type fresh from the Design Center. Lujack pushed forward.

"You're doing all this remodeling, all of a sudden Liz wants me to stop looking into Ginger's murder . . ."

"So you think Brownell and Yoshida have paid me off. You think the men who gave the orders that almost killed my oldest son, the men who did kill my niece, you think they wave money under my nose and I go away?" His face turned a strange shade of pink. Jimmy had seen Tommy upset, but this was different.

"Ten, eleven years I've known you. We've been partners more than five years. We share everything, winning and losing, good days and bad days, right, Jimmy? And now you think I sell my family's honor to a Nipponese murderer?"

"I told you I don't know what to think. Ever since I walked into that creep's room and saw Ginger's head and those markings on the wall. This whole thing's got to me. I'm sorry, man."

"Don't be, Jimmy. I haven't told you about my brother-in-law," Tommy said in a lowered voice.

"Ray?"

"When Liz called last week and told me to talk with you, I thought it was because she was afraid, but I didn't know what she was afraid of. Now I do."

Tommy paused and took another drag on his cigarette. "I told you Ray had been given a job in San Francisco and Liz was going up to see him. She went up last week, a day or two before you and the news lady. Ray lives down on the peninsula, he's running his own restaurant-bar in the Silicon Valley. He wanted Liz to move in with him. To try again. Liz asked where he got the money. Ray used to be a bartender. He said some of his old customers had come to him a few months ago and said they needed a good man to run their new place. They remembered Ray's winning personality. They said they'd make him a partner and put him up in a nice house."

"All he had to do was forget he ever had a daughter."

Tommy nodded his head. "They told him he should keep a low public profile. Not draw any unneeded attention to himself and his family. You were right, Jimmy. He sold the soul of his own daughter."

"His new partners. Do they have names?"

"One of them does. George Kim."

"The other was probably Micky Kim. Big fans of Ray's winning personality. Never met the asshole in their life."

"Another thing, Jimmy. This restaurant. It's next to the big Brownell Industries plant in Sunnyvale. They own the land, and the paper is—"

"Don't tell me. The paper is held by the Pacific National Bank."

"It used to be a Polynesian restaurant. Now they serve sushi and hard drinks. Ray always said he hated sushi."

"But he never had anything against sake or cash. What's Liz going to do?"

"She doesn't know what to do. She doesn't like her job anymore. With Ginger gone there's no reason to stay here. She doesn't really understand that she's being bought off. Liz doesn't think like that. Ever since Ginger's death she's not seeing things clearly."

"I guess it's her call, but she can't be that blind."

The Chinese decorator was now humming something as he matched a fabric to the wall.

"That's the strangest interior decorator I've ever seen," said Lujack.

"That's no interior decorator. That's Lin Pau. The geomancer. He's making sure the remodeling plans will be acceptable to the spirits."

"You're not serious."

"When the Chin Up first opened, my father thought

it was silly to do business the Chinese way now that he was in America. The first year business was horrible. The food was good, the waiters were good, he didn't know what the matter was. My mother called Lin Pau. Lin said the restaurant's front door was in a straight line with the kitchen's back door. The good food produced in the kitchen, which also produced the money, was going straight out through the front door. That is bad *feng shui.* My father moved the door to the right side and moved the cashier from the front to the back. Since then business has been good and Lin Pau has always been consulted."

"What happens if Mr. Lin doesn't like the new plans?"

"Then we will change them," Jackie Chin said, coming out of the kitchen. "*Feng shui* is very important to the Chinese," Jackie continued solemnly, leaving Lujack with the impression she was much closer to the Chinese spirit world than her husband.

"How's Miss Arnold?"

Lujack could do no wrong since he began dating Debbi Arnold. He didn't think it wise to tell Jackie that their romance was a bit rocky. "She's fine. She enjoyed meeting you the other night. Can't wait to bring her friends to the new Chin Up."

"Of course we won't be calling it the Chin Up anymore."

"Naturally."

"What do you think about Fukien Place? My family is from Fukien and the food from the province is very unique. Not overly hot like Szechuan or bland like Cantonese. There are many fish dishes, very low in cholesterol."

"I think it might lose a little in translation," Lujack observed. "Maybe you should ask Mr. Lin for a suggestion."

"Americans are so filthy-minded," Jackie said with a giggle.

"What's gotten into your wife?" Lujack asked after Jackie had gone over to consult with the old geomancer.

"I don't know. She's changed since Lionel's accident," Tommy said. "The other night she told me it was all right if Lionel didn't get into Harvard. She said he didn't even have to be a nuclear physicist."

"Maybe she looked at his report card," Lujack suggested.

"Chinese mothers have their children's report cards memorized from the first grade. I think she's just happy to have him alive," Tommy said.

"Can't blame her." Lujack wondered about Debbi and about his own family or lack of it.

"So what's our next step?" Tommy asked him.

"You're serious. You want to keep pushing? It won't make us too popular with the mayor, or with the president, for that matter."

"I didn't vote for them. You think Yoshida is guilty, right?"

"Of espionage, I don't know. Of murder, yes."

"Then he will kill again, don't you think?"

"Yeah, I do think. I think he's got a screw loose, Tommy," Lujack said, seeing Yoshida a little clearer. "He's smart and sophisticated and he's a numbers whiz, but he's missing a piece. I can feel it."

"Numbers," Tommy said. "You say Yoshida likes numbers."

"He loves numbers. His house, his gardens, everything is a mathematical equation."

"Maybe that's how we'll figure him out, with numbers. What was the date Ginger was killed?"

"August sixth," both men said at the same time, realizing the significance.

"The day the U.S. dropped the bomb," Tommy said.

"That can't be a coincidence."

"What was the date of the other girl?"

"March something," Lujack said, trying to remember. "It was the spring regatta. March twenty-third. I think it was March twenty-third. Does that mean anything to you?"

"No," Tommy said, "but I bet it does to Yoshida. Let me do some digging."

"And I'll see if I can get a look at Brownell's yacht. My guess is Yoshida has his own cabin. I'd like to check it for bloodstains."

"A boat like that can have a big cold storage hold. He could take the girls down to the hold. It would be easier to wash."

"Do you think Brownell knows about it?"

"For all I know, the two bastards are in it together."

"Doesn't say much for billionaires," Lujack observed.

"I wonder where Yoshida was during the war."

"Maybe he was in Hiroshima at the end."

"Or maybe he served in China. Remember, the two girls were Chinese-American," Tommy said, seeming more and more like his old vengeful, Japanese-hating self.

"I think I'm going to have a talk with Dolph Killian. It's about time that bastard picked his horse."

"What about Debbi? Will she help?"

"I'm not sure. Debbi's suddenly become very patriotic. Politicians can do that to you."

"She might be in danger," Tommy warned.

"We're the ones who are in danger, old friend," Lujack said. "I think I might need your friend to give me some magic dust."

"Not you, Lujack. The only dust you like is gunpowder."

"Coming from a Chinese, I'll take that as a compliment."

Lujack found Dolph Killian at his private dock in the Marina Shores. Lujack had picked the lock on the gate, just in case Killian wasn't receiving guests. Killian's sailboat, the *Midway,* was almost directly under the deck bar of the Shores. Lujack remembered the day he and Tommy had sat out on the deck and watched the *Southern Cross* tie up. The big white Feadship was nowhere to be seen on this day. That fact made Lujack more than slightly uncomfortable.

"Aren't you dead yet, asshole?" Dolph Killian said, looking up from his teak deck. Dolph was polishing the wooden deck. His two mercenary bodyguards moved toward Lujack.

"I can handle this," Killian said, motioning his two goons to the far end of the boat.

"I had a nice chat with your good friend Senator Rudlow yesterday."

"I heard," Killian said, still polishing.

"He said you were a patriot."

"And you said I was a murderer."

"Something like that."

"What do you want, Lujack?"

"I want you to help me prove that Kazuo Yoshida is a murderer."

Killian threw the rag down on the deck and laughed. Next he grabbed a beer from the six-pack that was sitting in a pail on the top hatch.

"You're out of your fuckin' mind, Lujack. You know that, don't you?"

"It kinda slips up on me once in a while."

Killian popped a beer and threw one to Lujack. The two mercs gave Lujack a suspicious look.

"Give me one good reason why I should help you arrest the man who has financed my company for the past five years."

"One reason is because he's guilty and you know it. Another reason is because you really don't want the Japanese government to have the technology in the B-3. But the best reason is that if you don't help me get Yoshida, your buddies Brownell and Rudlow have it set up so that you're the fall guy."

Killian ran a brown hand over his sunburned pate. Lujack had liked dealing with Killian better when he thought the old pilot was a murderer.

"First you want me to turn in my banker, then you tell me two of my closest associates are setting me up," Killian said, shaking his head. "Why?"

"Because you're a natural. You used to work Ginger over, you're compromised by both sides because you have no scruples, and if it comes down to Brownell making a choice between you and Yoshida, that's no choice."

"Thanks for the vote of confidence. What about Rudlow?"

"Rudlow's a politician. He's covering his ass. If his committee doesn't have the votes to stop the B-3 joint venture, my guess is he'll switch his vote and sweep the deck of all the right-wing crazies who lobbied against our trusted allies the Japanese."

"You're a cynical bastard, aren't you, Lujack?"

"Are you going to help me or not?"

"I'm not sure. Let's say you've given me food for thought."

"If I were you, I'd start chewing. The Armed Services Committee vote is next week."

"I know when the vote is, Lujack. Remember, I'm a weapons analyst. I work for the fucking committee."

Killian looked out on the channel. What Lujack told him had an effect. It wasn't easy to make a prick like Killian doubt himself.

"The B-3, it really is a bad deal."

"A weapons dealer with a conscience."

Killian ignored the comment. "Once the Japs get their hands on those avionics and composite materials, we'll have lost our edge. When our boys go up in the sky, they know they have an advantage over any bodies they come up against. Even the Israelis. After the B-3 trade they won't. The B-3 is the best of our fighter software combined with the best of our long-range material. We're giving away our edge."

"Brownell doesn't agree with you."

"Yoshida owns Brownell. He owns all of us."

"What about your friends in the CIA?"

"The company is run by politicians now. Everybody's afraid if we nix the deal the Japs will stop buying our paper."

"So do something about it yourself."

Killian looked at the two killers at the end of the boat. Lujack wondered how the two men could subcontract out to Colonel Martin. Then he understood. Yoshida did own them all.

"I don't know, Lujack. It's been a long time since I wanted to be a hero." He took another swig. The breeze was coming up. Lujack watched a plane climb above Playa del Rey across the channel. He knew what Killian meant. Sometimes it was easier to do nothing.

"Let me talk to Pete tomorrow. If he seems

squirrelly about that committee vote, I might help you."

"Tomorrow. Rudlow is back in Washington."

"You're slipping, Lujack. Senator Rudlow is at the Bonaventure. He's going to Catalina with me tomorrow for the regatta."

"What regatta?"

"Once a year the Shores has a race around Catalina."

"And Rudlow's going over with you."

"Yeah. I think he's bringing that news bitch. The one who broke up our last fight." Killian smiled at Lujack's chagrin. "That's right. You just saved her life a few days ago, didn't you?"

"This race, will Yoshida be in it?" Lujack said, suddenly not caring about Debbi and at the same time being afraid for her.

"Sure he will. He's the defending champ. That SOB is some competitor."

"Then that's where the *Southern Cross* is, right? In Catalina?"

"Left this morning for Avalon Harbor. She's the official race boat. She also has a new owner."

"Don't tell me. Kazuo Yoshida?"

"He wrote Larry a check for five and a half million."

"When's the race?"

"Wednesday the second."

"September second."

"That's right. Same day every year. Yoshida takes special pleasure in kicking our butts on the second. That's the day of the Japanese surrender."

"To MacArthur on the *Missouri,*" Lujack said and finished his beer. "When does everybody get out to the island?"

"Tomorrow night. We rent out the old ballroom and Casino. About fifty of us really dance up a storm. Some of the guys even bring their wives."

"Sounds like a hell of a party."

"Come on over. That way you can chaperon Pete and your girlfriend." Killian smiled.

"I just might."

# Chapter Sixteen

## *Who's Got the Telltale Gene?*

Lujack had to move fast and he didn't have much time. The race was on Wednesday. He guessed Yoshida and his entourage would arrive in Avalon the next night. Lujack knew he somehow had to get on the *Southern Cross* and stop the banker from butchering another girl. The problem, of course, was proof. He had none, and the police weren't in the habit of picking up billionaire bankers on a hunch.

Barney Milch answered on the sixth ring.

"Barney, Jimmy Lujack."

"You sound like you're on one of those car phones."

"I am."

"I hate car phones. Go to a phone booth."

Milch hung up. Lujack looked for a phone booth. There weren't any more phone booths in Los Angeles. Only those naked phones stuck back to back. Anything to save a buck.

"Lujack again."

"That's better," Milch barked.

"I want you to do me a favor."

"I'm listening."

"You know that semen trace you found on Ginger Louie?"

"Who told you about that?"

"Who do you think?"

"Kyle Thurgood."

"You can get a read on the DNA structure, right?"

"Right."

"Can you tell if a man is sterile?"

"Maybe."

"Was the sample you found on Ginger? Was that man sterile?"

"Maybe."

"It's important, Barney."

"The case is closed, Jimmy. It's over. I don't say it's over, the chief says it's over. The mayor, God bless his cheating heart, says it's over."

"It won't be over when another headless girl is found in Avalon Harbor this weekend."

"You know, I was the first guy they called in on the Natalie Wood case. Jesus, what a body. She'd been in the water all night, but what a body."

"Barney, tell me if the guy was sterile."

"Lujack, I don't know if the guy was sterile."

"You know the sample didn't match Chase Field."

"Maybe I do, maybe I don't. What are you getting at, Lujack?"

"The instrument used to cut off Ginger's head. Could it have been a samurai sword?"

"Yeah, sure it could. Why do I think I shouldn't be telling you all this?" he asked hesitantly.

"Thanks, Barney."

Tommy was waiting for him in front of the Chin Up. He was smiling, which usually meant he knew something or they had won a lot of money. The

Monday night football game had just started, so he knew Tommy's research had borne fruit.

"Yoshida served in China during the war. He was wounded in the evacuation of Shanghai and was in a military hospital in Hiroshima when the bomb was dropped."

"Jesus, you do have good sources in the Japanese community."

"No, I have good sources in the Triads. I called my cousin in Hong Kong. He says Yoshida has been in the Yakuza since before the war. Yoshida's father was one of the leaders of the Yamaguchi-gumi, and Yoshida worked with both Kodama and the CIA after the war smuggling tungsten out of China. The man knows where the bodies are buried."

"An apt analogy."

"Yoshida came here in the 'fifties. The polite Japanese banker who even then was washing money for the Yakuza and shipping back technology for LDP. The way I see it, the B-3 is his last hurrah. After this he can go home to Tonomara and retire with honor."

"Too bad he still likes young girls."

Lujack filled Tommy in on his conversation with Milch and added his own thoughts. "It could have something to do with being sterilized during the bombing, or maybe it's just some kind of sick ritual."

"I heard once of an old Yakuza practice of tattooing the inner thigh of a favored concubine," Tommy said. "It seems Yoshida has come up with his own variation."

"The ultimate *yubitsume.* It's going to happen again, Tommy, I know it. The Marina Shores is having a yacht race on Wednesday. Every year it's the same date, September second, which happens to be the day the Japanese surrendered to MacArthur on the *Missouri.*"

"So what do we do next?"

"Yoshida will be aboard the *Southern Cross* tomorrow night, he owns her now. Somehow we have to be aboard too."

"How did you find out?"

"Dolph Killian."

"Killian is with Yoshida."

"Killian is with Killian."

"Where are we going?"

"To see Kyle and Matsuda. I've told them to meet us at the Zodiac."

"Why the Zodiac?"

"Because it's the only place I know of where we can find a real live Yakuza after banking hours without a warrant."

The Zodiac was packed as usual. Chase Field's grotesque murder had given the place even more cachet than it had before. Similar to what a gangland killing would do for a New York Italian restaurant. He half expected some of the regulars to show up in Chase Field T-shirts.

Aristotle gave Lujack a toothy smile. "Everybody is waiting for you inside, Mr. Lujack."

"Everybody?"

"The cops and the robbers."

"Sounds like you put it on the bat line," Lujack said.

"What's the bat line?" Tommy asked.

"It's the number you call to find out what's happening."

"Don't any of these kids have jobs?"

"This is their job, Tommy." Lujack knew that Tommy was seeing his niece and maybe his son in the made-up, eager faces along the sidewalk.

Lujack led Tommy through the maze. It was lighter than usual, and Lujack half expected to find another body. So did the zoned-out regular who was walking in front of him.

"It happened right along here," the guy told his spiky-haired date. Lujack thought he recognized the voice. The barfing surfer from the night of Chase's murder.

"I was coming in and this cop dude and this Chinaman are like standing in the hallway checking out this body hanging from the wall."

"Far out," the girl said. "Was he dead?"

"It was Chase Field. The modeling honcho."

"Then he *was* dead."

"I hope he was, 'cause we buried him," Lujack said and pushed his way past the gawkers.

"That's him, that's the cop!" the surfer said.

"Wrong, kid, I'm a personal consultant."

"Friends of yours?" Tommy said as Lujack moved past.

Thurgood and Matsuda were the first people Lujack saw when he came out of the tunnel. They stuck out like sore big toes at the bar. Besides being the only two guys wearing wide ties and Brylcream, they obviously didn't want to be there.

"This better be good, Jimmy," Thurgood said. Matsuda nodded to Lujack and Tommy.

"I don't know if it's good or bad, but it's the truth. Once you hear me out, you can walk away or you can help, but I owe you the story."

"Do you owe us this rat hole?"

"You're lucky the band hasn't started. Let's move to the back."

Lujack led the two cops toward the back of the club. Henry Park and his so-called cousin were on duty.

Henry was standing near the doorway to the office. The cousin was near the back bar station. With any luck they might try something.

"How are you doing tonight, Henry?" Lujack said. "You remember Lieutenant Matsuda, and this is his friend Lieutenant Thurgood."

Henry nodded curtly.

"Lieutenant Thurgood here doesn't believe there are any Yakuza in LA," Lujack said. He grabbed Henry's left hand. The Korean was quick, but Lujack was quicker. He held Henry's hand up for Thurgood to see. Henry struggled, but Lujack was heavier and stronger.

"What happened to the end of your finger, Henry?"

"I cut it working at a sushi bar," Henry said contemptuously.

"Let him go, Lujack," Matsuda said.

Lujack let the hand drop. He nodded in the cousin's direction. "He lost his in a sushi bar too."

"You're losing it, Jimmy," Thurgood said when they'd taken over the back booth. "The chief tells you personally to lay off, and the next thing I know you're bothering Senator Rudlow and Dolph Killian. Telling them that Yoshida is a murderer. What kind of shit are you pulling?"

"I'm trying to help you jerk-offs, that's what I'm pulling. Yoshida has lost it. The guy's bonkers. He's going to do it again this weekend, and we have to stop him."

Both Thurgood and Matsuda stared at him. At least he had their attention.

Lujack ran down the dates. Yoshida's love of numbers. The military history. The family history. Hiroshima. Kodama. The B-3. The Brownell bribe. The sale of the *Southern Cross.* The Rudlow and Killian stories. It took him ten minutes.

"Tomorrow night there's a party in Catalina. The date coincides with the formal Japanese surrender. Before midnight the next night, another girl is going to lose her head. I'd bet my life on it."

"You might have to bet more than that, Jimmy, if this guy's clean," Thurgood said.

"You'll help us then?"

"I didn't say that."

"There's no judge in America who would give a warrant to search the *Southern Cross* based on what you told us. Even if Brownell and Yoshida weren't friends of the president's," Matsuda said.

"You're gonna do nothing then?"

"We didn't say that either," Thurgood said.

"Jimmy, I think someone wants your attention," Tommy said.

Lujack turned and saw Janis waving for him to come over. Janis had on a black leather vest and a miniskirt. Her lips were painted bright red. Lujack could feel the collective groin tighten up around the table.

"Jesus, will you look at that," Thurgood muttered. "If my daughter left the house looking like that . . ."

"She wouldn't leave the house," Lujack finished for him and walked over to Janis.

"Hi, Lujack."

"Hi, Janis."

"We called you the other night. Molly and me wanted to play."

"Molly and I."

"Whatever. Who're the guys you're with, cops?"

"Some of them."

"The fat one's kinda cute."

"I'll tell him you're a fan."

"Don't bother, Lujack. If I'm gonna start playing around with cops, it's gonna be you."

"I told you I'm not a cop."

"You want to buy me a drink?"

"Sure, what are you drinking?"

"A Cape Cod."

Lujack ordered a Cape Cod. He dared not look back at Thurgood and Matsuda. "How's Molly?"

"Great. She's doing a big spring layout this week for Calvin."

"She's not getting into any trouble?"

"It's hard to get into trouble on Catalina. The place is beautiful, but it's dead."

Lujack stopped. "Catalina?"

"You know, twenty six miles across the sea," she said off tune.

"Yeah, I know. When did she leave?"

"This morning. She and the other girls are staying on some big yacht. A friend of Mark Lyman's."

"Is Lyman with her?"

"I think so. Rumor is he's going to take over the agency himself," she said, then gave a playful sigh. "What a girl has to do in this world to get ahead."

"It's what the guys have to do that scares me," Lujack said and went back to the table.

"Is there any way to get to Catalina tonight?" he asked the two cops.

"Sure, swim," Thurgood said.

"Mark Lyman took four models including Molly Blair over to the island with him today. They're staying on the *Southern Cross.*"

"They'll be safe until Yoshida gets there," Matsuda said evenly.

"What if he's already there?" Lujack asked.

"He's not there, Lujack. He's at home in bed," Matsuda said.

"You mean you guys have a tail on him?" Lujack asked with a smile. "What about the mayor?"

"Fuck the mayor," Thurgood said. "We're going to get this bastard."

"You assholes believed me all along."

"Let's say we share your suspicions," Matsuda said.

"Sometimes you got to stand up and be counted, Jimmy," Thurgood said.

"What about Chief Bane?"

"The chief can take care of himself," Thurgood said.

# — Chapter Seventeen —

### *Here Come the Marines*

Tommy insisted on going. Thurgood and Matsuda were waiting for them at the Long Beach Marina the next morning. The trip to Catalina was unofficial in every capacity. If Chief Bane knew about it, which Lujack guessed he did, his knowledge was deniable. Both Matsuda and Thurgood were risking their careers, but both of them were standing next to the twenty-two-foot Bayliner that Thurgood had managed to borrow from his cousin. Matsuda had on a Hawaiian shirt and was carrying a camera. Thurgood was wearing a windbreaker over a pair of white ducks. Matsuda looked like a tourist. Thurgood looked like a weekend water warrior.

"What do you want to do, scare the fish to death?" Thurgood asked, admiring Tommy's hot pink sport shirt and canary-colored baseball cap. "I told you to dress inconspicuously."

"I'm an Oriental, Thurgood. No one ever notices Orientals. Ask your partner."

Matsuda made a mock bow. "He speaks the truth, most honorable Lieutenant."

"Jesus, I'm working with two bookies and a comic," Thurgood groused.

"Nice boat, Kyle," Lujack said, throwing his knapsack in the back of the aluminum Bayliner. Four people was near maximum capacity.

"Sorry, Jimmy, but my Hatteras is in the shop."

"We should have flown."

"Not with these we shouldn't." Thurgood pointed his Topsiders in the direction of the dark blue duffel bag underneath the fishing poles. "Two M-16s and an Uzi, courtesy of my private collection."

"We'll tell the Coast Guard were hunting great whites," Lujack said.

"In this tub." Matsuda laughed.

"Do you standup comics think you can interrupt your acts long enough to cast off?"

"Sure," Lujack said uncertainly.

"See that line running from the front of the boat to the dock? That's the bow line. Slip it off the cleat and bring it with you back on the boat."

"Piece of cake."

"Tommy, you get the stern line. Kamikaze, you make sure the boat doesn't hit the dock. My cousin Fred will kill me if I ding his boat."

Thurgood pulled at the cord to start the Evinrude outboard. After the second try the sixty-horsepower engine kicked over. Lujack and Tommy slipped their lines off the cleats and jumped aboard. Matsuda pushed off. They almost looked like they knew what they were doing.

"Does this boat have a name?" Lujack asked.

"Yeah, it's on the back," Thurgood said, one hand on the rear rudder, eyes watching the traffic in the Marina channel.

"Did anyone ever tell you you look like Dennis Conner?" Lujack asked.

"You know, he does. Especially in the jowls." Matsuda laughed.

"Fuck you," Captain Thurgood replied.

Lujack leaned over and read the name: *Joshua.* "Who's Joshua?"

"Beats me. I think he's in the Bible. My cousin Fred is a Bible freak."

"I thought boats were named after women," Tommy interjected.

"Like *Slut* and *Bitch,"* Lujack volunteered.

"That bad, eh?" Tommy asked, laughing.

Lujack hadn't thought of Debbi for all of ten minutes. When he'd called her that morning and said he'd heard she might be going to Catalina, she was very open, almost proud of her overnight trip with Dolph Killian and Pete Rudlow. She assured him that she would watch Yoshida, who was giving a cocktail party on the *Southern Cross* that night. The important thing, of course, was that the B-3 be defeated in congressional committee. Rudlow was going to approach Yoshida that night to see if he could persuade the Japanese government to back away from the deal. There was patriotism and adventure in her voice. Lujack told her to be careful. Debbi laughed and said now she knew why men loved politics. It was at that moment Lujack realized why he had fallen for her. She made ambition sound like virtue, as she had made sex feel like child's play.

"Face it, Lujack. Senators are more glamorous than bookies. Even married senators. Ask Donna Rice's old boyfriend," Tommy said.

"I think he was a bookie too." Thurgood smiled.

"No, he was a drug dealer," Matsuda corrected.

"Thanks, guys," Lujack said to one and all.

Thurgood maneuvered out past the jetty and headed into the open sea. The *Joshua* moved steadily through the swells. It didn't take long for Lujack to realize the Bayliner wasn't built for long offshore trips.

"How long does it take?"

"It's not the size of the boat, it's the motion of the ocean, as Hiram Hotel used to say," Thurgood said, smiling. "We should be there in about four hours. Sit back and enjoy the sunshine."

"What happens if I throw out a line?" Matsuda asked.

"We're going about six, seven knots. We might get a marlin, but that's a long shot."

"That's not the only long shot," Matsuda said. "We're not even sure Yoshida is going to show."

At that moment there was a crackling on the portable radio. "Kamikaze, this is Rising Sun," came a voice from the other end.

"Go ahead, Rising Sun."

"The Emperor's helicopter just left the pad. It's heading southwest," came the voice.

"Thank's, Rising Sun, over." Matsuda signed off.

"Who's Rising Sun?" Lujack asked.

"Billy Ito, he's on the Asian Task Force. He's been doing some volunteer work down at the Pacific National Bank Building."

"And the Emperor just took off in his helicopter for Catalina?"

"You got it."

"So much for long shots," Lujack said, and then to Kyle, "I'm going to collect that hundred bucks yet," referring to the bet they'd made about Mason's guilt.

Lujack tried to sleep on the way over, but the sun was too hot. The blue Pacific was like a desert, and the constant roar of the engine seemed to amplify the heat. After an hour Tommy and Matsuda constructed a tent out of a tarp they found in the bow. Lujack enjoyed watching the overweight, methodical Mr. Chin working with the muscled, intense Mr. Matsuda. It was in one way easy to see why their nationalities had built up thousands of years of enmity, but at the same time he couldn't help feeling there was a certain Asian fit.

"Leave it to us boat people," Tommy said, inspecting their handiwork.

"Yeah, so where's the air conditioning?" Thurgood griped, letting them know that when it came to fluorocarbons America was still king.

They approached the island a little after four. Lujack had been to Catalina only once in his life. When he was ten, he'd gone with his parents and remembered mostly the flying fish alongside the boat. There were no flying fish this day, and as the island loomed larger and the scenery became more picturesque, the mood in the boat grew more animated.

Once they were behind the long, rugged island the swells flattened out. The water along the southeast shore was a deep, clear blue. Lujack could see the rocks and an occasional fish as the visibility was easily twenty-five feet down. He put his hand in the water and was tempted to jump in. Tommy and Matsuda dropped their lines in the water and requested that Captain Thurgood slow up. Thurgood trolled the final quarter-mile to Avalon at under four knots, but the fish weren't biting, at least not at Tommy and Matsuda's lures.

They motored past Hamilton Cove, a fancy condominium development just north of Avalon. Some developer thought that Southern California real estate prices would carry across the water to Catalina, but the place had the look of a beautiful mausoleum, complete with bougainvillea and terra-cotta. As bad as the freeway traffic was getting, no one had yet invented a way to commute from Catalina to LA short of a hydrofoil or a helicopter.

"What a waste," Thurgood said, looking up at the empty homes.

"It reminds me of Palm Springs," Lujack said, reflecting back to where it all began eighty miles to the east.

"There's no water here either," Matsuda said.

"They could use Mark Lyman to move those condos," Tommy commented.

"Marina Shores West. I'll ask him about that tonight at the party," Lujack said.

The *Joshua* rounded the last bluff and approached the great Casino at the north end of Avalon Harbor. Built in the 1930s, the huge Casino with its Doric columns and circular roof was a monument to a different time. The whole town of Avalon, tucked away like a little seaport on a hill, was much more Mediterranean than Southern Californian.

"This place always gets to me," Thurgood said with affection. "I used to come here with the Boy Scouts when I was a kid. We used to ride bikes up to the old Wrigley place. It never seems to change."

"My dad brought me here once," Matsuda said. "We fished off the pier while everyone else rented boats and came around the point."

"How did you do?"

"We caught more fish than everyone else combined," Matsuda said, smiling.

"What kind of bait did your dad use?" Tommy asked, jiggling his rod.

"Baby worms, still wriggling. He always said live bait was the best way to fish."

"We'll soon find out," Lujack said as the Bayliner came around the breakwater and entered the harbor.

The buoys closest to the channel were for the biggest boats. The first boat they passed was by far the largest in the harbor. It was the *Southern Cross.* They came within fifty yards of the glistening white Feadship. Two men were standing on the bridge. Lujack recognized one of them as Colonel Martin, Larry Brownell's pit bull, and the other as George Kim, the Pacific National vice-president, who did a lot more for Kazuo Yoshida than trade dollars and yen.

Both men had recognized Lujack and probably knew Matsuda on sight. That was the way Thurgood had insisted they play it. If their theory about Yoshida was right, all the police surveillance in the world wouldn't stop him from fulfilling his tortured destiny.

Lujack waved. Neither man reacted.

"David against Goliath," Thurgood said, admiring the hundred-and-forty-foot yacht. "*Joshua* against the *Southern Cross.* It does have a biblical ring to it."

"We have more than slingshots," Lujack said.

"So do they," Tommy chimed.

"All right, boys. We all know the plan. Nothing is going to happen until midnight, unless our friend starts operating on Tokyo time, in which case we might already be too late."

"We're not too late," Lujack said as Yoshida himself appeared on the fantail. He was wearing a cotton shirt, and a pair of dark glasses dangled from his neck. He was followed by a man and two women. Both women were wearing fashionable white pants and blouses. They looked cool and beautiful in the late-afternoon sun. The man, a photographer, flitted about the two girls like a hummingbird. Lujack recognized one of the women as Molly. The other was obviously another model. Lujack didn't know her, but for a second he thought she was the ghost of Ginger Louie. She was Asian-American.

"Jesus Christ," Tommy said under his breath.

Matsuda muttered something in Japanese. There was no need for translation.

Yoshida saw Lujack staring at him. He followed Lujack's gaze. The billionaire banker took the scene in with eerie satisfaction. He seemed pleased to see Lujack in the little skiff. Unlike their meeting in Bel Air, this time Lujack felt a current of evil flowing from the Japanese man's presence. Yoshida stared at the little boat for another five seconds, then brought the sunglasses up to cover his eyes. It was a deliberate act to show that he was not afraid but simply bored.

"He sure is an arrogant bastard, even for a Japanese," Matsuda said with a mixture of pride and contempt.

"The bastard does seem to be enjoying himself," Tommy said with no contradiction in his voice.

Captain Thurgood brought the *Joshua* alongside the floating dock at the foot of Avalon Pier.

"We've got to get that Oriental girl off the boat," Lujack said. "I'll talk to Molly."

He and Tommy jumped onto the pier with their respective ropes. Thurgood shut the engine down and started offloading the "fishing rods."

An official-looking man came down the ramp to where they were docked.

"You can only stay here ten minutes, fellows. If you want to dock for the night, you're gonna have to rent a buoy and take the water taxi in."

"How much is a buoy?" Lujack asked.

"Fifty bucks a night. But we don't have any open tonight because of the big race tomorrow."

Thurgood reached into his windbreaker and pulled out his badge. "See this, mister? This is all the permission we need. Now beat it."

The man looked at the badge, then at the four of them, then at the bulging fishing rods. "Just keep it down at this end of the dock, then. Other people are gonna be usin' it," the man said meekly and walked off.

"So what's the plan?" Tommy asked when the man was out of earshot.

"You and Jimmy are going to the party on the *Southern Cross,"* Thurgood said. "Try to get downstairs and check out the staterooms. Make sure when you leave, the girls leave with you."

"How do we do that?" Lujack asked.

"I'm sure you can think of something," Thurgood answered.

"How about money?" Tommy suggested.

"I think Yoshida can outspend you," Thurgood said.

"Then it will have to be love," Lujack said.

"Once we make sure the girls are safe, Rick and I are going to introduce ourselves to the local cops and report a burglary in progress aboard the *Southern Cross,"* Thurgood continued. "Everyone will be at the dance, we should have the yacht to ourselves. Hopefully by then we'll know where to look."

"What happens when the locals discover the LA big shots have sent them on a wild-goose chase?"

"Why do you think we brought you along, Lujack?" Thurgood smiled.

"I'm the burglar?"

"You're the probable cause we need to get on the

yacht. The locals are the authority we need to make an arrest."

"Sounds like there are still a few loose ends," Lujack pressed. "What happens if we don't find anything?"

"Our only other move is to catch Yoshida in the act. You want to send those girls to the guillotine, Lujack?"

"No. We'll do it your way and hope he's as crazy as we think he is."

Thurgood booked two rooms in the Avalon Arms, a hotel right off the boardwalk. Lujack and Tommy's room could have fit into the *Joshua,* but Lujack wasn't planning on getting much sleep. It was five-thirty, and many of the tourist boats had gone back to Newport and Long Beach. The town was beginning to settle in for the night. Tommy insisted on the first shower. The boat ride hadn't done much for his mood or his stomach. He said he was flying back and suggested they get things over with as soon as possible.

"How do you think we should do that?"

"You and Thurgood know explosives. They blew up your car. We blow up their ship."

"And kill fifteen innocent people?"

"No one on that boat is innocent," Tommy said darkly.

"Go take your shower. I think the sun has fried what was left of your brain. Next thing you'll be telling me that you like Rick Matsuda."

Tommy smiled. "I got to admit, he's not a bad guy for a nip."

"You don't trust him, do you?"

"That's your call, Jimmy," Tommy said, disappearing into the bathroom.

From the window of their room Lujack could see the harbor and the Casino. He had no idea what the evening would bring, but it had to be played out. He didn't like playing such a dangerous game with so many people involved, but he had little choice. A girl's life depended on him. If Kyle and Matsuda were using him, which they admitted they were, that was all right as long as they got Yoshida. If Kyle and Matsuda were putting on a show to protect Yoshida and a bunch of crooked politicians, it was going to be worse than bloody and more than careers were going to be in jeopardy.

Lujack wasn't sure what was going to happen, but he knew it was going to start on the *Southern Cross.* Lujack and Tommy took the water taxi out to the yacht. It was a balmy September evening. September weather was always Southern California's best. The crew members of the Marina Shores yachts were readying their boats for the next day's race, while the owners put on their finery and took their launches over to visit their favorite banker.

Lujack looked from the taxi but wasn't able to see Dolph Killian's *Midway* in the rows of boats parked in the harbor.

"Hey, Lujack, what are you doing here?" Molly called out as Lujack and Tommy came up to the Feadship.

Molly was standing on the foredeck. She was still in Calvin's whites and looked fantastic. Next to her was the Oriental girl. She was very beautiful and was holding what looked to be a glass of champagne.

"Fishing," Lujack said, stepping on the makeshift dock alongside the big white boat.

"Did you catch anything?" Molly asked.

"Not yet," Lujack said as he came up the stairs.

Colonel Martin was standing at the top of the stairs, blocking Lujack's passage.

"Can I help you, Mr. Lujack?" Martin asked brusquely.

Lujack rubbed his head. "I'm just beginning to recover from the last time you helped me, Colonel. What are you doing here? I thought Mr. Brownell was in Europe."

"I work for Mr. Yoshida now. He's the new owner of the *Southern Cross.*"

"I heard," Lujack said, gauging his enemy. "I don't blame Brownell for selling. Being an accessory to murder might not play too well in the Oval Office, no matter how real the politics."

"You're a twisted man, Lujack, and you're not coming on this ship."

"It's all right, Martin. Mr. Lujack and Mr. Chin are my guests," Dolph Killian said, coming up behind him.

Martin stood his ground. "Does Mr. Yoshida know?"

"Yes, Martin, Mr. Yoshida knows," Killian said curtly.

Martin continued on his rounds.

"The Army isn't what it used to be, and it never was much," Killian said, welcoming Lujack and Tommy. "These Vietnam officers are all real head cases."

"I would swear you have a few of those same head cases on your security staff," Lujack said.

"You mean Kilgore and Murphy? They served with Martin in Nam and for a few years in Angola. They'd kill you as soon as look at you. Don't worry. I left them on the *Midway* with Senator Rudlow and your girlfriend. What are we drinking, boys?"

"Scotch," Lujack said.

"I think I'll go to the bar with you, Mr. Killian,"

Tommy said. "I'd like to look around this incredible ship."

"Call me Dolph," Killian said to his former sparring partner. Killian led Tommy toward the bar. Lujack had the distinct feeling he was very much out of his depth. Not a comfortable feeling, since they were still in the harbor.

"What are you really doing here, Lujack?" Molly asked, making her way back to him with her friend in tow. From the way Molly talked and walked, Lujack surmised she'd started the party without him.

"I'm here to look after you and your friend," he said, waiting for an introduction.

"Leslie Wing, meet Jimmy Lujack."

Leslie nodded politely. She had the kind of beauty that grew on you the closer you got. Her eyes were black, almond-shaped, her skin the color of watery cream, her lips thin and powerful like red brush strokes by De Kooning.

"Leslie lives in New York. She just came for the Calvin shoot."

"So, how do you like Catalina?"

"It's very nice, like the Italian Riviera," she said in a low voice that sounded more Bronx than Beijing.

"Lujack was a friend of Ginger's," Molly continued.

Leslie bit her lip.

"Ginger used to stay with Leslie when she went to New York," Molly added. "No investment banker on the island of Manhattan was safe."

"It was horrible what happened to Ginger," Leslie said sincerely. "It's hard to believe that Chase could do something like that."

"Lujack doesn't believe Chase did it, do you, Lujack?"

"No, I don't," he said, looking only at Leslie. "I think the killer is still at large."

"Are you a policeman?"

"He's a bookie," Molly volunteered.

"Really. I used to go out with a bookie. A Chinese bookie who hated the Mets and Yankees."

"You might like my partner. The cute guy over there in the yellow baseball cap with his hands in the hors d'oeuvre table. He hates all the home teams too."

Leslie watched as Tommy polished off seven or eight canapes. "I think I might like you better," Leslie said.

"I'll keep that in mind," Lujack said. "So how's the shoot going?"

"We worked like dogs yesterday, but it's been easier today. Did you hear Yoshi bought the *Southern Cross?*"

"Yoshi?"

"He's a doll, Lujack. As soon as he got here today, we started drinking champagne. To celebrate his new toy. He told Mark and Andre, the photographer, that if Calvin didn't like it he'd make a run on his company."

"These billionaires are a laugh a minute."

"Are you jealous?" Leslie asked.

"Not really. He's not my type."

"What is your type?"

"That's a good question," he said, watching Debbi and Senator Rudlow arrive in the water taxi. "Are you girls going to the dance?"

"Get real, Lujack. It's bad enough that we have to kiss up to these Marina Shores fogeys because of Mark and the agency, but we don't have to go dancing with them," Molly said with a little slur. Lujack wondered if she'd been into her cigarette lighter too.

"Have you listened to the music these guys like? I mean, Frank Sinatra, Glenn Miller. My grandfather didn't like Glenn Miller, and he's dead."

Lujack thought he saw some logic there somewhere, but he wasn't sure.

"How about if I meet you ladies later in town, say the No Name Saloon at around nine?"

"All right, Lujack!" Molly exclaimed. "Let's get down."

"Are there any more models staying aboard the yacht?"

"Aren't two of us enough for you?" Leslie asked.

"The other two girls went back to New York this afternoon. Mark wants us to stay for the race tomorrow."

"Mark's taking over the agency himself, you know," Molly said.

"So I heard."

"At twenty-five hundred a day, who's complaining?" Leslie explained.

"Not you two," Lujack said, knowing only that once he got the girls off the ship, he was going to do everything in his power to keep them off.

"Excuse us while we powder our noses, Lujack," Molly said, laughing. "Do you want to join us in our stateroom?"

"I told you, Molly, that shit is bad for your complexion."

"I asked my doctor, Lujack. He said you were full of it."

"So much for the Hippocratic oath."

"Jimmy, I thought that was you," Debbi said as she stepped aboard. "You didn't tell me you were coming over."

"Wouldn't miss a Marina Shores party."

"You remember Senator Rudlow."

"Sure I do. I just got a letter from the senator. Actually, it was from your campaign committee," Lujack said slowly. "You have a lovely family, Senator."

"Thanks, Lujack," the senator said stiffly. Lujack could feel Debbi glaring at him, but he didn't care. Rudlow moved away from trouble in the direction of Dolph Killian.

"I can't believe you said that," Debbi said after Rudlow left.

"I did get a letter from him, and it did have a picture of his family on it. They were asking for money."

"Pete and his wife are in the process of separating. It's been very hard for him."

"How do you think it's been for me?"

Debbi looked at him. As usual, she looked too good. Much too good for Pete Rudlow. Her hair was up, and she was tucked into a pair of beige linen pants.

"You don't think there's anything going on between Pete and me?"

"It crossed my mind."

"Jimmy, whatever happened between us," she started, then looked around to make sure she wasn't being overheard. "Whatever *happens* between us can't be as important as the future of our country."

"Aren't you taking this B-3 technology a little too seriously? From what I understand, these things are obsolete in a few months if they work at all."

"Jimmy, this is for the leadership of the Western world," she said, and from the way her big blue eyes looked at him, Lujack knew there was no way he could marry a girl who was that good an actress or that gullible a reporter.

"Have it your way, Debbi, but don't say I didn't warn you."

"Don't say you didn't warn me about what?"

"About Yoshida. We think he's going to try and kill again tonight."

An angry expression came over her lovely face. "Damn, I knew I should have brought a camera crew."

"Don't worry, babe, I'm sure the senator can arrange it."

"He thinks Yoshida is a spy, not a murderer."

"But you and I, we know better," Lujack said, feeling a sudden urge to mingle.

It was surprising how sixty guests could be so comfortable on a yacht. The number of people at least gave him a chance to move around the ship without looking too obvious. One thing you had to say about the Marina Shores sailors, they had good taste in women. Of the thirty or so guys at the party, no more than two or three of them were there with women within twenty years of their age. Lujack recognized the redhead from the Shores bar with an old horse owner and horse player he knew.

"Nice party, Mark," Lujack said to the Marina Shores founder. Lyman was the only guest Lujack had encountered who was actually wearing a blue blazer on this warm evening. He looked like a Schwepps poster.

"Dolph told me you were coming. I couldn't believe it. You never give up, do you?"

"I hear you're expanding your horizons and taking over the Field Agency. Chase would be proud of you."

"It's only temporary."

"So's an orgasm."

Lyman walked away disgustedly. Lujack moved discreetly toward the front of the yacht. He regretted turning down Larry Brownell's invitation to tour the ship when he had the chance but doubted Brownell would have shown him what he wanted to see. Yoshida knew why Lujack was there. But if Lujack was right, it wouldn't make any difference. The insane enjoy their little games. At some point, Yoshida would dare Lujack to stop him.

He walked forward to the bow. The yacht had three main levels. On the top level was a covered bridge and a staging area where the launches, jet skis, sail boards, and other water paraphernalia were stored. Above the covered bridge was a flying bridge. The bridges and staging area provided great visibility. If the yacht had to be boarded, it wouldn't be easy to sneak up on. During the party there was a lone watcher on the flying bridge. The man was Korean, and Lujack recognized him. It was Henry Park's cousin from the Zodiac. Two more men stood on the staging area to the rear of the bridge. One was Gerorge Kim, the other was Colonel Martin. They pretended to be chatting casually, but Lujack knew better. He couldn't see into the main bridge but figured the yacht's captain and at least one other guard were manning the Sat Nav, radar, and other electronic marvels the *Southern Cross* possessed.

The second level, the one Lujack stood on, consisted of the grand salon, the galley, an aft master stateroom, and the fantail. Most of the guests were in the salon or standing out on the fantail. Lujack had nudged the outside door to the large stateroom, but it wouldn't open and the windows were opaque. He assumed that was where Yoshida would be sleeping but wasn't at all sure that it was where he would be killing young girls. Assuming Brownell always had used the master stateroom, Lujack's best guess was that one of the six staterooms on the lower level was where Yoshida took his prey. The trick was finding the right room.

"You know Alan Bond, the Australian, once owned this yacht," Yoshida said, coming out on the foredeck. "He's the man who won the Americas Cup."

Lujack assumed Yoshida had come out of the stateroom door he had found locked. He bowed politely as Lujack turned.

"Took it away from the Americans," Lujack said.

Yoshida smiled. "That's right," he said. "The Americans didn't like that, and they won it back."

"And now you own it—the boat, I mean."

"Bought it yesterday. Larry's in Amsterdam ordering a new one."

"Is that why he sold it to you? Because he's getting a new one?"

"I paid him nearly six million in cash. That's why he sold it to me," Yoshida said. "Now he can build a new one for fifteen million. Larry likes new things. I like old things." Yoshida looked around. "They have certain memories." Yoshida's voice drifted with the memories, almost as if he were in a trance.

"That's why I'm here, Mr. Yoshida, to make sure there aren't any more memories."

"You still think I'm a mad killer, do you?"

"I wouldn't be here if I didn't."

"Maybe I should give you a sample of my blood after all. So you could sleep better."

"I don't think it makes any difference now, do you?"

Yoshida looked at him. "Why doesn't it make a difference?"

"Tomorrow is the anniversary of the Japanese surrender."

"But the war was over a long time ago," Yoshida said.

"Not for everyone," Lujack answered.

"It was on the USS *Missouri.* Shigemitsu Mamoru signed the agreement in the name of our Emperor. Even then there were those who thought it an act of treason," Yoshida said, not hiding his contempt.

The two were silent again. Laughter could be heard from the party in the rear. Lujack wanted to ask the old man why he was doing it or if he could stop, but the answers to those questions were either too obvious or too convoluted.

"The last time we talked, you didn't tell me that your father was a Yakuza."

"When my father was in the Yakuza, it meant something. He was a great *oyuban* in Yokohoma. He was a man worthy of much respect. A man of tradition. Now there are no such men."

"Not even Kodama?"

"He was the last. Now we have, what they call them here, bean counters."

"No one else has to die, Mr. Yoshida," Lujack said. "These young girls, what do they have to do with the way of history? What do they have to do with the changing times?"

"I was thinking, Mr. Lujack. What would you think if I put together a Japanese syndicate for the Americas Cup? Do you think I could win it?"

"I think where you're going, Mr. Yoshida, they won't have any yacht clubs."

# Chapter Eighteen

***Gotta Date with a Guillotine***

Lujack was sitting at a table in the No Name waiting for his dates. The No Name was the kind of bar where locals went to drink and mainlanders went to get laid. The cops were better at getting a drink. The last two hours hadn't gone like he'd expected. Not with Yoshida, not with Debbi, not with anyone. He'd been unable to get downstairs and into either the forward or aft cabins. Both stairways were being guarded by Yoshida's men.

Tommy had gone with Yoshida, Killian, and the others to the Casino for the dance. Leave it to Tommy to strike up a conversation with Yoshida about Tommy Dorsey. When Lujack had left the party they were best friends, and Tommy told him he was ready to boogie. Lujack told him to enjoy himself but to watch his back.

Thurgood and Matsuda came in looking more frustrated than happy. The burglary plan was looking like a long shot. Three men were still on the *Southern Cross.* One of them was Colonel Martin.

"It's hard to stage a robbery on a heavily guarded yacht. What happens if I swim naked out to the yacht and run around on the foredeck?" Lujack suggested.

"I've seen you in the shower, Lujack. That's not probable cause for search or seizure," Thurgood said.

"Wait 'til the girls get here. I think they might be the answer to all our problems."

"Does that mean you didn't get into the staterooms?"

"Something like that," Lujack admitted.

"I'm beginning to feel like the limb we're out on is breaking," Thurgood said.

"We can always go fishing," Matsuda added.

The girls sauntered into the No Name on cue. Every male and female head in the place turned in their direction. The Pointer Sisters' rendition of "Jump" came on the juke. The girls were all smiles until Molly recognized Thurgood.

"I know you're a cop," she said loud enough to move out a table of sunburned Raider fans two tables away. "You're the cop who came to our house with Lujack."

"Lieutenant Thurgood, Lieutenant Matsuda, meet Molly Blair and Leslie Wing," Lujack said.

"Why do I think we should have stayed on the yacht?" Leslie said in her most effusive New York manner.

"If you'd stayed on the yacht you would have ended up dead," Lujack said flatly.

"We think he may be right, ladies," Thurgood said, pretending to be William Shatner and/or Edward Olmos.

"If this killer is still on the loose, why isn't he in the papers?" Molly asked, looking through Thurgood and Matsuda and concentrating on Lujack.

"Because the man we're after is very powerful, he has friends who are very influential," Lujack said.

"You mean Yoshida," Leslie said blandly.

"Why do you say that?" Matsuda asked.

"Why would the LAPD send Japanese to Catalina if it weren't to go after another Japanese?" Leslie asked.

The three men looked at one another.

"You're right, we think it's Yoshida," Matsuda said.

"Two Cape Cods, please," Leslie said to the waiter, nonplussed by the revelation.

"If you'd seen what happened to Ginger, you wouldn't be so casual, Miss Wing," Thurgood said with more edge in his voice.

"It was awful, Les," Molly said, grabbing Lujack's arm. "You didn't see it."

"We think there's some kind of ritual involved, and we think whatever he does, it is done on the *Southern Cross.* What do you know about the staterooms besides the one you're in?" Thurgood asked.

Molly looked at Leslie, who offered no support. Molly knew Leslie didn't trust police and probably didn't trust men in general. That could happen to a girl who goes out with bookies.

"We're in the back," Molly said. "Leslie and I share a stateroom. Mark Lyman is in the other room, and the third room—the third room's . . . I made a mistake and tried to open it yesterday, but it was locked."

"What about the forward staterooms?"

"I think Colonel Martin and Mr. Kim and Henry and the rest of the crew stay up front."

"And Yoshida?" Matsuda asked.

"He's upstairs. He showed us his stateroom. It's huge. There's a Jacuzzi, a sauna, everything. He said his friend Mr. Brownell had everything specially built so you could live on the ship for months and never even have to go on deck," Molly said.

"We've got to get inside that locked cabin," Thurgood said.

"And we can't let these two go back to the yacht," Matsuda said.

"I'd like to see you stop us," Leslie said, staring daggers at Matsuda.

"They're right, Les," Molly said. "If Yoshida is the killer, I don't want to go back."

"If these bozos had any authority they'd have boarded the yacht this afternoon," Leslie said.

Thurgood looked at Lujack. "She's beginning to get on my nerves."

"I think I have a solution to all our problems," Lujack said.

"I knew you could do it, Lujack," Molly said, smiling.

"You better wait until you hear my solution, Molly."

Molly continued to smile.

"Molly, would you please light Kyle's cigarette?"

Molly frowned.

"I'm trying to quit, Lujack," Thurgood said.

"That's all right. Molly doesn't smoke either, but she carries a lighter."

Molly grabbed for her purse, but Lujack was faster.

"You bastard!" Molly yelled.

Lujack twisted off the bottom of the lighter and took out a small bottle. He poured the powdery white substance on the table.

Leslie made a move for the door, but Matsuda grabbed her arm and pulled her back to the chair.

"Maybe she doesn't smoke either," he said, taking an identical lighter out of her purse.

Matsuda didn't attempt to hide his pleasure as he unscrewed the cap and poured the contents of the bottle into a neat white pile next to the first neat white pile.

"I always wondered how models kept their girlish figures." Matsuda smiled.

"Asshole," Leslie spat.

"I think you're right, Lujack, our problems are solved. This gives us our probable cause to turn the yacht inside out, provided I can convince the local sheriff there are fifty kilos more of the stuff onboard."

"And it keeps the girls out of harm's way," Lujack said.

"Assholes!" Molly yelled.

"Rick, you and Lujack keep the girls company. Don't let them snort up the evidence."

Leslie lunged for the table, but Matsuda grabbed her. Lujack took Molly's hands and brought them behind her back.

"Sorry, girls, you shouldn't have tried that," Matsuda said. "See that brass railing under the bar? That's your date for the evening."

"Kyle, throw Lujack your cuffs."

Thurgood gave Lujack his cuffs.

"I'll send some of Avalon's finest down to fetch the prisoners. Let's hope the local sheriff believes in zero tolerance."

Lujack dragged Molly over to the brass railing. It wasn't going to do much for her white Calvin slacks, but her other obsession wasn't going to do much for her brain.

"I hate you, Lujack. I hate you."

"I know you don't believe me, Molly, but I'm saving your life."

Lujack cuffed Molly to the railing. Matsuda did the same with Leslie.

The guys in the Raider T-shirts came over to look at Lujack's handiwork.

"I like your style, boys," one of them said, squatting down to get a better look at Molly. "Maybe we can help you out a little."

Lujack pushed the guy backward with his shoe, and the guy landed on his ass. Hard.

"This isn't for your benefit, boys, so why don't you keep moving?"

The guy on the floor looked at Lujack, then at Matsuda, then at his two buddies. The trio thought better of it and walked out.

"I'm going to go check on Tommy. Meet you back at the *Joshua,"* Lujack told Matsuda.

"Thurgood wanted you here," Matsuda protested.

"There's something I have to check out," Lujack said and walked into the street, not waiting to argue and knowing Matsuda couldn't go after him with the evidence lying on the table and the suspects cuffed to the bar.

He went back to the rooms and grabbed one of the automatic rifles. He had a strange feeling something wasn't right. He couldn't put his finger on it, but something was bothering him. Yoshida had made no effort to keep the girls on the yacht. His mood most of the night had been upbeat. If the billionaire was daring Lujack to stop him, he was sure being casual about it. And then there was something Molly had said about the main salon being self-contained and one of the lower staterooms being locked. Was it possible Yoshida already had his next victim aboard? Lujack had to get into that locked stateroom, and he couldn't afford to wait for Thurgood to get the local cops to search a billionaire's yacht because two models were caught with two grams of coke. Lujack had a sudden sick feeling that he was a pawn, not a player, in the deadly game being played aboard the *Southern Cross.*

After stowing the rifle in the *Joshua,* Lujack ran along the waterfront all the way to the Casino. There was a funny-looking man at the door taking tickets, but Lujack pushed past him and found himself inside a huge auditorium. It was like running into a time warp. On the bandstand was the spitting image of a 1930s swing band. The song was "In the Mood," and the dancing was straight out of radio land. The only modern things were the Marina Shores bimbos.

Tommy was definitely in the mood, twirling the redheaded hostess for all she was worth. Lujack grabbed him in mid-dip.

"Tommy, what the hell are you doing? You're supposed to be watching Yoshida," Lujack yelled.

"I am watching him. He's right over there." Tommy pointed in the direction of the bandstand. Lujack followed his finger and saw Yoshida, still in his cotton shirt and pleated slacks, doing a very polite version of the swing with the Shores social director. Next to him, George Kim was also dancing up a storm. Henry Park and his cousin were a discreet distance away.

"What the fuck is going on?" Lujack asked. "Where's Killian?"

Tommy pointed in the other direction. Killian was standing on the edge of the dance floor talking with Rudlow. Both had drinks in their hands and seemed to be enjoying themselves. Lujack walked quickly across the dance floor.

"Where's Debbi?" Lujack demanded.

"She wasn't feeling well. My men took her back to the *Midway,"* Killian said.

Lujack began to feel the rhythm of evil working in his heart. He could feel the blackness flowing to him. He took a last look in Yoshida's direction. The banker let his partner twirl under his arm. Always the perfect, polite gentleman.

"Mr. Killian and I talked to Mr. Yoshida on the way over here," Rudlow said. "We're going to work out a compromise on the B-3."

"What about our national security, Dolph?" Lujack asked.

"It gives us another four or five years. We can live with it," Killian said.

"Everyone will be protected this way," Rudlow added.

"Not everyone," Lujack said, feeling it grow closer. The rhythm, the duplicity, the greed. "It's the Americans you should worry about," he repeated.

"What?" Rudlow asked.

"Some advice I should have taken."

"Go home, Lujack. That's the advice you should be taking," Rudlow said.

"That's what all you patriotic pimps keep telling me."

Rudlow didn't know what Lujack was talking about. He would soon enough.

"Dolph, do you know why Colonel Martin went to work for Yoshida? I thought he and Brownell went back a long ways."

"Surprised me too. I guess it was the same reason the rest of us go to work for the Japs. Money."

Lujack looked back at Yoshida grooving gently to the music. The perfect spy down to his love of prewar American music, but not a crazed murderer. Lujack felt a chill down his spine. He'd been wrong. Dead wrong.

Lujack waved for Tommy to meet him outside. Tommy looked confused but followed Lujack out of the Casino.

Tommy ran to catch up with him. Lujack was walking quickly along the quay, looking for the *Midway*. He found her in the second row, the fifth boat in.

She looked dark and deserted. He looked next in the direction of the *Southern Cross.* She was no longer at her mooring. He looked out past the breakwater and thought he could see her running lights. She was heading north out past the breakwater!

"What's going on?" Tommy asked, catching up with him. "Is that the *Southern Cross* going out to sea?"

"It sure is."

"What are we going to do?"

"I'm going to the boat, you're going to the No Name to tell Matsuda and Thurgood I've gone after Debbi."

"Debbi's on the *Southern Cross?* But Yoshida's still inside."

"Forget Yoshida, Tommy. We bet the wrong horse."

"Killian and Rudlow are in there too," Tommy said, trying to make sense of it.

"Tell Kyle it's better I do this alone. I don't need a judge's permission."

"Do what alone?"

"Kill the bastard," Lujack said.

"Which bastard?" Tommy demanded.

He left his partner dumbfounded at the foot of the pier. He ran down to the lower dock and jumped aboard the *Joshua.* The engine started on the first pull. There was just enough moon to see his way past the other boats in the harbor. If the *Joshua* had running lights, he didn't know how to turn them on. The last thing he was worried about was getting a ticket from the Harbor Patrol.

The sea seemed to be calm as he made his way out to the main channel past the ferry docks at the mouth of the harbor. It was after ten o'clock, and the ocean was cool and black. Lujack turned north and gave the little boat more gas. The hull slapped against the dark waves. He steered in the direction of the large shadow on the horizon. All he had to go by was the red light shining dimly in the distance.

It was eerie being out on the water at night. But the eeriness was lost on Lujack as his mind filled with the horrible vision of what was going on in the locked stateroom aboard the *Southern Cross.* He saw the walls of Dave Mason's apartment, he saw the headless body, the body-less head. He saw a limousine pull up and the men carrying the body bag. Dave Mason wouldn't have known it if they'd dumped an elephant in his bed.

All the time he had been focusing on Yoshida when, in fact, the Japanese banker had only been the polite, efficient, careful businessman that he appeared. A businessman and patriot who may countenance murder when necessary but was far too disciplined to commit it.

Lujack began to see the outline of the yacht as he drew closer to the light. The quarter moon shone on the huge white hull of the *Southern Cross,* giving it a ghostly pallor. Lujack could now make out what looked to be a flickering light coming from one of the aft cabins.

Lujack pushed the throttle down, and the *Joshua*'s hull came down in the water. He was now less than a hundred yards from the *Southern Cross.* The big yacht was sitting dead in the water, bobbing, rolling with the sea. The closer he got, the more his eyes concentrated on the flickering light.

His hand felt instinctively for the automatic rifle. The clip was in, and he tucked another in his parka along with his .38. He didn't know how many of them would be aboard. Maybe one, maybe four or five. It was hard to predict the depth of evil and the power of money. The corpses and the greed all led to the light.

Lujack saw a flash, then heard the bullet hit the aluminum hull of the *Joshua.* He ducked down behind the bow as another shot was fired. Another ricochet. Crawling back to the stern, he gently moved the rudder back and forth, working closer to the gunfire, keeping the shooters off balance. Four more shots were fired. The first shooter was on the flying bridge, the second on the second deck near the anchor. Lujack knew that when he popped above the boat's frame his shots had to count. There was no backup out in the Pacific.

Lujack maneuvered to within fifty yards of the big yacht. Using his knees for balance, he rose up and sprayed the bridge with bullets from the M-16. The gunfire silhouetted the white yacht. Lujack saw the black man, Kilgore, fall into the water. One down.

The other man, Murphy, didn't grieve for his friend. He simply stood on the top deck and fired until Lujack found him with the second half of the clip. Murphy fell back away from the railing with a thud. In a night fight, fire power was everything, and thanks to Thurgood's private collection, Lujack had it. Two down.

His advantage was short-lived. He heard the huge BTU diesels rev up and knew that Colonel Martin was about to use his power advantage. If Lujack couldn't get alongside the *Southern Cross* in the time it took the huge yacht to come around, the *Joshua* was going to be aluminum siding.

Lujack put the throttle down and drove for the stern of the yacht. The *Southern Cross* came around abruptly, and Lujack could see Martin at the controls. The David and Goliath match was all too real. Lujack saw the ten-foot bow of the *Southern Cross* coming at him, the angle getting critical. The yards were becoming feet. Fifty tons of steel were about to crush him.

Lujack's only hope was his maneuverability, and at the last second he swung the rudder hard right, then hard back, so that the *Joshua* missed the bow and was hit by the side of the giant yacht. The aluminum bent but didn't break. Lujack kept the *Joshua* hard against the metal hull of the *Southern Cross.* There was a horrible screeching noise as the boats scraped against each other.

Lujack threw the automatic rifle onto the main deck and made a jump for the lowest part of the railing at the back of the ship. He just caught the rear railing near the transom. He felt dizzy from the force of his collision but knew he couldn't lose his concentration or his grip. If he did, he would die. Slowly he pulled himself aboard.

The *Southern Cross* was doing seven or eight knots and turning sharply as Martin swung her back in the direction of the *Joshua.* It wouldn't be long before the colonel discovered he was chasing an empty boat. Lujack began searching the darkness for the rifle. Feeling along the deck, he couldn't find the gun. There was no time to waste. He pulled out his .38 and continued his way toward the stairway that led to the bridge.

Lujack's foot was on the second step when the *Southern Cross*'s engines shut down. Martin had found the empty *Joshua.* Now it was every man for himself.

"Kilgore?" the colonel shouted from the door of the bridge.

"Kilgore? Murphy?" he shouted again.

"They're swimming home, Colonel. Now it's just you and me," Lujack yelled back.

"Don't bet on it, bookie," Martin said.

From where he stood, Lujack knew there were only two ways to reach the bridge. He could guess which way Martin would be coming. Or he could make his move first. Lujack had been fortunate with the first two soldiers. They hadn't expected a guy in a Bayliner to pop up with an M-16. With Martin there was no advantage.

The steps of the staircase were gradual and wide for a yacht, but still they didn't allow much room to maneuver. Lujack used one hand to balance and kept his .38 poised in the other. The *Southern Cross* rocked slightly on the dark sea, not enough to throw him off balance but more than enough to make a good shooter miss. Ask Kilgore and Murphy.

That was when he heard the scream. It was a high, guttural shriek that chilled the heart in its desperation. He knew instantly that the scream was Debbi's, and he realized he had forgotten all about the candle-lit room below. The room he had caught glimpses of in his dreams for the past month. Since he first saw Ginger's body he had known there must be a special place where the killer carried out his ritual. A killing room where the smell and stain of blood could be washed away like in a hospital. The scream stopped short, and somewhere in the bowels of the ship he heard a door slam. There was no more sound, but Lujack knew she had not stopped screaming.

There wasn't much time. No film at eleven.

"Your girlfriend doesn't sound like she's enjoying the party," Martin said calmly from the door of the bridge.

Before Lujack's eyes could pick up the figure in the door, he saw the flash of Martin's gun. He felt a stinging swipe just above the ear. It felt like a tennis ball, but he knew it was a bullet. The shot had knocked him down. He could feel the cold epoxied deck under his cheek. He felt the top of his ear. The bullet had only grazed his skull, but his ear was a bloody mess. It was then he realized he was no longer holding his gun.

Lujack lay still on the deck. He could hear Martin walking toward him. Lujack moved his hand slowly in the darkness, feeling for his pistol. He was surprised when he found the still warm muzzle of his automatic rifle.

"Come on, bookie, don't play dead on me," Martin said, walking slowly toward him.

Lujack forced his eyes to adjust. He knew now what his mistake had been. When he came up to the top deck his head had been framed in the moonlight. But there was no light where he lay now in the shadow. The darkness was all he had to work with.

Lujack's eyes adjusted first, and he saw that Martin was going to trip. When the colonel's foot stepped on Murphy's leg, Lujack was rolling to the right, pulling the automatic toward him. He clicked off the safety, aimed, and fired in one fluid motion. By the time Martin realized he had tripped over the body of his own man, five rounds had found his chest. The colonel was dead before he hit the ground.

Lujack didn't have time to think. He wiped the side of his head and saw the blood. He didn't have time to look for the top of his ear. He found his .38 next to one of the *Cross*'s rubberized lifeboats. It was time for the descent.

Taking the steps by two, he reached the main deck. Remembering what Molly had told him, he knew in which cabin he would find the flickering lights. He descended to the lower aft staterooms. Everything was dark. None of the light switches worked, and Lujack figured the darkness was part of the ritual.

The first door opened easily, and the room was empty. Lujack walked down the narrow corridor to the second stateroom. He tried the door, but it was locked. Lujack pushed and jiggled the handle, but the door wouldn't move. He put his ear to the door but could hear nothing. The room was soundproof. The door was solid, like a wall. Impenetrable. Lujack had the ugly hunch that it had been built that way for a reason.

Lujack knelt down on the carpet and caught a whiff of something that gave him chills. It wasn't blood he smelled. It was wax.

Lujack tried the third door. It opened, but there was a connecting door between the two cabins. He began to feel desperate. He had to get into that cabin and he didn't have much time.

Lujack then remembered why he had come out to the *Southern Cross* in the first place. The upstairs cabin!

He ran up the stairs. The master stateroom door was locked, but Lujack broke the door with his shoulder. He ran into the sauna, the private sauna next to the Jacuzzi. Sure enough. He saw a light though a crack in one of the walls. He pushed on the crack and a panel opened.

Lujack took a tentative step. He could see the circular staircase that led into the torture chamber below. Slowly he descended, the smell growing more pungent, the moans clearly audible. Finally, he reached the bottom door. It was slightly ajar . . . he was quiet. The .38 was cocked. It was time to end the madness.

Lujack pushed the door open and found himself in a modern Hades. The killing room. A room filled with candles and swords and incense and death.

Debbi was gagged and tied on a Shinto-style altar. On the wall behind her were markings he instantly recognized. Eight, nine, and three. Above the markings was the symbol of the Yamaguchi-gumi. Before

Debbi a hooded man sat in a black robe. He held a samurai sword in his hand. The man did not turn when Lujack walked into the room.

Debbi's eyes opened wide with relief when she saw Lujack standing in the doorway. Eyewitness life.

"Leave it to an Occidental to fuck up an Oriental tradition," Lujack said, pointing his gun at the back of the hooded man's head.

The black hood turned. Lujack could see the front of the robe was open. This guy was big-time sicko.

"Good evening, Mr. Lujack," said a familiar voice.

Lawrence Brownell took off his black hood and smiled grotesquely at Lujack. "I've been expecting you."

Lujack debated whether to shoot him on the spot or listen to what the pathetic pervert had to say.

"So this is real politics."

"You never knew Kodama. Even Kazuo never really understood him."

"Yoshida and Kodama don't cut girls' heads off."

"Sometimes new traditions have to be forged."

"Since when did killing innocent young girls become traditional?"

"No woman is innocent. You should know that, Lujack," Brownell said, nodding in Debbi's direction. "She would do anything to save her own life. They all would."

Debbi struggled against the ropes, but Lujack could wait to hear her side of the story.

"You were in Japan after the war, weren't you, Brownell? That's what got you started with all this kinky Oriental shit."

"I was the OSS liaison at Sugamo prison. That's where I met Kodama. Kazuo's father was also in the prison."

"The beginnings of a beautiful friendship. The

ultranationalist admiral, the Yakuza godfather, and the American intelligence officer."

"We were patriots. We did more for our countries than most politicians could ever dream. We fought the Communists in Japan. We saved the country for democracy."

"And you got paid well for your patriotism."

"That came later."

"And the girls, when did they come? Did you think this little game up all by yourself?"

"There comes a time in a man's life when he has enough money, enough power," Brownell said, looking again at Debbi, then back to Lujack.

"The others were just party girls, but with Miss Arnold it will be different. You might call it mixing business with pleasure."

The old man gave Lujack a wet, licentious smile. Brownell was more than just a decadent pervert, he was a truly evil man. A devil incarnate.

"There's only one problem," Lujack said.

"What's that?" the old man asked with genuine curiosity.

"Me," Lujack said.

# Chapter Nineteen

## *The Final Scene*

For the month of September, Saint Orel kept throwing strikes and the Good Book kept paying off. On October 3 he broke Drysdale's record. Fifty-nine innings without a run. To make it worse, the Dodgers were going into the playoffs with one of the most ragtag teams in the history of baseball. Lujack knew they didn't have a chance, and his only solace was that the Mets or, if by some miracle Lasorda's Legions made it to the Series, the mighty A's would win him back all the money he'd been losing that month. At least some of it had gone to Sports. Enough to let him keep his car and Sports keep his teeth.

Molly was meeting him at the Hard Rock Cafe in the Beverly Center. She was late. He sipped at a Coke and tried to imagine Boy George was George Benson. It didn't work. Lujack wasn't surprised. He wasn't surprised by much the last few weeks. Susie said he'd snap out of it, but he wasn't sure. Now he knew how Anna must have felt.

For a successful personal consultant, he wasn't handling his own personality too well. The events the night of September 1 kept coming back to him in waves of anger and frustration. He remembered starting back for Avalon Harbor in one of the Avons stored on the top deck. Debbi was in the bow covered in a blanket, sobbing softly. Suddenly he saw a bright flash reflect on her face. He turned and saw the *Southern Cross* consumed in a giant fireball of flame. The force of the explosion almost capsized the little boat. Debbi didn't even flinch. Lujack thought he saw another boat heading for shore in the light of the flames, but he couldn't be sure. He wasn't sure of much that night.

The papers played it as politics and murder. "Billionaire's Yacht Explodes Off Catalina." There was a picture of Lawrence Brownell on the front page of every newspaper in the country. It was the lead story on the evening news. Every home in America saw the picture of Kazuo Yoshida holding back the tears as he described his good friend and business associate. Brownell was eulogized as "America's godfather of defense." The cause of the explosion was under investigation, and speculation was that the blast may have been meant for the *Southern Cross*'s new owner, Yoshida, in an attempt to scuttle the heretofore top-secret B-3 bomber co-venture with Japan. Only because Brownell had changed the dates of his planned European trip at the last minute did he become the "innocent victim" of such a heinous act.

The following week, the Senate Armed Services Committee, reacting to an impassioned plea by Senator Peter Rudlow not to be intimidated by anti-Japanese terrorists, passed the project out of committee on a unanimous vote. The president signed the bill, and Dolph Killian, the newly appointed president of Brownell Industries, said he only wished Larry could have lived to see this long-awaited day of U.S.-Japanese cooperation.

Right. If there was a compromise, Lujack didn't read about it. He assumed Rudlow and Killian had been lying to him, like they'd lied about everything else. All's fair in love and war and business deals over fifty billion dollars.

Debbi had the story of a lifetime, but she was never going to tell it. Some stories are too horrible to tell or to believe. In Debbi's case, maybe she didn't believe it herself, or she had wisely chosen to forget it. The official version was that she had gone for a boat ride with Lujack after the dance. Then, last week, Lujack read that she had gotten engaged to a movie director and was taking over the anchor spot on "Entertainment Tonight." No film at eleven. No Peabody award. As Tommy said, Lionel was better off without her.

"You never look the same, do you?" he said, watching her saunter through the front door, looking more like a lanky, attractive Madonna than the Grace Kelly look she'd been sporting the last time he'd seen her. But she looked good, she always looked good.

"And you always look the same—Levis, tennis shoes, beat-up sport coat."

"This is my good sport coat. It's Italian, I think."

"If that's Italian, I'm Mona Lisa."

She plopped down in the chair. Her long legs stretched out in front of her. For all her beauty, she still had that young colt quality about her.

"I need a drink. I did a ramp show downtown this afternoon in some rundown old building without air conditioners. They had us going up and down in those old iron elevators."

"That's the Bradbury Building. The place is a historic landmark."

"The place is a sweat box."

She flagged down a waiter and ordered a Cape Cod. The waiter seemed to recognize her, and it occurred to Lujack that Molly was a celebrity in certain circles.

"That's right, Lujack, I'm still drinking, but that's all I'm doing. No thanks to you."

"It was for your own protection."

"That's why I wore these," she said, pointing to handcuffs that dangled from her black vest. "But I've got the key."

"It wasn't that bad. They only held you one night."

"That's because all hell broke loose. We'd still be there if every G-man in LA hadn't come out to investigate the explosion."

"At least you had a good alibi."

"Better than yours. From what I heard, nobody ever did know what you were doing out there."

"Taking a midnight cruise. Don't you read the papers?"

"I read them enough to know your girlfriend is getting married to another guy. That must have been some cruise."

"It was," Lujack said, and Molly knew him well enough not to press him.

"So where's Thurgood?"

"Lieutenant Thurgood. He'll be here. He had to swing by his house after work to pick up his daughter."

"I can't believe I'm actually doing an interview for a high school paper."

"You sound like you never went to high school."

"La Mirada High, Class of '86," she said as if it were a thousand years ago, not two.

"Kids grow up fast these days, don't they?" Lujack said. He still felt close to Molly, closer than he had to

Ginger, but he didn't know why. A daughter he didn't have. A wife he didn't have.

"If they make it that far," she said.

"You made it this far. You're making it pretty good."

"You mean now that I'm off drugs."

"I mean considering what you've seen, where you've been. I don't think Janis or Leslie would help out a high school girl with her school paper."

"Leslie would, if you paid her ramp rates."

"I've known Chinese tank commanders nicer than Leslie."

"She's not bad, once you get to know her. She really was bummed out by what happened to Ginger. Models aren't always as tough as they look."

"I'll remember that," Lujack said. Kyle Thurgood walked in the front door. He was in his usual mafioso-style suit and tie. He could have been a capo taking his daughter to church, which in a way he was, the church of rock and roll. Tracy Thurgood looked more like her father than was good for her. She was a little overweight, with a round, intelligent face. Lujack could see resemblance, and it was unattractive. It was clear she was very excited to be with her dad in a place like the Hard Rock Cafe.

Lujack had never seen Kyle look so uneasy and proud at the same time. He nodded to Lujack and barely looked at Molly.

"Handcuff anyone to a bar lately, Lieutenant?" Molly said, offering him one of her decorations.

Thurgood managed a smile, but it was a struggle. He checked out the surroundings. "I thought Hard Rock was the name of a T-shirt company."

"I'm Molly Blair," Molly said and stuck out her hand to Kyle's daughter.

"I know," the girl said shyly, pulling a magazine from her purse with Molly's picture on it. "I'm Tracy Thurgood."

Molly took the picture. It was one of the covers she did when she looked like Grace Kelly. She was coming out of a New York museum and was drop-dead beautiful.

"I hated that shot," she said disdainfully. "Look at my eyes, they look like marshmallows."

"I think you look gorgeous," Tracy said respectfully.

"I was partying all night. I could barely keep my eyes open," Molly said, and Tracy giggled. This was the real story.

"Listen, ladies, why don't you do your story at the table while Lujack and I stroll over to the bar?" Thurgood said uncomfortably.

"That's fine with me, Dad," Tracy said.

"Don't worry, Lieutenant, I'll take good care of her," Molly said, laughing.

Lujack followed Thurgood to the bar. They were the two oldest guys in the place.

"It's kind of nice hearing someone call you Dad, Kyle. Especially when they're as nice as Tracy."

"She's a good kid. I appreciate you getting Molly to come down. She's been after me ever since the Ginger Louie case started. She loves models. She wants to be a model. Maybe Molly can give her a few tips on how to lose weight."

Thurgood saw Lujack smile. "Not that way, asshole," Thurgood said.

"Molly wanted to do it. She's a good kid too."

"Watch it, Lujack. She may look and act like she's thirty, but that doesn't make her a woman."

"Thanks, Kyle."

"Just lookin' out for ya, though I don't know why after what you did to my cousin's boat."

"I paid you for the damages."

"But you never told me what happened out there. Not all of it."

"I told you enough to keep you out of it. No one seemed to be interested in the truth anyway."

"That usually happens when the FBI and the CIA and the CID work together. That explosion had more security than the crash of a stealth bomber."

"Just as much money at stake."

"More. I've never seen anything like it. You'd think Brownell was the fucking president."

"Maybe it's just as well," Lujack said.

"Maybe," Thurgood said, looking around, making sure no one was listening. In the Hard Rock it was hard enough to hear yourself. "When did you know it wasn't Yoshida?"

"Something Molly said in the bar," Lujack answered, putting the pieces together in his own mind. "She mentioned that Brownell had designed the main stateroom so he could live there for months. The day I visited him on the yacht, he seemed inordinately proud of that ship. It was almost a mystical or romantic connection. It didn't make sense that he would sell her to Yoshida . . . for any amount of money. That's when I guessed Yoshida might be using himself as a decoy."

"So Yoshida knew what was going on?"

Lujack nodded in affirmation. "Damn right he did. He might not have been sure when Brownell was going to strike again, but he knew the old bastard was crazy. He knew Brownell killed Ginger, and he knew Brownell was going to keep killing. That's why he staged the phony yacht sale, to give Brownell an alibi.

Yoshida told me himself that night Brownell was in Amsterdam. All the time he was ten feet away watching us through the one-way glass from his cabin."

"I talked to Milch yesterday. He said the semen specimen on Ginger matched the DNA sample from Brownell's body. Of course, no one will ever know it."

"No one will ever know a lot of things about Larry Brownell. He was a monster who lived just under the surface of reality."

"What about the girl in San Francisco?

"Brownell could easily have been aboard the *Southern Cross* that weekend. No one saw him, but that's the way he liked it. He and Yoshida could make deals in private. Yoshida could sail in the race, and Brownell could have Colonel Martin go out and recruit his date for the evening.

"I did some research this past month. Remember I told you both Brownell and Yoshida were admirers of a Japanese ultranationalist and Yakuza godfather, Yoshio Kodama? On March 23rd, 1976, a Japanese porno actor, Mitsuytau Maeno, rented a Piper Cherokee from an airport near the home of Kodama. He was dressed as a kamikaze pilot. He circled Kodama's house and aimed the plane for Kodama's bedroom. Maeno missed Kodama by twenty feet and died instantly. Kodama survived the attack, but it was the beginning of the end of his power in Japan. I checked with a friend in the State Department. Brownell was on an official state visit to Japan at the time. There was a rumor that Kodama might implicate another U.S. defense contractor along with the Lockheed company. After the attack, Kodama never said a word. The date the girl was murdered in San Francisco was also March 23rd."

"So it was the dates? Hiroshima, the surrender . . ."

"More than the dates. I think it was some kind of

transference. Brownell thought he was the real Kodama, the real *oyuban.* The guy was bonkers city."

"And Yoshida?"

"Yoshida played along. He wasn't crazy, but he wasn't stupid either. One of the most powerful men in the American defense establishment thought he and Yoshida were part of some Nippon rightist cabal. Why not go along with the guy? He's making you the richest man in the world and he's helping your native country get top-secret technology. What's the life of a few girls when compared to economic and possibly even military domination for the next generation?"

"Jesus Christ."

"After Ginger's death, though, I think Yoshida realized something had to be done. Too many people had seen both him and Brownell with Ginger. Too many people at the Marina Shores were involved. Then, when Tommy and I started nosing around, things got even messier."

"So he had a bomb planted in your car?"

"I can't prove it, but I think Yoshida or his Yakuza lieutenant George Kim ordered a bomb put in my car, sent Micky Kim to San Francisco, had Dave Mason and Chase Field murdered, and finally blew up the *Southern Cross.*"

"Yoshida blew up his own ship?"

"Brownell's obsession was threatening the future of the B-3 coventure. The B-3 was the crowning achievement of Yoshida's career. Something had to be done. That ship blew up like a detonated building. The explosives were set before, not after, she left the Avalon Harbor that night. Yoshida was the only one who knew Brownell was aboard. You figure it out."

"He gets rid of Brownell and Martin and, if he's lucky . . . you."

"Why waste good explosives? Not to mention political capital. The bastard played it like a modern-day burning of the Reichstag."

"What about Killian and Rudlow?"

"They take Brownell's place. One's a defense contractor, the other's a politician. That way neither is too powerful. Yoshida keeps control."

"A new improved version of the Yoshida theory."

"It's more than a theory."

"But you can't prove it."

"No."

"How about Miss Anchor? She might have heard something that night. If Brownell mentioned Yoshida?"

"I don't think she remembers much, Kyle. She's better off forgetting."

"She's not the only one, is she?" Thurgood said with an enigmatic smile.

"Meaning?"

"Meaning, when I was talking to Milch the other day, he said there was something else interesting about the bodies they found near the *Southern Cross.* The three Viet vets were all shot by an unregistered automatic. The kind of gun a cop might use. Milch asked me if I knew about such a gun, and I told him no."

"Is that a roundabout way to remind me that I owe you a new Colt?"

"Consider the rifle a gift. I'm only sorry I didn't have the pleasure of using it."

"You would have gotten all wet."

"Milch said Brownell wasn't shot by an automatic. He was shot by a .38. From the angle of entry, he figured the man who shot him was less than ten feet away."

Lujack looked at the lieutenant, then looked at his daughter and Molly talking at the table.

"Since when did Milch get to be a firearms expert?"

"He isn't, and he didn't send the bullet on to the firearms lab. The powers that be would just as soon close the book on this mess and fast. As far as they're concerned, Brownell was killed by the explosion. I'm only telling you so that"—he hesitated—"so that you'll know I would probably have done the same thing."

"You mean you would have shot him in the forehead like you're saying I did. Even though he was holding nothing but a sword and was ten feet away."

Thurgood thought a minute. He was deadly earnest. "Like Joshua in the Bible. Sometimes you have to stand up and be counted. Sometimes you gotta do what you gotta do."

"That's the difference between you and me, Kyle. If you had to cross the Red Sea, you'd try to part it. I'd let the current carry me across."

"What's that supposed to mean?"

"It means I don't believe you, but thanks anyway."

Thurgood nodded and looked over at the two girls who were happily chatting away and eyeing the waiters.

"You know, Lujack, maybe you owe that girl an apology."

Lujack knew the girl he was talking about. She wasn't in the Hard Rock.

"That night you barely looked at her. You dumped her on the shore like she was a piece of meat."

"Rudlow was there for her."

"Rudlow is an asshole. That girl could have told her story to the world and won a Pulitzer prize. But she'd have to give you up to do it."

"That's one way of looking at it," Lujack said, but he didn't see it that way. He saw it like an invitation to a club. A club that granted forgiveness and absolution.

All you had to do was say it was an aberration, a mistake, and promise not to do it again. Lujack couldn't join that club.

The girls came bouncing up to the bar.

"Daddy, Molly can get us into a new club. It's called Enter the Dragon and it's supposed to be raging."

"I don't know, Hon," Thurgood said.

"But Daddy, I can use it in my story," Tracy pleaded. Lujack had never seen Thurgood so powerless.

"I'll tell you what. I'll go if Lujack goes."

"Oh no, I have a rule against private clubs," Lujack protested.

"What about the Zodiac?" Molly teased.

"That was business."

"And Riviera?" Thurgood said.

"That's business too."

"Please, Mr. Lujack. We'll have you home by twelve."

"Eleven," Thurgood corrected.

"So much for Lujack's rules," he said. He got up, and Tracy took both his and Kyle's hands.

It's a good thing your old man owes me a hundred bucks," Lujack said.